RE-HAUNT

CHILLING STORIES OF GHOSTS & OTHER HAUNTS

EDITED
BY

KELLY A. HARMON AND
VONNIE WINSLOW CRIST

Pole to Pole Publishing
Baltimore

Re-Haunt
Chilling Stories of Ghosts & Other Haunts
Copyright © 2019 Pole to Pole Publishing

Published by Pole to Pole Publishing
Edited by Kelly A. Harmon and Vonnie Winslow Crist
Cover layout copyright © 2019 Pole to Pole Publishing
www.poletopolepublishing.com

ISBN: 978-1-941559-33-8

The Cold Girl © 2016 Michael Fassbender, first published in *Hypnos Magazine*.
Down the Myrtle Tree © 2016, first published in *Writing Wicket: Horror for Teens*.
The Idlewild Letters © 2017 H.R. Boldwood, first published in *Killing It Softly 2*.
The Red-Haired Girl © 1903 S. Baring-Gould, first published in *The Windsor Magazine*.
You Are Such A One © 2009 Nancy Springer, first published in *Fantasy and Science Fiction Magazine*.
The Strange Bequest of Simon Bray © 2008 Tom English, first published in *Bound for Evil*.
The Haunted Patrol Car © 2001 Jody Lynn Nye, first published in *Blood and Donuts*.
Glitter © 2007 Jacqueline Seewald, first published in *Maguszine*.
Dark August Rain © 2015 Nicole Kurtz, first published in *Rain Anthology*.
Finders Keepers © 2016 Kelly A. Harmon, first published in *A Blue Collar Proposition*.
When Crows Come Calling © 2008 John Wolf, first published in *The Phoenix*.
The Scarecrow © 1918 G. Ranger Wormser, first published in *The Scarecrow And Other Stories*.
Battlefields © 2018 Vonnie Winslow Crist, first published in *Fantasia Divinity Magazine*.
One More © 2015 Gregory L. Norris, first published in *Dreamscapes into Darkness*.
Red Leaves © 2013 Marc Sorondo, first published in *Pavor Nocturnus Dark Fiction Anthology*.
The Spirit of the Back Stairs © 1991 Darrell Schweitzer, first published in *Fear*.

Library of Congress Control Number: 2019949440

RE-HAUNT

The boundaries which divide Life from Death are at best shadowy and vague.

- Edgar Allan Poe

Table of Contents

Cold Girl
Michael Fassbender

Vasili *adjusted the brim of his hat against the rain blown* into his face. It was a delicate balance he had to strike: too low and his vision would be obscured, too high and the rain would get into his eyes. The Cold Girl would show tonight; somehow, he just knew it. He needed to stay alert to any change in the environment that might herald her appearance.

A bright flash illuminated the canopy of leaves above him, swallowing up the puny efforts of his heavy-duty flashlight. In another moment followed the expected peal of thunder. Accursed rain; southern Indiana struck him as surprisingly tropical for its geographical location. Granted, he only knew the summer months, when he flew in from St. Petersburg to teach Russian in the SIU Intensive Language Program. His students had spoken of winters that outdid those of St. Petersburg in harshness. Vasili was not impressed. He had studied in Moscow, where winter savagery mocked anything in the contiguous United States. No, to Vasili, the college town of Beecher's Run might as well have been in the Yucatan.

Vasili ducked under some low-lying branches to light a cigarette. He took a good, hard drag and set out again into the open. It was dangerous, he knew, to be under trees during a storm, and this one promised to be a healthy one. It was only in the rain that she appeared, however. The Cold Girl haunted rainy nights, and he, Vasili

Aleksandrovich Bessmertnykh had figured out why. He alone in this town had been able to do so.

He shifted the broad beam of his flashlight to the left when movement registered in his peripheral vision. He took a deep, slow breath when he saw it was just a young evergreen, swaying in the wind. *Plenty of those in the taiga.* On he trudged, muddying his expensive leather shoes. He did not expect to see anything until he reached the gully.

The entire student body knew about the Cold Girl. She was, without doubt, the most popular phantom on a college campus considered somewhat more spectrally active than most. Like one of America's many Vanishing Hitchhikers, she appeared only to men, and only to one at a time, on rainy nights in or near the woods east of campus. She seemed completely solid, not an ethereal apparition glowing with unearthly light. More importantly, she was young and beautiful, and if not for the strangeness of her dress, she might seem just an attractive junior or senior.

On the subject of her dress, no one was capable of offering a useful description, save that it was tattered and dripping wet. As if that were not enough, she always seemed disoriented, even dazed, when witnessed, and this tended to evoke chivalrous and predatory impulses in equal measure. Many times, she would ask for help in finding something, never specifying what she sought; nor did she ever seem to find it, and before long she would vanish in frustration.

The town of Beecher's Run relished her mystery. She had been seen since 1935, and at least half a dozen explanations had been floated, but no one pursued any of them with any ardor. Perhaps they feared a prosaic explanation that would cheapen her image. If Vasili were right, they needn't have worried. As far as he knew, Beecher's Run had something unique in the Western Hemisphere.

Vasili slowed his pace as he began to scale a steep slope. At 47, he remained in good shape, old habits from his stint in the Soviet Army governing his lifestyle, but the ground was becoming treacherous as the rain continued, and he did not wish to lose his balance. Vasili prided himself on his cautious approach to problems.

He probably wouldn't have believed in the Cold Girl in the first place, if it weren't for a student in his conversation class who had seen her. Jerry Hixon wasn't the sort of student who sought out attention. More often than not, Vasili had to make an effort to draw him out. It was, after all, a conversation class; oral participation was the whole point. Jerry had also admitted to having a bit of a buzz going from a few shots of whiskey when he had wandered out to the woods, knowing that it made his testimony rather less impressive.

What had captured Vasili's imagination was Jerry's description of where he saw her. A deep gully ran through the woods, ranging from six to ten feet in depth, and Jerry had seen her standing on the embankment to the near side. She told him she was looking for something (in his addled state he had failed to catch exactly what that was) and asked him for help. Jerry hadn't realized he was seeing a ghost. He thought she might be some sorority girl even more blitzed than he was, and saw a chance to score some action for the night. He didn't balk when she led him down into the gully, and made a game show of looking for whatever it was supposed to be, until she vanished and left him wondering just what was going on.

Vasili had reached the top of the embankment, and looked down into the gully below. Three to five centimeters of water sat in the bottom, and the storm had hardly gotten into full swing. He smiled; tonight it was. He had no doubt that the Cold Girl would appear. Annoyed, he looked up at the sky. Devil take it, it really didn't matter how much water got dumped on him while he waited. The session was over, and in two days he was going to fly back to St. Petersburg for the year. Who really cared if he had the sniffles on the flight? What mattered is that this would be his last chance to check this matter out until next June.

He shuffled along the embankment, careful not to slip into the gully. That was what had convinced him in the first place, why it all made sense. There was a perfectly rational reason why the ghost appeared in 1935: that's when they built the reservoir. In the process, they changed the course of the Beecher River. Once that river had flowed through these woods. In 1935, that stretch of the river dried up. The unclean dead don't like change.

The rain pelting him grew into a torrent. He stopped walking and scanned the woods about him for some sign of the girl. Movement was everywhere, but it seemed only the movement of branch and leaf. The young lady was taking her time in putting in an appearance.

"*Blyad'*," he cursed under his breath. A sharp intake of breath followed, and then in silence his light darted from side to side. He hoped she hadn't heard. It was never a smart move to criticize the unclean dead, above all when one sought their favor. And was that not, after all, what he sought? For her to gift him with her attention, and the opportunity to observe her, to study her? In the end, this was science in its primal form.

It was Professor Taykhman, his parapsychology teacher at MGU, who had opened his mind to this sort of inquiry. Yevgeniy O. Taykhman had been in the KGB back when the Soviet Union still existed, and when he wasn't monitoring the "lunatics" who were being treated for dissidence, he was involved in the whole gamut of secret experiments undertaken in the name of espionage. Such a tragic career, Vasili thought.

In 1990, Taykhman was a man of status in the KGB, on the cutting edge of the study of the human mind; by 1994, he was a junior professor at MGU. Then, sometime in 1998, he had gotten into a highly lucrative undocumented business with a handful of former comrades, a business that made him a very wealthy man until 2002, when six bullets robbed him of all earthly possessions during a visit to Rostov-na-Dnu. Vasili wondered whether the assailants had really been members of a rival Ingush gang, or nominal comrades dissatisfied with the math.

Taykhman's efforts had ended with tragedy, but Vasili could hardly blame the man for his choices, and like many of his countrymen he was indifferent to the idea of an unlawful career. Taykhman was a brilliant scientist who followed the rubles, dollars and deutschmarks to a more lucrative career in Russia's shadow economy. Was Vasili any better? He was a trained professor of psychology who taught Russian to spoiled American kids because it paid better than his real job. And in the end, maybe that's why he needed to see the Cold Girl while he was here. For a change, he felt like a real scientist hard at work on an important research project.

Taykhman had taught him to be open to legends and folklore. Peasants and other common types may not be especially well-equipped to interpret why phenomena occur, but they do a surprisingly fine job of telling one what they saw or heard. They are splendid information gatherers, paving the way for the scientist who is ready to make sense of the data. Under Taykhman's influence, he read extensively in Russian peasant folklore, prepared to accept that on some level, everything from the household spirits, or *domovye*, to the blood-drinking *upyr'* had some foundation in reality, even if science did not yet understand where they belonged. Vasili had dreamed of being the one to roll back the frontier of ignorance, to extend the borders of science into the dark corners of superstition.

Then, he became a language tutor, because that was where the money was.

He sighed and pulled the flask from his pocket. He needed to keep his mind and senses clear, of course, to detect and record all that happened when he reached his goal, but he was getting cold and wet and depressed, and he needed a dose of fortitude, too. Just a quick swig of vodka, and then he felt a little warmer, and didn't care so much about being wet, and if he were still a bit depressed, he was less inclined to think about it.

Hey, a lot of pilots fly their jets after drinking a whole lot more than that, and most of them manage to land without tragedy.

Feeling a bit warmer now, he continued trudging along the crest of the embankment, following the old course of the Beecher River. It was close, he told himself, but he found it difficult to suppress his irritation. She moves around, too, when she walks; she could just as easily have met him somewhere along the way. The warmth in his stomach gave way to a slight chill as he wondered if perhaps she had chosen some other prospective suitor elsewhere in the woods, nearer the campus. Maybe this whole enterprise would be for nothing. The thought of next year brought no comfort.

Soon enough he happened upon the remains of the old footbridge. Although by now a familiar sight, he stopped to appraise it once again. This was the key to his reconstruction of what had happened.

He had seen it when Jerry Hixon took him to see where he had met the Cold Girl. Jerry hadn't known anything about it, but a little bit of research worked wonders. Much of the modern college campus had been part of town in the mid-nineteenth century, and the resources of a large forest were necessities for the population. Moreover, the nearest neighboring town of any size was twenty miles east, on the other side of the woods. In those days a trail was maintained between Beecher's Run and its neighbor, Emmett's Hollow. A footbridge crossed the Beecher where the trail met the river, and it was a vital fixture of local commerce through the middle of the century. Its use declined when the railroad came to Beecher's Run, and maintenance suffered accordingly.

In 1864, following an unusually heavy rainstorm, a large section of the bridge was found to have collapsed. The river ran high that year, and repair was deemed neither safe nor necessary. Instead, the bridge was abandoned, and a covered bridge was built further north, where the embankments to either side of the river rose higher.

Curiously, the newspaper telling of this event held another story that captured his interest. During the night of that rainstorm, the local doctor died of a heart attack, and his daughter vanished. Both the good doctor and his lovely, exotic daughter were much missed in the community. In her case, no body was ever found, and opinion was divided over whether she died or ran away.

To Vasili's mind, by far the most likely scenario was that she had found her father dead or dying and ran out into the storm to seek help. The nearest doctor was twenty miles away, on the other side of the trail that crossed the Beecher. Had she tried to cross the bridge, only to fall into the swollen river when the neglected planks gave way? It would explain a lot.

Vasili crouched down to peer into the gully. This was where she fell. The body would have been carried some distance downriver. If it had gotten pinned among some rocks, or buried with silt, it might never have surfaced. So, she rested in a watery grave, until the river's course changed. The river bed dried up in 1935, and ever since, she has been restless.

Every time her grave becomes wet again, she rises.

Vasili stood up, basking in self-congratulation. He understood what the others would not, could not, understand. Anyone else who had done his research would conclude, and reasonably, that her spirit is unquiet during storms like that which claimed her life. The Americans made no distinction between the unquiet dead and the *unclean* dead. Hers was by far a different purpose, and the construction of the reservoir in 1935 had robbed her of her ability to perform it.

She is a *rusalka,* and her purpose is to lure men to drown in her own watery grave.

Who would have thought it? Here, deep in the American heartland, along a small river far from the mighty arteries of the Don, Dnepr, and Volga, a *rusalka* had been created, and seventy-one years later she had been trapped by the dislocation of her environment! Like an adder defanged, she could now be studied without fear. Should he succeed in his quest, and confirm his belief, he could make provisions for a more thorough investigation next year. Now *that* would be exciting!

As long as the Girl showed, he could imagine no other result. It all fit together. Her disorientation, universally attested by witnesses, flows naturally from the irony of her situation. She was a landlocked river spirit, a beached mermaid, one might say. The core of her being urged her to swim up through the waters that claimed her life and drag down others to share her fate, and now all of that was gone. She had lost her livelihood, even her identity. Little wonder that she seems confused!

Excitement rose in him as he began to walk again. In his heart, he was certain he was right. The improbability of this situation was allayed when one realized that this *rusalka* was transplanted. Dr. Arkady S. Shaposhnikoff had come to this country with his daughter Lidiya in 1858, seeking a new start. His wife, her mother, died of typhus while he served the soldiers in the Crimean War, and the loss weighed deeply on his heart. The implications were staggering. Surely Lidiya Arkadevna had known the stories, most likely from the family's servants. Could it be that the death of a young woman by drowning is not enough, that an understanding of the possibility of becoming a *rusalka* is a prerequisite of making the transition? If so, poor Lidiya may well be unique in the entire Western Hemisphere, although one could not discount the prospect of others appearing among the Ukrainian emigre communities of Canada, for example.

He quickened his pace in spite of the heavy downpour, buoyed by the expectation of success and revelation. He paused only to light another cigarette. He breathed the smoke in deeply, like a diver before making the plunge. He grinned at the thought; it was apt enough in this case.

Before long the gully took a sharp turn to the right. Looking down into the bottom, he saw the tips of rocks peeking up through the now marshy soil. It could have been here, he thought. Beneath the silt deposits of seven decades, the girl's bones may rest right there. If it came to that in next year's investigation, this would be his first choice to dig. Vasili frowned at the prospect. He didn't like the possible consequences. A *rusalka* in the New World was enough of a treasure, let alone one rendered harmless. He didn't want to take the chance of consuming his subject during the experiment.

Then a fresh eruption of lightning above the tree canopy shed a moment's illumination all around him. Amid the varied hues of green and brown, he saw a flash of white. Or rather, it had seemed white at first blush. In the dark that followed, he recognized that much of much of it was gray. A sodden dress, perhaps white when new, could easily seem gray, and her skin was likely of a similar shade.

Heedless of his footing, Vasili darted around the corner of the embankment for a better look. Perhaps twelve meters away, he spotted a pale figure passing through the opportunistic underbrush that had taken root when the basin drained. Not wanting to alarm her with a beam of light in the face, he aimed his flashlight down, before her feet. Its reflected light was sufficient to let him watch as she stepped into a clearing, pushing a small shrub aside in the process. His first thought was to note with delight that she fully interacted with her environment: if not truly a corporeal entity, at least she functioned as one. No specter this, she was fully capable of dragging a man down to share her watery grave.

His second thought was one of irritation: Devil take it, she would turn up down there in the bottom of the gully. She might have kept to the higher ground; after all, it would have made it easier for her to spot a likely lad. Seeing no help for it, he took a moment to assess a descent of more than two meters, then carefully made his way down to the bottom.

As he had feared, it was marshy, and a good eight centimeters of water stood above the earth. He could feel it seeping into his expensive leather shoes and soaking his socks. Under the circumstances, however, he had no right to complain. He tossed the butt of his cigarette into the pool around him and focused his attention on his quarry, now so near.

She had plainly noticed him, too, even if her gaze seemed oddly vacant. Like one in a trance, she drew nearer; Vasili thought of the hypnotism experiments he had witnessed at MGU. In the next moment, he noted how silently she moved. Glancing down at her feet, he saw that she excited scarcely a ripple, as if she were gliding through the water, where he had so coarsely splashed about. Then she broke the silence, asking in a frail voice, "Where is the river?"

From her, it sounded more like "reaver." Even three years ago, he might have pronounced it the same way. The passage of a century-and-a-half after her death had done nothing to efface her accent. Small wonder that in his drunken state, Jerry Hixon could not determine what she really sought.

Vasili chose not to answer just yet. In spite of the poor light, he sized her up. She was, indeed, a lovely creature, even if her skin looked distressingly gray in the shadows. She seemed about twenty years old, with a graceful, girlish figure and, most importantly of all, an unquestionably Slavic face. Her clear blue eyes peered out through lids that carried the slight Asiatic tilt that so many southern Russians had inherited from the Tatar invaders. In that moment, he could see how easy it was to become lost in those eyes, and to willingly follow them into the depths. Her hair—chestnut, perhaps?—and her torn clothing were as sodden as his socks had become, and clung to her form in a most becoming manner. A new excitement threatened to take form in his mind, but he was smart enough not to let *that* take over. The possibilities posed by her physicality, whether real or illusory, were not lost on him; it was precisely that impulse, however, that guided so many men to their doom at the hands of *rusalki*.

No longer mindful of the weather, he removed his hat and bowed to her. Best to start simply and politely. "Good evening, Miss." She responded with a weak imitation of a curtsy. Well, she was a product of the mid-nineteenth century; perhaps a bit of Victorian chivalry might get to her. "You seem cold and wet. Perhaps you would care for my coat?"

Before he could remove the garment, she shook her head. Although she looked as if she were on the verge of shivering, she said, "No sir, I am quite dry."

Vasili smiled. Quite dry, indeed. He reached out his right hand, palm up, as any well-bred young man might when meeting a young lady. "Have I the pleasure of meeting Miss Lidiya Arkadevna Shaposhnikova?"

Her eyes, heretofore dreamy and unfocused, drilled him sharply. She extended her own hand for him to kiss it. "You have me at a disadvantage, sir."

Vasili could see the caked mud beneath her utilitarian fingernails. He paid that no heed as he took her hand, saying, "I knew

Doktor Shaposhnikov in the Crimea." In his gentle grip, her hand felt completely solid. Splendid. He kissed it, and then slipped into Russian. "*Ochen' priyatno*." A pleasure.

She gazed at him with furrowed brow and mouth agape, then muttered her response. Vasili worried that he might have pushed this too far. He wanted to prove that the apparition, whatever its nature might be, was that of the Russian girl, Lidiya. Prodding her to access too many memories could become dangerous. Best to return to idle pleasantries.

He didn't even notice how hard the rain was falling.

Returning to English, he asked, "Tell me, how is the good doctor?"

Once again, he was met by that distressed expression. Surely, he thought, it was just her disorientation at work, the very same confusion that everyone had reported, and that he had so elegantly explained. Even so, it failed to quell the unease that rose in the pit of his stomach. But then, what is to be done now?

The girl sobbed and turned away from him.

Vasili sighed. At least the Victorian gallantry angle was helping him. He stepped forward, his feet beginning to sink into the nasty muck below. He didn't even want to think about what it was doing to his shoes. Instead, he tried to affect more *bonhomie* in his voice than he felt as he patted her right shoulder. "There, there, miss, everything is going to be all right."

She snatched his wrist with an eagle's grip.

Alarmed, Vasili watched her turn back toward him, twisting his arm up in the process, driving him down to his knees. He no longer heeded the clammy porridge that engulfed his lower legs. There was now a brightness in her gaze, a playful quality that eclipsed all other sensory data. The scientist in Vasili drifted away, even as Lidiya, for the first time, became truly *aware*.

"*Ya khochu tantsevat'*," she said; I want to dance.

Vasili could not piece together a coherent thought as she wrenched his arm around, driving his face into the marshy soil of the river bed. The water had become deep enough to cover his head entirely, but he did not struggle as the Cold Girl held him under. What remained of consciousness dimmed, framing only his exultation at being chosen.

Down the Myrtle Tree
A.P. Sessler

*T*he digital alarm clock read 1:20 a.m., and Connor's parents were fast asleep in the neighboring room. He knew that because "The Late Show" had been turned off in the middle of the monologue almost an hour ago. He knew *that* because the Bridell home had thin walls. An occasional sleeping snort from his father also confirmed the coast was clear.

He took his clothes from beneath the bed and put them on in the dark. He slowly slid his bedroom window open and climbed out onto the small section of pitched roof. Once his tennis shoes found their grip on the shingles, he eased down until the large tree branch came into reach.

He hung from it, and found the foothold in the trunk he had used to climb onto the roof several times, but this was his first going down without first going up. And it was night. Halloween night.

Branch by branch, foothold by foothold, he descended the peeling crepe myrtle into the night-damp grass of his lawn. He made his way through the narrow passage between the house, the tree, and his neighbor's tall, wood fence to the front yard, where he nervously glanced over his shoulder at the black rectangle of his parents' bedroom window, afraid a light would explode within at any moment, but it didn't.

It was then he realized their unusual psychic sense to catch him in any mischievous act was completely dormant while asleep. He turned to face the street, where in the middle stood Brad Turner, his best friend, holding the plastic bag of candy he had gathered earlier.

Connor didn't say a word until they met.

"How long have you been here?" he whispered.

"Like five minutes," whispered Brad, looking at his watch.

"Just standing in the road?"

"Yeah."

"What if you got hit by a car?"

"I guess no one drives this late at night."

Connor looked up and down the street. "Okay."

"Let's get moving before your parents wake up," Brad said, and led the way.

The two walked down the middle of the two-way street, Connor still turning his head on occasion to look for cars.

"This is awesome!" said Connor.

"Why haven't we done this before?" Brad asked, reaching into his bag of candy, now dangling from his wrist by its handles.

"There's a first time for everything."

Brad unwrapped a chocolate football, placed it in his mouth and took another from the bag. "You want one?"

"Heck yeah," said Connor, and held out a hand.

"Here you go."

Connor took the piece of candy and began to peel the foil wrapper off.

"Dang it, I can't see," he said, and walked into the light of the next streetlamp.

His fingers fumbled to remove every piece of foil, which he let fall to the street. He popped the football in his mouth and rolled it about with his tongue.

"These are so good," he said, his mouth full.

"I know."

"You ever wondered what makes Halloween so fun?"

"It's the candy," said Brad as he shook the bag.

"But you can get candy anytime."

"Not free candy."

"Yeah, but that's not it."

"Wearing costumes?"

"That's fun and all. But remember the time we had Halloween at the Community Center?"

Brad nodded. "That was lame."

"Exactly."

"I don't know. Going door to door?"

"We did that for fundraisers in broad daylight and that was even more lame."

"I give up."

"It's the only night we get to wander the streets at night. That's why it's so cool—the dark. Playing a game of Horse until 8 o'clock? Driving home from Grandma's at night. That thirty seconds you spend outside between the car and your house. That's where the magic happens."

It was the most he could articulate. He couldn't define the true mysteries of night. He made no mention of its cool, crisp air, how it tickles and tingles the nerves; its sterile cleanliness—that refreshingly, invigorating air void of smog and noise. Or how its misty depths, beneath the surface where no light reaches, lie the things of old—things of fable and fairy tale.

A light appeared from behind.

"Car," said Brad.

The boys took to the sidewalk and hid behind a holly bush. Beneath the canopy of maples that lined the block, they waited for the car to pass. The blinding white eyes of the car rose and fell with each dip in the road until the car slowed to a stop. The door opened, and out stepped a silhouetted figure, its head a twisted mass of snake-like things.

It walked to the front of the car, where its shadow lie flat on the street like a giant victim.

"Who is that?" Connor whispered.

"Bradley Turner! You are in so much trouble, young man," the woman shouted.

"Busted," said Brad.

"Do you think she saw me?" Connor asked.

"Just stay here unless she says something."

Instead of a head of writhing snakes, the Medusa's crown was lined with pink, plastic curlers, but her unblinking gaze had nearly the same effect as a Gorgon's stare. Bradley stood stone-cold frozen in his steps.

"You get over here right this minute!" she said. "Did you think I wouldn't hear you making all that noise?"

Brad sprung to life from behind the bush and went to his mother, his head humbly bowed and back bent. Connor watched the two get in the car and shut the doors, then drive up the street past him.

He suspected she had spotted him, but sat still behind the bush until the car turned into a driveway across the street, did a U-turn, and drove down the street, past his house to their own.

"Dang it. What do I do now?" Connor asked aloud.

"Stay with me," a voice came from behind.

Connor leaped forward with a yelp, turning midair to face the girl. A striped toboggan and scarf hid the majority of her hair, the color of Fall's last leaves. She seemed familiar, like an old locker combination.

"You scared the crap out of me," he grumbled as he dusted himself off.

"Halloween tradition. Who are you?" she asked, and offered a hand to help him up. It was cold when he took it in his own.

"Connor Bridell. Aren't you the new girl?" he asked as he stood to his feet and released the cold hand.

"It's Amy Drake. And I've been here two years. I'm in the eighth grade now."

"You showed up at homeroom in seventh grade, then you were gone. How come you stopped coming to school?"

"I got real sick. I couldn't be around too many people or I'd get sicker, so Mom and Dad pulled me out."

"Then how'd you get to the next grade?"

"Home school."

He wore a satisfied smirk, then his expression dulled. He looked away, fighting the desire to ask, but curiosity clawed at him until he caved. "What did you have?"

"An autoimmune disorder."

"Are you better?"

"I'm out here, ain't I?"

"Yeah," he said, putting on that same smirk.

"Sorry your friend got dragged off."

"And it was the first time either of us snuck out at night."

"Fun, isn't it?"

"It was 'til he got caught," he said, kicking at the crack in the sidewalk. "Guess I should just go home."

"You're already out. Come with me instead."

He smiled at her and wished he had the nerve to tell her it was a far better alternative.

"Where do we go?" he asked.

"Anywhere we want," she said and smiled back, walking away from his house.

"This isn't your first time?" he asked as he walked beside her.

"Nope."

"Cool."

"It is, isn't it?" she asked as a brisk breeze blew down the street, rustling the maple leaves above them—a handful came drifting down around them.

He stopped and reached out until one landed in his palm. He twiddled the red leaf in his fingers, then handed it to her.

She stuck it in the folded brim of her toboggan.

"You look like a Canadian," he said.

"Take off," she said.

They laughed.

When the night silence settled, they soaked it in like sweet music for just a moment.

"Guess we shouldn't stand here all night," she said, and continued walking.

"So when you're out here, where do you normally go?" he asked.

"Braid Cemetery."

"Why there?"

"It's Halloween. You're not supposed to hang out at the Post Office or someplace boring."

She took a right the next street. He followed her lead.

"You ever see anything?" he asked.

"Like what?"

He didn't want to answer.

"Like what?" she repeated.

"You know," he paused until he had the courage to say it. "Weird stuff."

"You mean like zombies and witches?"

He nodded his head.

She laughed. "Not yet. Just people like you."

"What's that mean?" he asked, his face contorted.

"Curious people. That's all," she said, mirroring his expression.

His guard lowered. "Oh. Okay."

They came to Braid Cemetery. A streetlamp illuminated the iron bars of its gate.

"So this is your favorite hangout?" he asked, gazing up at the dark, gnarled trees that lined the property's perimeter.

"You'd prefer the playground?"

"Okay. But we better see some zombies."

She laughed as she crossed the threshold, tramping leaves underfoot. "Nerd."

He followed her into the moonlit graveyard, slowly and unsure, carefully watching where each foot landed, while she kept her same, steady pace.

When she was well ahead of him, she stopped. "You're dragging behind," she said.

"It's dark. I don't want to step on anyone's grave."

"Guess you should be careful of that," she said, her head cocked slightly.

"Why?" he asked.

"You know what happens on Halloween, right?"

He shrugged, thinking only of the conversation he and Brad had earlier, and that somehow his answer would be insufficient.

"It's All Hallow's Eve. The night when the veil of spirits is thin. The spirits of the dead roam the earth from nightfall 'til sunrise," she said. "Stepping on someone's grave might make 'em really mad."

He looked around at the empty graveyard.

"I guess ghosts aren't real, either," he said.

"Sure they are. When the veil of spirits is thin it becomes like a two-way mirror."

"What's that mean?"

"They can see out, but you can't see in, and sometimes it's the other way around. Sometimes it's so thin you can see each other."

He laughed. "Whatever. I just wanna see a zombie."

"Tell me you didn't really expect to see monsters on Halloween."

"I don't know."

"Aren't you like fourteen?"

"Yeah, so."

Something stirred in the brush. He jumped, bumping into her.

"What was that?" he gasped.

"Your manhood," she teased him.

"Sorry, I don't spend all my free time in graveyards like you do."

Her expression went blank, followed by the furrowed brow of offense. She turned away and marched ahead. The squish-squish of damp grass grew soft as she disappeared in shadow beneath the canopy of a giant oak.

"Hey!" he yelled. "What's wrong?"

She didn't answer.

"Did I say something?" he asked, but received no answer. "Dang it. Wait up!"

He marched after her, fearfully flinching at every chirp and croak around him. With each step the canopy grew nearer, and with it the fear of what lie in its shadow.

"Amy?" he asked, stopping short of the shadow.

He reached his hand into the dark and stepped beneath the canopy. The darkness was thick. Its coolness tickled his hands and face.

"Amy?" he called again and took another step.

He bumped into something. It stood erect, but gave way to his momentum.

"Oh man!" he blurted out, but swallowed his pride and reached out for the shape in front of him.

"Amy?" he asked.

"Wimp," her voice came.

"What are you doing here in the dark?"

"Same as you," she said.

He felt her breath on his cheek. It grew cool. "Is it okay for you to be this close?"

"Why wouldn't it be?"

"I thought you'd get sick."

"I'll be fine."

"Should we keep walking?"

"There's no rush," she said. The mist of her breath settled on his lips.

He swallowed and reached into the pitch black for some part of her. He found her sleeved right arm, and followed it down to the cold hand.

"I'm sorry if I made you mad," he said.

She said nothing, but took his hand in hers. His hand warmed hers, like a slow-burning ember. He felt her body grow close to his, breasts brushing against his chest then pulling away. Hand in hand, his arm extending as she pulled him to the edge of the shadow, near the center of the cemetery.

"So what do you think of your first night out?" she asked.

He stepped forward beside her and squeezed her hand. "It's all right."

He wanted to say more, but he didn't want to sound soft. She would just look down on his childish expressions.

"Are you mad there aren't any monsters roaming the streets?" she asked.

"I am slightly disappointed," he admitted.

"You can kiss me if you want."

He flinched, then swallowed before speaking. "What about your dis— Won't you get sick?"

"You worry too much."

"But what if—"

"You don't have anything that could hurt me."

"How do you know?"

"Shh," she whispered.

Though they were both in the dark he closed his eyes and leaned forward. He felt her breath, then the moist lips, first top then bottom, press against his own.

He opened his eyes. She giggled into his mouth. Her breath felt like night air. She pulled him out of the shadow into the moonlight, and smiled at him.

"That kinda makes up for not seeing any monsters," he said.

"You *can* say you saw a ghost," she said.

His head jerked side to side in search of the phantom.

"Where?" he asked.

"Over there!" she pointed.

He let go of her hand and followed the direction of her pointed finger, only to find a trio of headstones.

"Here? There's nothing here," he said and turned to face her, but she was gone. "Amy?"

He returned to the shadow of the canopy, thrusting hands in every direction and height.

"Where are you?" he asked.

There was no answer. He left the shadow and looked where she had pointed: the three headstones. Dread fell upon him, pulling him irresistibly forward. He wanted to stop, to turn back, but he couldn't. In a moment he found himself standing at the foot of the three graves, where a long, horizontal stone lie. It read:

... A THREEFOLD CORD IS NOT QUICKLY BROKEN.
Ecclesiastes 4:12

He gazed at the first headstone, and read each from left to right, as the sickening dread stirred in his gut:

ARNOLD DRAKE   AMY DRAKE   CINDY DRAKE
1981-   2000-2013   1984-

In the center plot, the red maple leaf he had caught for her rested, pressed gently into the moist earth. His heart beat fast. He turned to flee. From where he stood to the tall iron gate of Braid Cemetery, the entire graveyard was full of moving shadows and forms, from barely visible to corporeal.

His legs froze in fear as Amy's words played in his mind.

"When the veil of spirits is thin it becomes like a two-way mirror... They can see out, but you can't see in... Sometimes it's so thin you can see each other."

He screamed until his legs broke free from their icy grip, and ran, dodging the solid forms that stood in his path. His arms flailed, thrashing, passing through the phantoms, fanning them away like smoke, their faces breaking apart the way a reflection does when stirring the water's surface.

"Come back!" some cried.

"Don't leave!" said others.

"Please stay!" pleaded more.

He ran screaming until he passed beneath the gate of Braid Cemetery, back onto the empty street. He kept running, now holding his peace, fearful of every sound or movement until he reached the small, grassy yard of his two-story home, where he climbed the peeling crepe myrtle onto the roof, went through his bedroom window and slammed it shut.

He leaped into the solace of his bed and buried himself beneath his blankets, praying the man-made veil would be dense enough to obscure his presence from the things of night once more.

The Idlewild Letters

H.R. Boldwood

*F*rom the missives of Catherine Morgan Chase:

Idlewild Estate
October 1, 1912

Dearest Abigale,

 For reasons unbeknownst to me, The Fates continue to pluck my strings. Barely one year ago, the twisted trio left me widowed and dependent on God's good humor. Now, the fickle sisters return proffering a bountiful olive branch. Their newfound generosity is unsettling, and I find myself pondering that old proverb about Greeks bearing gifts. Still, I marvel at the unexpected windfall that coincided with the arrival of a letter from one Charles Emerson Wilcott, Esquire, of the Colorado Bar Association.

 My spinster aunt, Helena Elizabeth Morgan, passed on rather unexpectedly. An accomplished horsewoman, Helena had gone for her daily ride and not returned. In time, the horse made its way home without her. An extensive search was undertaken, but her body was never recovered. Such a tragic death!

 According to Mr. Wilcott, I am the sole heiress of my aunt's worth, inclusive of her thousand-acre estate. And so it is I write to you as the mistress of my new home, Idlewild, nestled deep within the Rocky Mountains. It should be noted, however, that this blessing comes with its own dark cloud.

Mr. Wilcott warns that I should be wary of a loathsome opportunist named William Telford who wishes to purchase the estate. He is known to be an unscrupulous speculator, relentless in his attempts to swindle unsuspecting victims. As they say, forewarned is forearmed, but a tiny fly, such as Mr. Telford, cannot diminish my anticipation of the new life that awaits me.

Dearest friend, this reversal of fortune leaves me reeling. I pray nightly that The Good Lord looks upon my Aunt Helena with tenderness and mercy; and so, too, I thank Him for this boon. Were I to continue to live in the home I shared with Edmund, memories of our life together would surely swallow me whole with the passage of time. I shall write again soon.

All my love,
Catherine

Idlewild Estate
October 8, 1912

My Dearest Abigale,

I arrived at Idlewild yesterday to find a sprawling, gleaming manse of purest white, with twin stairways cascading to the porch on either side. Guest houses, staff quarters, and stables are within walking distance of the manor. I saw countless elk grazing peacefully in the meadow and multicolored magpies making mischief in the trees. The leaves were ablaze with the fiery hues of autumn, their beauty marred only by the absence of friend or family with whom to share their glory.

Tiny Beatrice frolicked through the carpet of shimmering leaves, her poodle fur a tangle of golds and reds. It is our intention to know every nook and cranny of these grounds.

The interior boasts freshly polished brass and the richest hardwoods, not to mention the most exquisite hand-carved mantles and facades. Such luxury sounds most inviting; and yet, having passed my first night in this new abode, I must confess that I did not sleep well.

The darkness inside these walls is akin to pitch. Perhaps my tired eyes deceived me, but I was certain, if only for a moment, *something* moved within that blackness—something fluid, something without discernible shape, something more elusive than the shroud of night. And then, as if this *something* had not sufficiently caused my heart to palpitate, it whispered my name so softly that the sound whirred inside my ear like a tiny fly. I will disclose to you, though to none other, that this *something* struck me as unnatural.

No doubt, you think me daft! Surely, this episode was triggered by exhaustion; yes, exhaustion borne of this recent upheaval, and nothing more. Pay no heed to my lunacy. A good night's sleep should cure my ills.

How I miss your reassuring smile! I shall write to you often, imagining that you are here with me—my written words but testimony to the conversations we share, my smiles but a reflection of yours as we chatter like a pair of crones seated beside each other on the sofa, wondering where the day has gone.

Yours,
Catherine

Idlewild
October 15, 1912

Dear Abigale,

Though proper introductions have taken place, I endeavor daily to acquaint myself with each of the staff. Having never before been the mistress of a household, I know not how they should regard me. I find them civil yet aloof, with the exception of Mrs. Dunwoody, the English cook, who can always be counted on for a smile or some hysterically inappropriate breech of etiquette. That is, without a doubt, her most endearing quality. She was most sincere in her grief over Aunt Helena's death, and I found her to be my only friend at this new place. I am afraid, given the abominable turn in the weather, that I have monopolized her time.

Rain has fallen each day with a certainty that rivals that of death and taxes. Today at last, the sun returned, and so, I thought to take in the magnificent walled gardens of which Mrs. Dunwoody boasts. It would also be the perfect opportunity to visit the gazebo Mr. Wilcott erected in memoriam of Aunt Helena. The stone walls, eight feet tall and blanketed by English ivy, beckoned me. The paths inside promised new territory to be explored. How devastated I was to find the massive wooden door locked!

Unable to locate Mr. Rousey, the gardener, I left word with his young apprentice, Gilford, requesting Rousey present himself as soon as practicable. He arrived some several hours later, looking none too pleased at having been summoned.

"I have chores need tending to, Mrs. Morgan Chase. How may I help you?"

"You may give me the key to the garden door, sir."

"I don't have it. My boy Gilford could've told you that. If there's nothing else then," he said, turning on his heel.

"Mr. Rousey," I said. "One moment please. We have not yet finished our conversation."

He sighed mightily.

"You are the gardener, are you not? If you do not have the key, then who does?"

"Mr. Wilcott, ma'am."

"Any why, pray tell, would Mr. Wilcott have the key?"

Rousey huffed like a bellows. "Came and got the key from me weeks ago, he did. Said I needn't *concern* myself with the garden 'til spring. He put the new gazebo in the center of the maze, without so much as a by-your-leave, and said he wanted to give it time to settle. If you don't mind me saying, that was rather cheeky of him, undertaking such a project without my input."

I nodded. "Thank you for your concern, Mr. Rousey. That will be all."

Wanting to draft a formal request for a meeting with Wilcott, I ascended the stairway to my study and caught wind of a ghastly odor, so noxious as to cause me to retch. It was at once sickly and sweet, filling my mouth with a vile tang.

So taken aback was I, that I stood stock still, and heard an otherworldly voice whisper, *"Find me!"* Afraid to move, yet maddeningly curious, I followed the source of this spectral plea only to find that it emanated from a portrait of my Aunt Helena! And as God is my witness, I could not lie about such things, upon closer inspection of the portrait, I saw round, wet tears streaming from her eyes! Roiling in waves of nausea and ready to swoon, I grasped the banister to steady myself. I closed my eyes for only a moment. Upon reopening them, the fetid odor had disappeared and the sea of tears had gone bone dry!

Bedeviled to my core, I made for the study and drafted my note to Mr. Wilcott for delivery the following morning.

At last, I lie in my bed beneath the lamplight, sharing my innermost secrets with my dearest friend. Dread gnaws inside my bones, refusing to be squelched. What causes such visions as these? Can this eerie apparition have been self-induced? I have no answers. I know only that the line between reality and fantasy diminishes more each day. Even as I write, the solitary trumpet of an elk breaks the night and yields a mournful moan as if to warn me of danger. It strikes me as a call to arms, though against whom or what, I have yet to learn. Pray that clarity returns.

Yours,
Catherine

Idlewild
October 30, 1912

Dear Sweet Friend,

Imagine my unease when I was informed that a handwritten note from Mr. William Telford arrived for me this morning. It read:

> *Mrs. Morgan Chase,*
> *I am eager to discuss the purchase of your newly inherited estate. You will find that I am a man of singular determination in pursuing that which I want. I shall return at noon tomorrow to discuss this personally.*
> *Sincerely,*
> *William Telford*

Such unmitigated gall! That note, coupled with the fact that I remained unable to access the gardens until Mr. Wilcott appeared, key in hand, left me in need of quick diversion. Beatrice and I set our sights on the curiosities that might lie hidden in the cellar. Imagine my furor at encountering yet another locked door! Mrs. Dunwoody, bucket and mop in tow, happened by as I stomped my foot.

"Ballocks! How is it every door in my house is locked, and I without the key?"

She laughed nearly dropping her bucket. "A bit tightly wrapped today, are we? Ask me, nothing a good grinding wouldn't cure."

I snickered. "Mrs. Dunwoody, you're incorrigible."

"Good Lord! Don't pick that plug-ugly wanker, Wilcott. The man's as mad as a bag o' ferrets."

"Mrs. Dunwoody, please!"

After a protracted bout of tittering, she produced a large key ring from her apron. "Mr. Bag o' Ferrets be damned, I may not have the garden key, but there's not a door inside this house I cannot access. Here you go, dearie, though why you want to play in that dirty hole defies me." She lit the lantern hanging in the doorway and left Beatrice and me to our adventure.

We descended the steps and found ourselves in a tomb-like world where the air was close, smelling of dampness and soil. My footsteps echoed against the stony walls of the cellar, and I felt a cool zephyr threading through the air. Countless crates of castaways, relics, and heirlooms surrounded me and yet, it was the source of the zephyr that intrigued me most. I traced it to a large mahogany chiffonier that lined one of the walls. I leaned against it and pushed sideways. There before me was the obsidian mouth of an earthen tunnel!

Beatrice charged ahead, following her nose, darting to and fro. Having caught a scent, she lifted her head and scampered toward a shaft leading away from the main tunnel. When I caught up to her, she was licking the business end of a pick axe. I took it from her as to examine it more closely and saw a dark stain covering its head. The air grew frigid. Beatrice looked above my head and began to bark. An enormous jolt surged up my arm as if it had been electrified.

What happened next is at best fantastical. I recovered from the galvanizing shock to see Aunt Helena racing through the cuts in the tunnel, breathless, whimpering, and desperate to escape the evil that nipped at her heels. I felt a searing pain as the pick axe tore through her shoulder, and saw her blood burst forth in a spray. The bloodied head of the axe gleamed in the lamplight. My eyes fluttered once, twice, and when they finally closed, I saw a vision of her lying inside a tomb dazed and bleeding. Her faced was screwed in agony, and her moans pricked my ears. All that came after was the scent of flowers and the steady rasp of my breaths.

Upon awakening, I had no time to mourn the sanity that had abandoned me, or wonder whose reflection might greet me when next I glanced into a mirror. I gathered Beatrice into my arms and fled that dark dreadful tunnel, careful to return the chiffonier to its place lest my intrusion be discovered.

Shortly thereafter, Mrs. Dunwoody announced that Mr. Wilcott would be returning within the hour. I retired to change my gown and groom my hair, carefully removing all traces of the tunnel's dust and grime. I watched through the window as he approached and noticed the sky had taken on a nasty hue. I stood at the top of the staircase as Mrs. Dunwoody bade him enter.

"Brought some weather along for company, did you?" she said. "Best stay with us for sup. Wouldn't do to turn you out into a maelstrom."

The delight in his voice was unmistakable. "I accept your kind invitation, ma'am. As it so happens, I have additional matters to discuss with your mistress. Thank you for your courtesy."

As if she sensed my ire at her invitation, Mrs. Dunwoody cast a glance up the stairway in my direction. "Of course. 'Tis not a bother. Besides, me mistress says I have the manners of an Irish cow. She'll be pleased to see my progress. I wanted to thank you too, sir, for taking care of Philip, the stable boy, when old Molly kicked him a good one. 'Twas decent of you to see he lost no pay while on the mend."

"Good lad, Philip," Wilcott said. "Think nothing of it."

I descended the staircase, hiding the blush of embarrassment behind my fan, silently rebuking Mrs. Dunwoody's raucous sense of humor. After welcoming Wilcott, I made no haste in reporting Telford's bold note.

His face turned magenta. "The nervy maggot! He'll not set foot on these grounds. I'll see to it myself. No need to worry, Mrs. Morgan Chase." He offered his arm and escorted me to the dining room.

Supper was served without so much as a peep from Mrs. Dunwoody, who made a hasty retreat to her quarters when the storm began to howl, leaving me alone with Mr. Wilcott.

I folded my napkin neatly on the table and addressed my concerns.

"May I inquire as to why, when you relinquished the estate to me, you failed to turn over the key to the garden door? I attempted to visit my aunt's memorial and was unable to enter."

He paused as if deliberating. "My most humble apologies, madam. Although I attempted to finish the gazebo and the surrounding walkways in time for your arrival, I was unable to do so. Work continues in the area. I retained the key for that purpose."

"There is something else I don't understand. Would you not consult the gardener on the placement of a gazebo? And why order him to suspend his duties in the garden all together?"

Wilcott furrowed his brow. "I did not believe his guidance was necessary. As for his tending the garden, I was being frugal with the funds from your inheritance, and I wished to allow the gazebo to settle before disturbing the surrounding soil. Frankly, knowing something of a woman's mind, I assumed you would have your own tastes as to design and plantings anyway."

"Is that so?" I asked.

"It is."

"You profess to know my mind?"

He squirmed. "Not *your* woman's mind, per se, but the mind of a typical woman."

"You find me atypical?"

"Yes. No. Mrs. Morgan Chase…may I call you Catherine?" His gaze softened. "I find you … intriguing. I am not a young man, but I am a man of considerable means. Please know that I hold you in the highest regard, and would be honored if you would allow me to call upon you."

"'Tis a high compliment you pay me, Mr. Wilcott."

"Please, call me Charles."

I demurred. "Mr. Wilcott, I am freshly widowed, and as you well know, my inheritance leaves me fiscally solvent. I think it best to defer such social activities for the time being."

"In fact, you have been widowed for more than a year." He strolled toward my chair. "A young woman, such as yourself, should consider her future."

I rose to my feet and stared into his eyes. "I trust you can find your way to the room Mrs. Dunwoody prepared for you. The storm should pass soon, leaving you free to travel at first light."

"Yes, of course."

"Mr. Wilcott, one more question, please. May I ask the purpose of the tunnels beneath the estate?"

His eyes widened. "That vermin ridden cellar is no place for a lady. Whatever you may need, I am certain the staff can retrieve for you. But to answer your question, the tunnels were built long ago as underground passages to the stables and residence quarters for use during inclement weather. The snow gets quite deep here in the mountains. Over the years, they have been used for storage as well. Will there be anything else, madam?"

"The key, Mr. Wilcott."

"I beg your pardon?"

"The key to the garden door. I would have it now."

"As you wish." With a paper-thin smile, he placed the key on the dining table and proceeded to his room. I climbed the steps to my suite and locked the door behind me.

Sweet Abigale, I know in my heart the garden holds the key to these preternatural events. I hastily pen this letter, biding my time, waiting for Wilcott to slumber. Storm or no, I intend to steal into the garden tonight to solve this mysterious riddle. Pray for my protection.

Yours,

Catherine

Idlewild

October 31, 1912

Dearest Abigale,

When all was quiet, I crept out to the garden. The rain slowed to a steady drizzle; the wind was brisk, and the night cold. Unlocking the garden door, I held my lantern high to see what lay inside. Row upon row of yew bushes, no more than five feet apart and eight feet tall, woven in elaborate pathways stood before me. And at the heart of this maze towered a gazebo, gleaming white, its latticework edged with intricate trim.

Mr. Wilcott had not misled me. Clearly, the construction was ongoing. Mounds of dirt and open trenches remained. Though visibility was poor, I worked my way to the center of the configuration in much the same way a seamstress threads her needle through densely woven cloth, pushing first here, then there, looking for the path of least resistance.

I climbed the steps to the gazebo and rested my hand against one of its pillars. The wind began to swirl, slowly at first, growing until it reached a frenzy, and finally trapping me in the center of its vortex. Amidst the raging gale, three unmistakable words assailed my ears.

"I am here!"

The heavens let loose; rain burst forth in torrents; thunder pealed and lightning breached the night in a thousand brilliant tendrils. A familiar voice rang out from behind.

"I would have been a good husband to you."

I spun around as another flash of lightning streaked across the sky, to find a man silhouetted against its eerie glow. "Mr. Wilcott!"

His eyes were cold. "I'm afraid you have wandered where you don't belong, my dear. An excavation site is such a dangerous place, what with all the holes. A person could get hurt…or worse."

"What are you doing here?" I cried.

"What do you think? So much like your aunt, you are—sticking your nose into things better left unexamined. As you may have guessed, it cost her." He moved toward me, rope and shovel in hand. "As it will cost you, too."

My cheeks burned. "What a fool I've been! There was no riding accident. There was no accident at all!"

"Of course not. But it was an easy tale to spin. I stabbed her and then carried her through the tunnels. She is buried here beneath this lovely gazebo—a dazzling memorial, if I say so myself." He paused, admiring the details of his handiwork. "Since Philip's injury kept him from the stables, with no one near I simply saddled her horse, led him out unnoticed, and let him find his way home. Voila! Helena fell victim to a tragic death by misadventure. Come, come now. Don't cry. There are far worse places to spend eternity than beneath a lovely garden." He drove the shovel into the ground.

"But why?" I asked. "What had you to gain from her death?"

"Mineral rights, you naive child! This property is a veritable gold mine of minerals." He smiled at his unintended pun. "*Gold mine of minerals.* Witty, don't you think?" He closed the distance between us. "Your aunt caught me mining the tunnel." He hesitated and stared into the driving rain. When he spoke again, his voice barely registered above the storm. "Your aunt was a remarkable woman with an unshakeable sense of honor. She took offense to my stealing the gold out from under her nose. It was my fault. I should have done a better job of concealing my activities, but she threatened to have me arrested. I couldn't have that now, could I? If she'd looked anything like her beautiful niece, I might have romanced the gold out of her, but, truthfully...well, she was a bit long in the tooth for me."

I slapped his face. "How could you?" My mind replayed every moment since arriving at the estate, wondering how I had missed this deception. And it came to me. "To think you named Mr. Telford as the wolf at my door!"

"Silly girl, there is no Telford! He was but a ruse I concocted to frighten you—so you would turn to me." His fingers moved to brush my cheek, but I pulled away. "I thought to woo you, but you spurned my affections. Had you accepted my courtship, we could have shared the wealth. That would have been my preference, but it bears no lasting consequence, for in the event of your death the estate falls to me." He laughed and leaned against the shovel. "A brilliant move, if I say so myself. A tiny codicil buried deep within your trusting aunt's will— one that she failed to read. Enough talk. Time to dig. Oh, not you, my sweet. I may be a murderous thief, but even I would not make a woman dig her own grave."

He trussed my arms to the pillar and pulled large shovelfuls of dirt from the rain-soaked ground. As the hole grew deeper, he became incoherent, railing at the night that Morgan women were as hard as oaks to fell. When the hole reached sufficient depth, he untied me from the pillar and wrestled me into the grave.

"Time to join your auntie, dear. Give her my regards, won't you? This might hurt a tad. So sorry." He raised the shovel high above his head but stopped when he caught sight of a specter churning and swirling in the raging sky atop the gazebo. It hovered in a roiling mass, twisting and turning before finally settling into a transparent likeness of Aunt Helena.

"No! This cannot be!" he screamed. "You are dead!"

So transfixed was Wilcott that he stood like a statue, the shovel still raised high above his head.

Noting his distraction, I clawed at the sides of the grave, pushing my hands and feet deep into the saturated soil over and over, hoisting myself out and away from the hole. Just as quickly as the specter had materialized, it faded, and a blinding flash of lightning descended like the finger of Zeus, striking Wilcott's shovel.

Wilcott flailed at the grave's edge like a beach-stranded fish, wearing a grotesque death mask I shall ne'er unsee; eyes popping, mouth agape, hair aflame. The stench of his burning flesh stung my nose as he toppled face first into the open grave. The displaced dirt began to flow like a river of mud, rolling and sliding, returning to the hole, backfilling the grave until no trace of him remained.

Wet, cold and spent, I stumbled back to the manor wondering if my eyes and ears had deceived me, or if sleep would alter my perspective of the night's events. And I marveled at the tenacity of Aunt Helena, who had crossed the void in spectral form to save me.

Astonishing as it may sound, morning has now dawned, and the facts remain unchanged. Perhaps, The Fates have finally made their peace with me, for even as I write, snow lays the first of winter's blankets on Idlewild, burying the malignant ghosts of the past. And life begins anew.

Today, with head held high and heartbeat strong, I claim my place among these mountains. I belong to this land even as it belongs to me, for the blood of Helena Morgan runs through my veins. Only now, do I understand the true depth of my inheritance.

I am Catherine Morgan Chase, niece of the extraordinary Helena Elizabeth Morgan. And I am the rightful mistress of Idlewild.

Your loving friend,

Catherine

The Red-Haired Girl
A Wife's Story
S. Baring-Gould

In 1876, we took a house in one of the best streets and parts of B—. I do not give the name of the street or the number of the house, because the circumstances that occurred in that place were such as to make people nervous, and shy—unreasonably so—of taking those lodgings, after reading our experiences therein.

We were a small family—my husband, a grown-up daughter, and myself; and we had two maids—a cook, and the other was house-and-parlor maid in one. We had not been a fortnight in the house before my daughter said to me one morning: "Mamma, I do not like Jane," —that was our house-parlor maid.

"Why so?" I asked. "She seems respectable, and she does her work systematically. I have no fault to find with her, none whatever."

"She may do her work," said Bessie, my daughter, "but I dislike inquisitiveness."

"Inquisitiveness!" I exclaimed. "What do you mean? Has she been looking into your drawers?"

"No, Mamma, but she watches me. It is hot weather now, and when I am in my room, occasionally, I leave my door open whilst writing a letter, or doing any little bit of needlework, and then I am almost certain to hear her outside. If I turn sharply round, I see her slipping out of sight. It is most annoying. I really was unaware that I was such an interesting personage as to make it worth anyone's while to spy out my proceedings."

"Nonsense, my dear. You are sure it is Jane?"

"Well—I suppose so." There was a slight hesitation in her voice. "If not Jane, who can it be?"

"Are you sure it is not Cook?"

"Oh, no, it is not Cook; she is busy in the kitchen. I have heard her there, when I have gone outside my room upon the landing, after having caught that girl watching me."

"If you have caught her," said I, "I suppose you spoke to her about the impropriety of her conduct."

"Well, caught is the wrong word. I have not actually *caught* her at it. Only today I distinctly heard her at my door, and I saw her back as she turned to run away, when I went towards her."

"But you followed her, of course?"

"Yes, but I did not find her on the landing when I got outside."

"Where was she, then?"

"I don't know."

"But did you not go and see?"

"She slipped away with astonishing celerity," said Bessie.

"I can take no steps in the matter. If she does it again, speak to her and remonstrate."

"But I never have a chance. She is gone in a moment."

"She cannot get away so quickly as all that."

"Somehow, she does."

"And you are sure it is Jane?" again I asked; and again, she replied: "If not Jane, who else can it be? There is no one else in the house."

So, this unpleasant matter ended, for the time. The next intimation of something of the sort proceeded from another quarter—in fact, from Jane herself. She came to me some days later and said, with some embarrassment in her tone—

"If you please, ma'am, if I do not give satisfaction, I would rather leave the situation."

"Leave!" I exclaimed. "Why, I have not given you the slightest cause. I have not found fault with you for anything as yet, have I, Jane?

On the contrary, I have been much pleased with the thoroughness of your work. And you are always tidy and obliging."

"It isn't that, ma'am; but I don't like being watched whatever I do."

"Watched!" I repeated. "What do you mean? You surely do not suppose that I am running after you when you are engaged on your occupations. I assure you I have other and more important things to do."

"No, ma'am, I don't suppose you do."

"Then, who watches you?"

"I think it must be Miss Bessie."

"Miss Bessie!" I could say no more, I was so astounded.

"Yes, ma'am. When I am sweeping out a room, and my back is turned, I hear her at the door; and when I turn myself about, I just catch a glimpse of her running away. I see her skirts—"

"Miss Bessie is above doing anything of the sort."

"If it is not Miss Bessie, who is it, ma'am?"

There was a tone of indecision in her voice.

"My good Jane," said I, "set your mind at rest. Miss Bessie could not act as you suppose. Have you seen her on these occasions and assured yourself that it is she?"

"No, ma'am, I've not, so to speak, seen her face; but I know it ain't Cook, and I'm sure it ain't you, ma'am; so, who else can it be?"

I considered for some moments, and the maid stood before me in dubious mood.

"You say you saw her skirts. Did you recognize the gown? What did she wear?"

"It was a light cotton print—more like a maid's morning dress."

"Well, set your mind at ease; Miss Bessie has not got such a frock as you describe."

"I don't think she has," said Jane; "but there was someone at the door, watching me, who ran away when I turned myself about."

"Did she run upstairs or down?"

"I don't know. I did go out on the landing, but there was no one there. I'm sure it wasn't Cook, for I heard her clattering the dishes down in the kitchen at the time."

"Well, Jane, there is some mystery in this. I will not accept your notice; we will let matters stand over till we can look into this complaint of yours and discover the rights of it."

"Thank you, ma'am. I'm very comfortable here, but it is unpleasant to suppose that one is not trusted, and is spied on wherever one goes and whatever one is about."

A week later, after dinner one evening, when Bessie and I had quit the table and left my husband to his smoke, Bessie said to me, when we were in the drawing room together: "Mamma, it is not Jane."

"What is not Jane?" I asked.

"It is not Jane who watches me."

"Who can it be, then?"

"I don't know."

"And how is it that you are confident that you are not being observed by Jane?"

"Because I have seen her—that is to say, her head."

"When? Where?"

"Whilst dressing for dinner, I was before the glass doing my hair, when I saw in the mirror someone behind me. I had only the two candles lighted on the table, and the room was otherwise dark. I thought I heard someone stirring—just the sort of stealthy step I have come to recognize as having troubled me so often. I did not turn, but looked steadily before me into the glass, and I could see reflected therein someone—a woman with red hair. Then, I moved from my place quickly. I heard steps of some person hurrying away, but I saw no one."

"The door was open?"

"No, it was shut."

"But where did she go?"

"I do not know, Mamma. I looked everywhere in the room and could find no one. I have been quite upset. I cannot tell what to think of this. I feel utterly unhinged."

"I noticed at table that you did not appear well, but I said nothing about it. Your father gets so alarmed, and fidgets and fusses, if he thinks that there is anything the matter with you. But this is a most extraordinary story."

"It is an extraordinary fact," said Bessie.

"You have searched your room thoroughly?"

"I have looked into every corner."

"And there is no one there?"

"No one. Would you mind, Mamma, sleeping with me tonight? I am so frightened. Do you think it can be a ghost?"

"Ghost? Fiddlesticks!"

I made some excuse to my husband and spent the night in Bessie's room. There was no disturbance that night of any sort, and although my daughter was excited and unable to sleep till long after midnight, she did fall into refreshing slumber at last, and in the morning said to me: "Mamma, I think I must have fancied that I saw something in the glass. I dare say my nerves were over-wrought."

I was greatly relieved to hear this, and I arrived at much the same conclusion as did Bessie, but was again bewildered, and my mind unsettled by Jane, who came to me just before lunch, when I was alone, and said—

"Please, ma'am, it's only fair to say, but it's not Miss Bessie."

"What is not Miss Bessie? I mean, who is not Miss Bessie?"

"Her as is spying on me."

"I told you it could not be she. Who is it?"

"Please, ma'am, I don't know. It's a red-haired girl."

"But, Jane, be serious. There is no red-haired girl in the house."

"I know there ain't, ma'am. But for all that, she spies on me."

"Be reasonable, Jane," I said, disguising the shock her words produced on me. "If there be no red-haired girl in the house, how can you have one watching you?"

"I don't know; but one does."

"How do you know that she is red-haired?"

"Because I have seen her."

"When?"

"This morning."

"Indeed?"

"Yes, ma'am. I was going upstairs, when I heard steps coming softly after me—the backstairs, ma'am; they're rather dark and steep, and there's no carpet on them, as on the front stairs, and I was sure I heard someone following me; so I twisted about, thinking it might be Cook, but it wasn't. I saw a young woman in a print dress, and the light as came from the window at the side fell on her head, and it was carrots—reg'lar carrots."

"Did you see her face?"

"No, ma'am; she put her arm up and turned and ran downstairs, and I went after her, but I never found her."

"You followed her—how far?"

"To the kitchen. Cook was there. And I said to Cook, says I: 'Did you see a girl come this way?' And she said, short-like, 'No.'"

"And Cook saw nothing at all?"

"Nothing. She didn't seem best pleased at my asking. I suppose I frightened her, as I'd been telling her about how I was followed and spied on."

I mused a moment only, and then said solemnly,

"Jane, what you want is a *pill*. You are suffering from hallucinations. I know a case very much like yours; and take my word for it that, in your condition of liver or digestion, a pill is a sovereign remedy. Set your mind at rest; this is a mere delusion, caused by pressure on the optic nerve. I will give you a pill tonight when you go to bed, another tomorrow, a third on the day after, and that will settle the red-haired girl. You will see no more of her."

"You think so, ma'am?"

"I am sure of it."

On consideration, I thought it as well to mention the matter to the cook—a strange, reserved woman, not given to talking, who did her work admirably, but whom, for some inexplicable reason, I did not like. If I had considered a little further as to how to broach the subject, I should perhaps have proved more successful; but by not doing so I rushed the question and obtained no satisfaction.

I had gone down to the kitchen to order dinner, and the difficult question had arisen how to dispose of the scraps from yesterday's joint.

"Rissoles, ma'am?"

"No," said I, "not rissoles. Your master objects to them."

"Then perhaps croquettes?"

"They are only rissoles in disguise."

"Perhaps cottage pie?"

"No; that is inorganic rissole, a sort of protoplasm out of which rissoles are developed."

"Then, ma'am, I might make a hash."

"Not an ordinary, barefaced, rudimentary hash?"

"No, ma'am, with French mushrooms, or truffles, or tomatoes."

"Well—yes—perhaps. By the way, talking of tomatoes, who is that red-haired girl who has been about the house?"

"Can't say, ma'am."

I noticed at once that the eyes of the cook contracted, her lips tightened, and her face assumed a half-defiant, half-terrified look.

"You have not many friends in this place, have you, Cook?"

"No, ma'am, none."

"Then, who can she be?"

"Can't say, ma'am."

"You can throw no light on the matter? It is very unsatisfactory having a person about the house—and she has been seen upstairs—of whom one knows nothing."

"No doubt, ma'am."

"And you cannot enlighten me?"

"She is no friend of mine."

"Nor is she of Jane's. Jane spoke to me about her. Has she remarked concerning this girl to you?"

"Can't say, ma'am, as I notice all Jane says. She talks a good deal."

"You see, there must be someone who is a stranger and who has access to this house. It is most awkward."

"Very so, ma'am."

I could get nothing more from the cook. I might as well have talked to a log; and, indeed, her face assumed a wooden look as I continued to speak to her on the matter. So, I sighed, and said, "Very well, hash with tomato," and went upstairs.

A few days later the house-parlor maid said to me, "Please, ma'am, may I have another pill?"

"Pill!" I exclaimed. "Why?"

"Because I have seen her again. She was behind the curtains, and I caught her putting out her red head to look at me."

"Did you see her face?"

"No; she up with her arm over it and scuttled away."

"This is strange. I do not think I have more than two liver pills left in the box, but to those you are welcome. Only I should recommend a different treatment. Instead of taking them yourself, the moment you see, or fancy that you see, the red-haired girl, go at her with the box and threaten to administer the pills to her. That will rout her, if anything will."

"But she will not stop for the pills."

"The threat of having them forced on her every time she shows herself will disconcert her. Conceive, I am supposing, that on each occasion Miss Bessie, or I, were to meet you on the stairs, in a room, on the landing, in the hall, we were to rush on you and force, let us say, castor-oil globules between your lips. You would give notice at once."

"Yes; so, I should, ma'am."

"Well, try this upon the red-haired girl. It will prove infallible."

"Thank you, ma'am; what you say seems reasonable."

Whether Bessie saw more of the puzzling apparition, I cannot say. She spoke no further on the matter to me; but that may have been so as to cause me no further uneasiness. I was unable to resolve the question to my own satisfaction—whether what had been seen was a real person, who obtained access to the house in some unaccountable manner, or whether it was, what I have called it, an apparition.

As far as I could ascertain, nothing had been taken away. The movements of the red-haired girl were not those of one who sought to pilfer. They seemed to me rather those of one not in her right mind; and on this supposition I made inquiries in the neighborhood as to the existence in our street, in any of the adjoining houses, of a person wanting in her wits, who was suffered to run about at will. But I could obtain no information that at all threw light on a point to me so perplexing.

Hitherto, I had not mentioned the topic to my husband. I knew so well that I should obtain no help from him, that I made no effort to seek it. He would "Pish!" and "Pshaw!" and make some slighting reference to women's intellects, and not further trouble himself about the matter.

But one day, to my great astonishment, he referred to it himself.

"Julia," said he, "do you observe how I have cut myself in shaving?"

"Yes, dear," I replied. "You have cotton-wool sticking to your jaw, as if you were growing a white whisker on one side."

"It bled a great deal," said he.

"I am sorry to hear it."

"And I mopped up the blood with the new toilet cover."

"Never!" I exclaimed. "You haven't been so foolish as to do that?"

"Yes. And that is just like you. You are much more concerned about your toilet-cover being stained than about my poor cheek which is gashed."

"You were very clumsy to do it," was all I could say. Married people are not always careful to preserve the amenities in private life. It is a pity, but it is so.

"It was due to no clumsiness on my part," said he, "though I do allow my nerves have been so shaken, broken, by married life, that I cannot always command my hand, as was the case when I was a bachelor. But this time it was due to that new, stupid, red-haired servant you have introduced into the house without consulting me or my pocket."

"Red-haired servant!" I echoed.

"Yes, that red-haired girl I have seen about. She thrusts herself into my study in a most offensive and objectionable way. But the climax of all was this morning, when I was shaving. I stood in my shirt before the glass, and had lathered my face, and was engaged on my right jaw, when that red-haired girl rushed between me and the mirror with both her elbows up, screening her face with her arms, and her head bowed. I started back, and in so doing cut myself."

"Where did she come from?"

"How can I tell? I did not expect to see anyone."

"Then, where did she go?"

"I do not know; I was too concerned about my bleeding jaw to look about me. That girl must be dismissed."

"I wish she could be dismissed," I said.

"What do you mean?"

I did not answer my husband, for I really did not know what answer to make.

I was now the only person in the house who had not seen the red-haired girl, except possibly the cook, from whom I could gather nothing, but whom I suspected of knowing more concerning this mysterious apparition than she chose to admit. That what had been seen by Bessie and Jane was a supernatural visitant, I now felt convinced, seeing that it had appeared to that least imaginative and most commonplace of all individuals, my husband. By no mental process could he have been got to imagine anything. He certainly did see this red-haired girl, and that no living, corporeal maid had been in his dressing room at the time I was perfectly certain.

I was soon, however, myself to be included in the number of those before whose eyes she appeared. It was in this wise.

Cook had gone out to do some marketing. I was in the breakfast room, when, wanting a funnel to fill a little phial of brandy I always keep on the washstand in case of emergencies, I went to the head of the kitchen stairs, to descend and fetch what I required. Then, I was aware of a great clattering of the fire irons below, and a banging about of the boiler and grate. I went down the steps very hastily and entered the kitchen.

There I saw a figure of a short, set girl in a shabby cotton gown, not over clean, and slipshod, stooping before the stove, and striking the fender with the iron poker. She had fiery red hair, very untidy.

I uttered an exclamation.

Instantly she dropped the poker, and covering her face with her arms, uttering a strange, low cry, she dashed round the kitchen table, making nearly the complete circuit, and then swept past me, and I heard her clattering up the kitchen stairs.

I was too much taken aback to follow. I stood as one petrified. I felt dazed and unable to trust either my eyes or my ears.

Something like a minute must have elapsed before I had sufficiently recovered to turn and leave the kitchen. Then, I ascended slowly and, I confess, nervously. I was fearful lest I should find the red-haired girl cowering against the wall, and that I should have to pass her.

But nothing was to be seen. I reached the hall, and saw that no door was open from it except that of the breakfast room. I entered and thoroughly examined every recess, corner, and conceivable hiding place, but could find no one there. Then, I ascended the staircase, with my hand on the balustrade, and searched all the rooms on the first floor, without the least success. Above were the servants' apartments, and I now resolved on mounting to them. Here, the staircase was uncarpeted. As I was ascending, I heard Jane at work in her room. I then heard her come out hastily upon the landing. At the same moment, with a rush past me, uttering the same moan, went the red-haired girl. I am sure I felt her skirts sweep my dress. I did not notice her till she was close upon me, but I did distinctly see her as she passed. I turned, and saw no more.

I at once mounted to the landing where was Jane.

"What is it?" I asked.

"Please, ma'am, I've seen the red-haired girl again, and I did as you recommended. I went at her rattling the pill box, and she turned and ran downstairs. Did you see her, ma'am, as you came up?"

"How inexplicable!" I said. I would not admit to Jane that I had seen the apparition.

The situation remained unaltered for a week. The mystery was unsolved. No fresh light had been thrown on it. I did not again see or hear anything out of the way; nor did my husband, I presume, for he made no further remarks relative to the extra servant who had caused him so much annoyance. I presume he supposed that I had summarily dismissed her. This I conjectured from a smugness assumed by his face, such as it always acquired when he had carried a point against me—which was not often.

However, one evening, abruptly, we had a new sensation. My husband, Bessie, and I were at dinner, and we were partaking of the soup, Jane standing by, waiting to change our plates and to remove the tureen, when we dropped our spoons, alarmed by fearful screams issuing from the kitchen. By the way, characteristically, my husband finished his soup before he laid down the spoon and said, "Good gracious! What is that?"

Bessie, Jane, and I were by this time at the door, and we rushed together to the kitchen stairs, and one after the other ran down them. I was the first to enter, and I saw Cook wrapped in flames, and a paraffin lamp on the floor broken, and the blazing oil flowing over it.

I had sufficient presence of mind to catch up the coconut matting which was not impregnated with the oil, and to throw it round Cook, wrap her tightly in it, and force her down on the floor where not overflowed by the oil. I held her thus, and Bessie succored me. Jane was too frightened to do other than scream. The cries of the burnt woman were terrible. Presently my husband appeared.

"Dear me! Bless me! Good gracious!" he said.

"You go away and fetch a doctor," I called to him. "You can be of no possible service here—you'll only get in our way."

"But the dinner?"

"Bother the dinner! Run for a surgeon."

In a little while we had removed the poor woman to her room, she shrieking the whole way upstairs; and, when there, we laid her on the bed, and kept her folded in the coconut matting till a medical man arrived, in spite of her struggles to be free. My husband, on this occasion, acted with commendable promptness; but whether because he was impatient for the completion of his meal, or whether his sluggish nature was for once touched with human sympathy, it is not for me to say.

All I know is that, so soon as the surgeon was there, I dismissed Jane with, "There, go and get your master the rest of his dinner, and leave us with Cook."

The poor creature was frightfully burnt. She was attended to devotedly by Bessie and myself, till a nurse was obtained from the hospital. For hours she was as one mad with terror as much as with pain.

The next day she was quieter and sent for me. I hastened to her, and she begged the nurse to leave the room. I took a chair and seated myself by her bedside, and expressed my profound commiseration, and told her that I should like to know how the accident had taken place.

"Ma'am, it was the red-haired girl that did it."

"The red-haired girl!"

"Yes, ma'am. I took a lamp to look how the fish was getting on, and all at once I saw her rush straight at me, and I—I backed away, thinking she would knock me down, and the lamp fell over and smashed, and my clothes caught, and—"

"Oh, Cook! You should not have taken the lamp."

"It's done. And she would never leave me alone till she had burnt or scalded me. You needn't be afraid—she don't haunt the house. It is *me* she has haunted, because of what I did to her."

"Then, you know her?"

"She was in service with me, as kitchen maid, at my last place, near Cambridge. I took a sort of hate against her; she was such a slattern and so inquisitive. She peeped into my letters, and turned out my box and drawers, she was ever prying; and when I spoke to her, she was that saucy! I reg'lar hated her. And one day she was kneeling by the stove, and I was there, too, and I suppose the devil possessed me, for I upset the boiler as was on the hot-plate right upon her, just as she looked up, and it poured over her face and bosom, and arms, and scalded her that dreadful, she died. And since then, she has haunted me. But she'll do so no more. She won't trouble you further. She has done for me, as she has always minded to do, since I scalded her to death."

The unhappy woman did not recover.

"Dear me! No hope?" said my husband, when informed that the surgeon despaired of her. "And good cooks are so scarce. By the way, that red-haired girl?"

"Gone—gone forever," I said.

You are Such a One
Nancy Springer

You *could not be a more middle-aged, middle-class,* middle-American, menopausal woman. You know this because you are driving alone and dutifully to the funeral of a family member whom you never met, and you are counting your hot flashes to pass the time. (Twelve so far.) You know how middle-everything you are, because you had trouble getting time off, and you have worked at the same bank for twenty-three years, and you are still a teller while a guy who trained along with you is now the vice-president, yet you process millions of dollars with your tastefully manicured hands and never sneak one for yourself. You have been married even longer, and you have never cheated at that job either, and know you never will, just as you know that when you sleep tonight you will dream—and even your dream is predictable. Nearly every night for years and years you have dreamed the exact same vivid dream, a night sweat of the mind, a hallucinatory hot flash to be disregarded like your other symptoms; nobody wants to hear about it.

The cell phone on the passenger seat next to you remains silent as you drive. During personal heat wave *du jour* number thirteen, a broiler, torrid enough to make you yearn to shred your navy-blue suit, you see your exit and get off the interstate. You have planned ahead, made yourself a motel reservation, but several miles later you start to worry; was that perhaps the wrong exit? You are driving down the middle of a rudimentary road, a country lane in Nebraska, where you have never in your life been before.

You would swear a court deposition to that fact.

Yet, rounding a curve, you flash not hot but sweaty cold, for before you manifests the intimately, impossibly familiar.

The house.

You slam on the brakes.

You stare through your trifocals.

It *is* the house from the dream.

Your dream. Your repetitive nightly dream. Always the same, always eidetically clear, the dream in which you enter this house.

Not what one would usually consider a dream house. A modest dwelling—yet unmistakable. You recognize it in the holistic, coded-into-your-DNA way you would recognize your mother's face if she were alive, yet you would have just as much difficulty describing it. Except for disjunctive details. The gazebo. The sundial, the birdbath, the celadon-green gazing ball. Circular things. Over the front door, a stained-glass rose window. Somewhere inside, you know, is a spiral staircase. Every night in your dream you walk up the trapezoidal steps, wearing a soft gown that petals you as if you were a lily, barefoot—

A horn toots briefly, politely. Behind you, a local in a pickup is waiting for you to get out of the middle of the road.

You pull over in front of the house to let him pass, and thus decide that you are going to stop for just a few minutes, see whether anyone is home, ask questions. You get out of your car, telling yourself that there must be an explanation, that perhaps your parents brought you here when you were two or three, that you are having a déjà vu experience beyond conscious memory—but what would your parents have been doing here? In this state of Nebraska and confusion?

Although you don't like to call attention to yourself—no, it's more than reticence; admit the truth: you are irrationally afraid. Although feeling spooked, you walk toward the house. In the navy-blue business suit that absolutely does not petal you like any flower, you stride across the lawn before you lose your nerve. The place is neither landscaped nor unkempt. Bushes, inert and taupe now in winter, stand at random distances from one another, ovoid or globular. Husks of last fall's chrysanthemums flank the front door. You look for a doorbell; there is none. You knock. Solid wood, the door barely acknowledges. You knock again, harder, then hear footsteps within.

The door is opened by a rather short, unremarkable man, dark of hair and skin, perhaps Latino. Ordinary—and you cannot admit even to yourself how relieved you are to see just an ordinary man— except that when *he* sees *you*, the generous russet and olive tints of his face fade like old shingles to gray.

"Please excuse me for intruding," you say, concerned by his reaction and trying to put him at ease, for you are the sort of person who is always thinking of others, "but I wonder if you would tell me something about this house. Is it yours?"

The man swallows twice before answering, "No, senora. I am the, how you say, the caretaker."

"Really?" You are surprised, for the residence seems middle-class, like you, not upscale enough for the sort of people who would have servants. "Do the owners live here only in the summer, then?"

"The owners live here not at all."

"What? Why not?"

"Because the gringos, they call it, how you say, *haunted*. But to my people—"

Involuntarily you echo, "Haunted?"

"Yes, senora."

"But—but what do you mean, haunted?"

"You should know, senora. *You* are the ghost."

§

Only yesterday, you were joking with one of the other tellers about being invisible. Short, graying, and perhaps potty trained a bit too early, you had stood unnoticed at a lunch counter while half a dozen other people rushed in front of you and were served. This sort of thing has been happening to you for years. Asked why you do not speak up, you say you don't like to make a fuss.

This is true. You are a very civilized person. So why, now, are you barking like a chimpanzee, "*What?* What did you say?"

Humbly the Latino man attempts to explain. "I have many times myself seen you on the escalera, senora. You are the ghost who—"

Why, now, are you interrupting? Shouting? "I am not a ghost!"

"Pardon, senora—"

"I am not a ghost!" Your fists curl, your head lowers, your chin juts, you step toward him. Yet, because you know your middle name is Meek, you are surprised when he yelps, says something prayerful in Spanish, and retreats, shutting the door. You hear the click as he locks it.

You now learn what it means to be "beside oneself." Who is this woman pounding on the white door with both fists, shouting "Open up! I am not finished with you! I am not a ghost!" Beside yourself, you discover that you know how to curse. Beside yourself, you learn that shouting feeds upon cursing as you stamp back to your car, yelling, "I am not a ghost! God damn it all to hell! I am not a ghost!" Beside yourself, you spray gravel as you rev out of there.

In a few moments you reduce speed, cease shouting and begin instead to weep. You now know that you are not, after all, going to your great-uncle whatshisface's funeral, but you have no idea why you are crying.

§

In the nearest town you find a cheap motel where you book a room, paying with cash. You do not bother to cancel your reservation at the other motel and save the money that will otherwise be charged to your credit card. Any such practical considerations seem to have flown out of a circular stained-glass window. Lying atop a linty chenille bedspread, you eye your cell phone, which remains silent. Your husband has not called. You will not call him. Many times he has made it clear that he does not want to hear about your "damn stupid dream." He will not care whether you are a ghost or not.

You turn the cell phone off and let it drop to the floor.

You now stare at the ceiling. Cheap tiles. Square. No circles anywhere.

Menopausal heat comes and goes. You are a geyser that spouts sweat at irregular intervals; you are no longer keeping track of the eruptions.

In your cavernous gut, hunger crawls. But not the sort that food would satisfy. So, you just lie where dust mites roam. For a long time. As day turns to dark.

And as you slowly, slowly go to sleep, making the transition so gradually that you become mindful of what you are doing.

Therefore, things are subtly different. This time, even though the dream is, as always, ineffably right—the starry night in which you can see without any other light, your lily-petal gown so soft, flowing to your bare feet that feel no cold, that stand upon the compass-rose tiled floor of the gazebo, where you always begin—even though this is perfection, you feel muted resentment, because you should not be a ghost. Why are you haunting? Yet, as if you have no control of your own body—or no, not body, for you are floating, incorporeal, and you sullenly love your freedom from glands and heat and weight—as if you have no control over your being, you glide into the nightly ritual. Issuing forth from the encirclement of the gazebo, you circle the house, caressing the gazing globe the color of a Luna Moth, the birdbath, the sundial, and—

And it is winter; you are tired of winter; you want wild green grass and the heady fragrance of springtime blossoms. Since you are asleep and this is just a dream, why can't you have them? It's about time you had something you want. You touch a sere, bulbous bush, and it bursts into yellow bloom; forsythia. There. Under your feet, lawn like emerald fire springs up, and puffball mushrooms; you stand at the center of a ring of them fit for pixies to dance in.

The white puffballs are a gift; you would never have thought of them. But a gift from what? Or from whom? Bemused, you continue your rounds, wafting into the house through the rose of stained glass.

Inside, things are not professionally decorated but not a dump either, just tidy and boring except for the circular pedestal table with antique doily, which—as always—attracts you down to ground level, as if it were put there for that reason. This time, however, as you stand admiring the detail of the doily, an area rug springs up beneath your feet, its lilac-and-daffodil yang/yin circle quite at variance with the otherwise staid furnishings.

As is the stairway, its open spiral an unusual feature in a middle-class house like this. Drifting over there, you wonder what's upstairs. Even though you have climbed the spiral in a thousand dreams or more, you do not remember what you find at the top. The difference this time is that you know you are dreaming, so you know that you should know, and your own blankness annoys you. The mystery at the top of the spiral is, after all, the hub of the matter, and why did you not realize this before?

You begin to climb. You could simply waft up there the way you wafted through the rose window, but you enjoy the novelty of ascending the stairway without effort, unlabored by the mass of your own body, as if each bleached wooden riser were a springboard. With one hand clinging to the central pillar you swing, ascending, with your long weightless gown fluttering; you are white ribbon unwinding, unwinding up a maypole to—where? At the top of the stairs, you can see now, is a closed door, quite a curious and fascinating wooden door, painted shrimp pink, its arched top carved with a circular motif. Distracted like a child from play, you hurry the rest of the way. The carving on the door is rather like the doily on the pedestal table, radial symmetry at its most intricate and beautiful, but unreadable.

You try the door. It is locked. Which is not fair, because this is *your* room, you know with sudden ontological certainty. Don't the idiots realize that's the whole reason you keep coming here, to get into your room? How dare they try to—

Wait a minute. They can't keep you out. There's a carved circle on the door. You can waft right through, the way you flew into the house through the rose window. You're a ghost.

No. No, you're not a ghost. Not.

Suddenly furious, like a cop on TV you kick the door, meaning to break it down. Your bare foot feels no pain from the impact, for there is none. Instead, your impetus carries you halfway through the door. Your foot comes down inside. Your head stops approximately in the middle of the carved circle.

You are looking at your room.

Yes, it is your room.

Square.

Bare.

Windowless.

Colorless.

Unpainted, uncarpeted.

Small.

Low.

Empty.

§

Driving past the house the next day, you see a forsythia bush in full bloom, although winter reigns all around. You see a patch of emerald-green grass wearing its own white pearl necklace. You see the Latino caretaker standing in the front yard peering at these manifestations. And for the first time since you woke up weeping in the night, you begin to sense that you need not despair.

You begin to feel inklings of possibility.

You feel a heat in you, but it is not just another hot flash; it is white fire kindling at your core, so that the fountain can burst forth.

But this is daytime, and daytime is rife with doubt. Can you—will you truly do it? Any of it? Things you never knew you had within you?

As never before, you long for night, for sleep.

§

A few days later, driving past the house, you see that a cupola has sprouted, as round and sudden as a mushroom, from its roof.

Smiling, you drive in as if you own the place—which in effect you do—and park in front. The caretaker, when he opens the door, bursts into a torrent of distraught Spanish and tries to shut you out, but anticipating this move, you have, in time-honored style, inserted your foot, protectively clad in a hiking boot that goes with your new blue jeans and colorful nylon jacket. Gesturing with palms down, you gaze at the man with the expression of benevolent and competent concern that has served you well from behind the teller's window. You are a nice person. A civilized person. It is a shame for anyone to shout at you. The caretaker's spate falters, and you address him with great sincerity, "I believe we can help each other. Did I understand you to say that your people know all about ghosts?"

His passion wheels like a condor on a changing wind. "Si! Si, senora, in my lifetime I alone, four ghosts I have met. Mi tia, sister of my father. . ."

Sometime later, inside, seated on the beige sofa and drinking an execrable South American brand of powdered instant coffee, you have learned that his aunt after dying at four in the morning, had gone to sit on the beds of all the neighbors in her village, unwilling to leave. He is from Chile, where people live all their lives in the one village so poor. Here in the *Estadas Unidas* he is rich, he has the automobile, he sends money home to his sisters. His grandmother after death had come back as a cold miasma terrorizing her family until all the babies were christened. Here in the *Estadas Unidas* he lives in the house very nice and his employers are good to him; he does not know what to tell them about the new room upstairs. His mother, who died in childbirth, came back every night to pull the hair of his father sleeping.

"But I am alive," you point out after a while. "How can I be a ghost?"

"How do I know that you are alive, senora?"

"You are sitting here talking with me."

"Stranger things have happened."

You explain to him about the sleeping, the dreams, the coincidence that led to your finding the house.

"It was no, how you say, coincidence, senora. Your great-uncle now dead, he led you here."

"But I didn't even know him. I was just going to his funeral because I thought I ought to."

"He led you here, maybe, same reason. Family is family."

"But I am not a ghost!" Seeing his face stiffen, quickly you soften your tone. "I do not want to be a ghost. Do you think your mother wanted to be a ghost?"

"No, senora, of course not. The ghosts, they, how you say, *haunt*, because they are unhappy."

"Oh," you say rather weakly, because once again it is too true, although you have seldom acknowledged your unhappiness; discontentment, like larceny or adultery, you have allowed no mental compass.

"Why, senora, have you caused the circle room upstairs, with the bed in it?"

You do not tell him how the empty shoebox of a room made you wake up to find yourself in a cheap motel bed weeping, or attempt to explain the white fire fountain that ensued within your chest, the manifestations you yourself do not fully understand. Instead, you say, "When I sleep somewhere else, in my dream I come here and haunt this house, is that not true?"

"Si, indeed I have seen it many times with my own eyes. So?"

"So, if I sleep here, in my very own room, then what is there for me to haunt?"

§

Everything about your room makes you feel exalted: the dome ceiling with circular skylight, the countryside view from your six arched windows, the glass bubbles floating and emanating a firefly glow above your head, the soft round rug with its pattern ever gently shifting like a pastel kaleidoscope, the similarly changeful mandala mosaics on the walls, the flower-shaped pillows on which you will rest your head, the sheer undeniable reality that it is daytime yet you have climbed the spiral staircase and opened the arched door and there is your condign dwelling just as you have shaped it in your dreams.

The caretaker remains at the bottom of what he calls the "ladder," the stairs. He will approach no nearer. Most reluctantly he has agreed to this experiment. "For one night only," he repeats for perhaps the fifteenth time, shouting up from his distance, although he knows as well as you do that it will not be for one night only. "You need anything? I am leaving."

This raises your eyebrows. "Are you frightened?"

"But *si*, yes." He does not deny it the way an American man would. "Are you not?"

"No, not at all! I am very…" With astonishment you realize what you are saying, and how true it is. "I am very happy."

"*Ai caramba!*" Complaining to Madre Maria, he goes away.

You truly do not need anything from him; once more you do not require food. The bed, a great water lily, floats on its kaleidoscope carpet pad, and you wish only to recline into its white softness. You do so, lying like a compass pointing five ways, and you gaze, gaze up through the skylight, watching blue and white turn to puce, greige, twilight and night. Unsleeping, you have nevertheless passed into a state in which you know no time. You gaze at the indigo sky, and like your reflection in a dark mirror the moon gazes back at you, a middle-aged moon in all her full-circle glory, wheeling luminous into her waning.

You are such a one. Why, oh why, does the world find you invisible? The world must be sleeping.

You sleep. You do not realize you are asleep until you find yourself outside of a house. A development house, triangles on top of rectangles, taupe, of course. The new houses are all taupe unless they're tan or beige. And all the others on the street are dark except for their little Malibu lights ranked along their foundation plantings. But in this one, you are surprised to see the living room lights still on at this time of the night. You fumble your keys out of your purse—for some reason you are once again carrying the black purse, wearing the navy-blue suit—and attempt to let yourself in, but the lock does not respond. You step inside anyway, through the hollow-core door, blinking when you see your husband and teenage children sitting in their usual places, fully clothed, yet not watching the TV. They look bewildered and somewhat aggrieved.

"Hi, I'm home," you say.

They do not hear you or look at you. Shrugging, you go on with your usual routine, your nightly ritual, hanging up your coat, setting your purse on the hallway table, glancing at the mail—junk, bills—then heading for the kitchen. The sink is piled with dishes. You open the dishwasher, find clean dishes still in it, and start putting them away in the cupboards.

You hear your husband talking to the children. "C'mon, guys, think. Where could she be that she's not using her credit cards?"

"Dead," says one of the kids.

"That's stupid," says the other. "Who would want to kill Mom?" They sound bone tired and uncommunicative, as if returning from a sleepover.

"It's a possibility we have to face." Your husband sounds the same way. "But until they find her or at least her car, I'd rather think she ran away. Where would she *go*? Did she ever say anything to you?"

"Just about that dumb-head dream of hers."

Meanwhile, handling the dishes, you notice what satisfying discs they are, what attractive circles in this otherwise angular place. And you like their stylized folk pattern, cornflower blue, but why in the name of the moon goddess must they all be the same? You would like each plate be lovely and unique, like the mandalas—*womandalas?*—you have recently created in your dumb-head dream.

Dumb? You're dreaming now. You can do things.

And with the awareness comes resentment, mixing oddly with your joy as your mind caresses onto each plate its own radial symmetry, its unique primal pattern. As you ensoul each circle of pottery, you load the dishwasher, put detergent in it, slam it closed, and turn it on. No one hears, of course, or pays any attention, and why should they, when this has been going on for years and years?

Yet, generally people do notice ghosts. The way slugs notice salt.

It's obvious, then, that what you have been saying all along is true. You are not a ghost.

"I can't see what her idiotic dream has to do with anything," your husband is saying. "Well, I guess we might as well face it, the phone's not going to ring. Let's try to get some sleep."

"Good night," you call automatically, and you drift into the living room to watch them trudge upstairs, wondering whether they will notice when they get up in the morning that you took care of the dishes for them.

The Strange Bequest of Simon Bray

Tom English

*It is for this I am Catholick in church and in thought, yet do let
swift Mood weave there what the shuttle of Mood wills.*
— Enoch Soames, *Negations*

He caught himself once again reading the engraved plaque that ornamented the top of the marble tomb: "...A Life Among Books...." It was typical of a bibliomaniac not to want to part with his books, but having his body entombed here, just outside the stacks, was a macabre touch only Simon Bray could have conceived. And it only added to the strangeness of the whole affair.

Dr. Ray Leeman finally turned away from the tomb with a reluctance he was unable to account for. "I still can't for the life of me understand why he would leave such a valuable collection to such a small university," he said.

An attractive woman in her middle years looked up from where she knelt by one of the shipping boxes. "Why wouldn't he give it to us? *He* was proud of Rathburn."

"So am I, Ms. St. Clare. All I'm saying is that there are a hundred more logical places these books could have gone, big-name institutions with larger libraries, better facilities. Surely you can see it's an unusual bequest?"

She removed a muslin-wrapped book from the box and stood up. She was a good half-foot taller than Leeman. "Dr. Bray donated

71

hundreds of books while he was president. Cole Library was his passion, that's all."

"Well he wasn't doing us any favors. We simply don't have the security measures in place to handle such a priceless acquisition. And until we do," he paused, studying the entrance to the RARE BOOKS room, soon to be the SIMON BRAY COLLECTION, "no one is to have access to these books."

"I was hoping you'd change your mind," she said. "These books were Dr. Brays' life. He wanted them to be studied, to be available to—"

"All in good time, Ms. St. Clare. And what about these?" he said, pointing to a row of flimsy, putty-colored, steel cabinets. "They're ugly and they're rickety. They're not suitable for the display of such valuable books."

She took a deep breath. Dr. Leeman was, after all, the new university president, even if his deportment did not befit the role. "Perhaps they could be displayed in better cabinets, but this is what was in his own library, and the bequest specifically stipulated that these units be used to display the books *here*, too."

"And you don't find that odd? The man was rich, and he used these cheap cabinets to display his most prized possessions."

Veronica St. Clare shrugged and turned to face one of the empty cabinets. She really did not care how the books were presented—so long as her library got "the Simon Bray Collection of Decadent Fiction." She carefully unwrapped the muslin from the book she held and drew a quick, short breath.

"What have you got there?" Dr. Leeman asked, rising up on his toes and craning his neck to see over the librarian's shoulder.

She gently ran her cotton-gloved hand over the leather cover. "It's one of the Enoch Soames books."

"*Negations*?" Leeman asked.

"You know about this book?" Veronica said, surprised.

Leeman sighed. "Yes, Ms. St. Clare, my mind simply brims with golden nuggets of utterly useless information." He extended his hand palm up. "May I?"

She hesitated, then reluctantly handed the book over. Dr. Leeman straightened his glasses and began to carelessly examine the book. He opened the volume to the preface, and read, "'Lean near to life. Lean very near—nearer.'" He sniggered. "Enoch Soames was weird, but I'm starting to think Simon Bray was even weirder to want to collect him."

At this Veronica stiffened a bit, her mouth tightened.

"I'm sorry, Ms. St. Clare. How tactless of me," Leeman said, genuinely apologetic. "I had forgotten how close you were to Simon."

"I only knew him professionally," she said defensively. "After he hired me to catalog the collection."

"Yes," he said, slightly drawing the word out. "You know, I've always wondered: didn't it ever bother you to immerse yourself in a subject that, by its very nature, was diametrically opposed to your faith."

"Books represent ideas, Dr. Leeman," she said stiffly, "and my faith in God is strong enough to withstand even the strangest of ideas."

Slowly and gently, but firmly, she pulled *Negations* from Dr. Leeman's grasp. "You obviously are familiar with Enoch Soames."

"Oh yes. The Catholic Diabolist. In league with the devil. Ridiculous stuff, this belief in the supernatural," he said. "But even presupposing such a belief, Soames' religion was…shall we say confused?"

"*Catholic* can be taken in the cultural sense. The same way *Jewish* denotes both a religion and an ethnic group. Historically, the only way someone left the Catholic Church was if they were denounced, excommunicated."

"In other words: once a Catholic, always a Catholic?"

She nodded. "So, Soames could justifiably say he was both Catholic and a Satanist. Today, though, the Church makes the distinction, with *practicing* Catholic."

"Yes. Well that's more your department," Leeman said. "Anyway, Soames was said to have mysteriously disappeared. Eighteen ninety-seven, as I recall. Sold his soul to the devil for the chance to visit the British Museum a hundred years later." He snorted. "To see if posterity would remember his writings."

"He was a tragic figure, Dr. Leeman."

"He was a fool, Ms. St. Clare. Why should Bray want to collect him? And why in these flimsy cabinets," he said, pacing back and forth in front of the row of steel units. "And why here of all places?" He rubbed his hands together. "I have a one o'clock luncheon appointment with Congressman Phipps. While I'm away, please remember: this collection is off-limits." He started for the door. "I'll drop in afterwards to see how things are progressing."

§

Upon his return, Leeman found the head of campus security standing at the foot of Bray's tomb. "A queer duck, if you ask me," Leeman said. "In spite of the fact he left us the books, he hasn't exactly released his hold on them—making us carry out all these bizarre arrangements to get them."

Bob Serviss eyed the university president for a brief moment before saying, "I can't claim to understand the academic mind, but I know his life was tied up in these books. Guess I can't blame him for wanting things just right."

"Just right? That's the problem: they're all wrong. They're actually downright weird. He's got this library looking like a cross between a storeroom and a funeral parlor."

Serviss nodded slowly. Dr. Bray had always been very kind to him. But with Bray's sudden death there had been a changing of the guard, and Serviss remembered he was only two years away from retirement. "I guess you're right," he said.

"If you ask me, this is all about control," Leeman said. "Not to mention an inability to let go of the world. Pretty materialistic of the old altar boy."

Serviss made a conspicuous show of looking at his watch. "I'm sorry, I gotta run. I'm doing an inspection in a few minutes. Nice talking to you, Dr. Leeman."

"Don't forget to increase library security, Bob."

"No sir," Serviss said as he headed for the door.

Leeman walked over to where Veronica St. Clare was arranging some of Bray's books and mementos. He stopped in front of one of the cheap metal cabinets. It was filled with rare volumes from the *fin-de-siécle* school of literature, all carefully displayed unopened on slanted bookstands. "What goes here?" he asked, pointing at an empty plastic stand placed on a shelf at eye level.

"Bray's missing book," Veronica said.

Dr. Leeman huffed. "Don't tell me we've already lost one of these books."

"No, no, this book's been missing for years. It was taken from Dr. Bray's house the night of a faculty party, more than a decade ago."

"You mean stolen?"

"Yes. Undoubtedly by someone who taught at the university. No one else was there that night. Just faculty…and spouses, of course," Veronica said. "So much for Bray's book curse."

"Book curse?"

Veronica nodded. "After the Middle Ages, book theft was one of the biggest problems facing Christian monasteries. For hundreds of years faithful monks had been tasked with the job of preserving the accumulated knowledge of the Western World, and they accomplished the task by hand-copying what documents they were able to save," she said. "And by creating books. Later on, when bibliomania began to infect the civilized world, they were faced with a new problem: stopping book thieves."

"I know *that*," Leeman said. "They would make books with iron-strapped bindings, and then chain them to reading tables so they couldn't be removed. But what about this curse?"

"Well, the Church soon found that the best deterrent to theft was to inscribe the front of a book with a curse. Something that threatened excommunication. Or something even worse, like having your eyeballs pop out. These curses worked pretty well among pious people and—"

"Yes, yes, I *know* all that," Leeman interrupted. "What does all this have to do with Bray?"

"I'll show you." She opened the glass doors of one of the steel cabinets and removed *Negations* from its stand. She carefully opened the cover to reveal an extremely ornate bookplate that read:

Ex Libris
Dr. Simon Bray

Leeman shrugged. He had seen Bray's bookplate before. "So?"

"Look closer," Veronica said, pointing to the tiny border of ornamentation that ran along the edges of the bookplate.

Leeman took the open book and raised it closer to his eyes. He blinked hard, then moved the page farther away until at last he was able to focus on the tiny, tightly-spaced block lettering that edged Bray's bookplate. The lettering seemed to melt together into a solid design. "Text of some sort. I still can't quite make it out," he said. "Hieroglyphics would be easier to read. Why isn't it more plain?"

"And tip off the thief to the fate that awaited him?" Veronica smiled. "Dr. Bray took a fiendish delight in the curse being apparently hidden from sight, yet in plain view. And he put more faith in that curse than in any burglar alarm."

"And to what effect?" Leeman asked. "Obviously these squiggles did nothing to prevent someone from stealing one of the books. And right under his very nose."

"No, they didn't," Veronica sighed, "which is sad, because the book that was taken that night was the rarest, most valuable volume in his collection." She carefully returned *Negations* to its shelf, then gently closed the glass doors.

Leeman stood in front of the dingy, yellow-gray cabinet, staring through the glass at the Soames book. It was incredibly rare. Only two or three copies were believed to exist, and he was looking at one of them.

"It really angered Dr. Bray that someone would take his hospitality as an opportunity to rob him of his dearest possession," Veronica said. "*Fungoids* was irreplaceable."

"Another Soames book," Leeman said, absently.

"The rarest. According to the Max Beerbohm story, Soames' publisher managed to sell only three copies of the book. So, who knows if another copy even exists?" she said. "I think you missed your calling, Dr. Leeman; you should have been an English Lit. professor."

"Yeah, well, at the time political science was beckoning. But why the vacant spot on the shelf?" he asked, thumbing over his shoulder at the empty bookstand.

"Another stipulation of the bequest," Veronica said. "Dr. Bray never gave up hope that someday he'd recover the book. How, I don't know. He didn't call in the police when the theft occurred—didn't want Rathburn associated with a scandal. He said he would handle the matter in his own way."

"But clearly, he never did recover the book," Leeman said. "Most thefts of this nature are rarely solved. Which is why security is so important, why this collection is off-limits for the time being."

Veronica no longer seemed to be listening. She stood there gazing at the tomb just beyond the stacks. "He was never able to figure out who it was, but Lord knows, he tried. Although he never accused anyone—never even announced the book was missing—he secretly suspected everyone. And he quickly found one excuse or another to visit the homes of all who'd been there the night of the theft. Once in their homes, he would excuse himself for some reason so he could prowl about their back rooms."

"Not exactly the most brilliant modus operandi," Leeman said.

"No," she said, "As would be expected, he found nothing. Then he started searching through book catalogs, on-line databases, corresponding with hundreds of antiquarian booksellers. Nothing. The book never surfaced."

"I'm not surprised," Leeman said.

"He brooded over it for years. He was still talking about it when I went to work for him three years ago. It was something that was never completely out of his mind; something that lay just below the surface, welling up in the conversation at the oddest times. He once told me that he'd have no peace until he got the book back."

"Sounds like bibliomania to me," said Leeman.

She glared at him. "I watched it eat away at his soul, Dr. Leeman." She turned back to the display cabinet. "And oddly, he never lost faith that someday he would recover the book—even solve the mystery of who took it; that *Fungoids* would once again be the crown jewel of his collection. Hence," she gestured to the empty bookstand, "he always reserved a special place in his library: this exact same bookstand, empty and awaiting the book's return."

"You're not serious," Leeman laughed. "I *hope* you're not serious."

"It's just another stipulation that has to be followed," she said, quickly adding, "and I will not allow something as simple as placing an empty easel on a shelf to cause us to lose this collection to another library. Or don't you think that every museum in the country will come nosing around to see if we've met all the requirements of Bray's bequest—regardless of how bizarre they may seem to you?"

Veronica's forehead and cheeks grew crimson with embarrassment. She had lost any detachment she had been hoping to maintain. "I'm sorry, Dr. Leeman," she said. "I know Dr. Bray was eccentric, maybe even obsessed. That's the sad part of this whole affair, that he would allow himself to grow so bitter over something that had no eternal value." She took a deep breath. "I often warned him to guard his heart—not to let hate consume him."

"Well, it's over and done with," Leeman said.

"Yes. I only pray that he's finally found peace," Veronica said, "even if he does know at last who took the book."

Leeman stared at her. "Then, he *did* find out?"

"No. At least not in *this* life. But Dr. Bray was always certain he would someday learn the truth, and if not in life, then why not in death?"

"Ms. St. Clare, death is just *that*: the termination of existence, the extinguishing of consciousness. Once you die, it's over. Done. Finished. Period. *Thee* end. I've been trying to tell you for quite some time now that there is nothing beyond this physical world."

"And I've been trying to tell you, Dr. Leeman, that there *is* more than this physical world. And this life."

Leeman frowned; his shoulders drooped. He knew what was coming, because he had heard it all before.

"There's a whole other dimension called the spirit world," Veronica said. "A dimension that exists right alongside your physical world, and permeates it. When our physical bodies die, our spirits continue on, eternally, in this realm. But the question is whether your spirit will reside in the presence of a loving God or in the presence of—"

"Yes, yes, so you've told me a dozen times. But what's that got to do with Bray knowing who took the book?"

"We can't see into the spiritual world as long as we're anchored by life to this physical world. But after death the blinders will fall off, and we'll see, I mean truly see, for the first time, the things of the spirit. Hidden things. Secret things. To the very depths of the soul," Veronica said, her face glowing with enthusiasm. "Doesn't it stand to reason that this newfound ability to see and move about within the spirit world would also enable us to look back into this physical world and see everything?"

Leeman grunted. "In other words, Ms. St. Clare, you think the dead are watching us?"

"Yes, I do. The Bible even speaks of it in the *Book of Hebrews*," she said. "'Since we are surrounded by so great a cloud of witnesses, let us lay aside the sin which so easily ensnares us and run—'"

"Oh *please*, Ms. St. Clare!" Leeman spun on his heels and walked briskly through the stacks, picking his way through the boxes of books that still littered the floor. "I don't have time for such nonsense. You'll excuse me." He headed quickly for the exit but stopped abruptly at the foot of Bray's marble tomb. He glared at it with visible disgust before forcing his way past a janitor at the exit.

§

Leeman could no longer see the spire of Cole Library from his office window. He had sat at his desk for hours now, trying to write the speech he was to give to the Chamber of Commerce in two days, but his thoughts had continually strayed from the task at hand and he had written almost nothing. He had watched the sun drop behind the huge old oaks that dotted Sorority Row, and the streetlights come on, and most of the cars leave the faculty lot.

It was 10:06 pm. The lights had long been out at the Cole Library, the last student booted out more than an hour ago. Even Ms. St. Clare would be gone by now.

Leeman pulled open the middle drawer of his desk and withdrew a large magnifying glass and a flashlight. "The game is afoot," he said as he walked through the outer office and past the secretary's desk.

The long corridor outside his office was quiet, most of the administrative staff having gone home long ago. As he walked the length of the now dimly-lit hallway, he took in the portraits that lined the east wall: first was his own, followed by those of all the previous presidents and ending at the main entrance with Harris Knowles Rathburn, who had founded the university in 1913. Leeman was very happy with his own portrait, as the artist had painted the hairline thicker and a bit lower than it actually was. He grinned, pleased with both the portrait and himself. But as he passed Bray's portrait his smile sagged. There, in all his self-righteous, Technicolor eccentricity stood Bray in front of a wall of books. In his hand he held a bronze plaque commemorating the expansion of Cole Library.

"You missed your chance, Bray. You could have got it renamed after you."

Leeman continued out the door, then walked briskly toward the library several hundred yards away. The night was cool and still, the moonless sky brilliant with stars. When he reached the library, he fished a key from his coat pocket and unlocked the main door. He was surprised to find the lights still on in the Rare Books room, but the door was locked and he assumed Ms. St. Clare had left them on as an added security measure. He placed the flashlight on the Circulation Desk, selected another key and unlocked the door.

He walked slowly toward the stacks, eyeing over his shoulder the tomb on the side of the room. He stopped in front of the ugly steel and glass cabinets. One of the units was still empty. He grasped it by the sides and gave it a gentle shake. The thin metal shuddered as the cabinet twisted slightly at its middle.

The units were clearly unstable, and already Leeman could see it coming: a student tries to get a book down from the top shelf and manages to pull the whole damn cabinet down on top of himself instead. That was all he needed, a big, fat lawsuit.

"What in hell were you thinking of, Simon Bray?"

He would have maintenance look at the cabinets in the morning. Perhaps they could attach some brackets and bolt the units to the floor.

Leeman moved to the cabinet where *Negations* reposed, opened the glass doors and removed the book. He pulled the magnifying glass from his pocket and started to examine Bray's bookplate. He moved the lens over the page, struggling between enlargement and clarity. What to his unaided eyes had appeared to be a decorative border was indeed an unbroken line of tiny block letters—and words that seemed to crawl along the edges of the bookplate like a trail of ants.

Reading the words took patience and concentration as several factors worked together to hinder their legibility. Not only were the component letters extremely small but, proportionate to their size, they were also extremely narrow, like the typeface consistently used at the bottom of movie posters to credit the cast and crew. Furthermore, there was practically no spacing between the individual words, and the resultant text lacked punctuation of any kind.

After several minutes Leeman had succeeded in reading the words, a malediction that had lay hidden in the front of the book for years:

...LET THE WRETCH WHO STEALS THIS BOOK DRAW NEAR TO DEATH FOR IN THAT HOUR AN EVIL EYE SHALL BE UPON HIM AND DOOM TRAIL HIS STEPS UNTIL THE DAY OF RETURN WHEN HIS FATE IS PRONOUNCED HIS THROAT CLEAVED HIS EXTERMINATION ACHIEVED ... LET THE WRETCH WHO STEALS THIS BOOK DRAW NEAR TO DEATH....

The words of the curse were repeated several times by the spidery letters encircling Bray's bookplate. Leeman stood there, slowly rotating the page, as he read the words over and over, trying to glean from them their full implication: day of return…throat cleaved?

He almost dropped the book when a loud *thump* sounded from somewhere in the stacks. The sound of a book being forcefully clapped shut. So, he was not alone in the room after all, he thought. He dropped the magnifying glass into his pocket and quietly replaced the book, then called out, "Is that you, Ms. St. Clare?" but there was no answer.

He was unsure from which direction the sound had come. Outside the stacks? Probably one of the study tables. "I see I'm not the only one burning the late-night oil," he called out.

Silence.

"Hey, don't worry about it," Leeman said. "This room is supposed to be off limits, but I can't fault a person for wanting to see the Bray books. They're keeping me here, too." He stepped lightly down the aisle in the direction of the study area. "I for one don't believe curiosity *ever* killed the cat. Matter of fact, it's probably good for the cat." He stepped out of the stacks.

The study area was empty. Six small tables clean of any books or documents. A dozen reading lamps, all of them cold to his touch. Leeman yelled out: "I won't tolerate any horsing around in this room. If you still want to be attending Rathburn in the spring, you'll get out here on the double." Silence.

Then the lights went out.

§

By the time Leeman had fumbled his way through the darkness and found the illuminated EXIT, he was drenched with sweat. He had made his blind sprint across the room in less than eight seconds, leaving in his wake several overturned chairs and at least one spilled wastepaper basket. He pushed through the door, breathing hard and rubbing his thigh where he had banged it on the corner of a table.

Outside in the cool night air he caught his breath. Someone was having a good laugh at his expense, and when he found out who it was, there'd be hell to pay. He wiped the sweat from his forehead and started back for his office. He just wanted to get his briefcase and go home now. His speech could wait until tomorrow.

As he limped down the sidewalk, he heard something rustling in the photinias that lined the path. "Who's there?" he said, twisting around in time to see the small trees shaking under the faint glow of a street lamp. "I said, who's there?" He took several paces backwards, never taking his eyes off the moving branches. "Come out, damn you!"

The green branches began to part, and Bob Serviss stepped through. "Dr. Leeman, are you all right?" he asked as he approached.

Leeman could feel his heart racing. His shoulders sagged, his arms dangling useless by his sides. "What the hell? What were you doing in there?"

Serviss realized he had startled the man. "I'm sorry, Dr. Leeman. It's a shortcut from Lambert Hall. I didn't mean to scare you."

"You didn't scare me," Leeman said hatefully. "Why don't you use the designated routes and stay outta the damn bushes?" He turned and limped away.

§

Back at his office, Leeman slumped into the chair behind his desk. The cool leather sighed softly as his body sank into the cushions. He was not sure if he would be able to get up again.

Mrs. Davis had been thoughtful enough to leave a thermal carafe of hot coffee on his desk before going home hours ago. He poured himself a cup and took a careful sip. It was only lukewarm now, and he gulped it down, grateful for something to wet his parched throat. He leaned back, put the foot of his bruised leg on the desk and sat there listening to the rhythmic chirping of crickets outside his window.

He had begun to nod off when something brought him back to full attention. He sprang from his chair, slamming his foot to the floor, and a raging current of pain shot up his sore leg.

He slapped a hand over his mouth and listened. Someone was rattling the doorknob to the outer office—repeatedly. It had to be Mrs. Davis, he thought. She had forgotten something; driven back in from Brentwood. But she had a key, why didn't she come on in?

He sat frozen behind the desk, not breathing, straining to hear. The rattling had stopped, and a few seconds later Leeman heard footsteps slowly trailing away down the corridor.

Security, he thought, inhaling deeply. He rubbed his face. "Too much coffee." It was time to go home. Time to put an end to a day filled with the bizarre affairs of an insane book collector and the weird opinions of a self-righteous librarian. He pushed himself up, threw a sheaf of papers into his briefcase, then headed for the door.

After locking the outer office, he walked quickly toward the main exit, frequently scanning the dimly lit corridor behind him. He was almost at the front door when he stopped abruptly and turned back. There was something wrong with Bray's portrait, something changed: no longer was Bray holding a bronze plaque. In its place was a book stamped with the title *Fungoids!*

Leeman drew closer to the canvas, felt the layers of paint, the brushstrokes. How could such an elaborate trick be pulled off? He raised his eyes to Bray's face. Gone was the noble gaze, the benevolent smile. In their place were blind hatred and malignance!

Leeman bolted out the door and hurried towards his car. Behind him in the parking lot he could hear footsteps on the blacktop. He whirled about, and seeing no one, broke into a run.

Leeman made the seven-minute drive to his home in Rathburn Heights in less than five. He rushed inside and locked the door. Then he hurried from room to room, searching each, until he was perfectly satisfied he was totally alone, and that every light in the house was burning.

In the study, he moved to a tall, narrow bookcase filled with old textbooks. He grasped the left edge of the case and pulled firmly. The bookcase swung slowly open and Leeman entered the room hidden behind it. He switched on the light, breathing hard. The walls of the room were covered from floor to ceiling with crowded rows of old books, their musty smell thick in the room's cool air.

At the center of the room stood a small table with several glass-topped display boxes. Leeman lifted the lid of one and removed a leather-bound volume with the gilt title, *Fungoids*. He flipped the front cover open and pulled the magnifying glass from his pocket.

"No!" he cried. He dropped the book on the table and drew back. The imprecation lay there like some venomous snake, tightly coiled, waiting to strike when he least expected. He could sense Bray's malignant stare, his evil incantation, smoldering beneath the leather cover.

§

Leeman angled the flashlight so the beam illuminated the steel cabinet. He could see his haggard face faintly reflected in the glass as he pulled *Fungoids* from under his arm. He was holding a hot potato and the time had come to pass it on.

"No offense, Bray," he said hoarsely. He wiped his sweaty palm on his trousers, then reached for the glass doors. In a few moments everything would be set right and the whole unfortunate affair behind him. As to the reappearance of the book, he would beat Ms. St. Clare to the punch; he would demand she explain how it got here. Perhaps she'd had the book all along. She might even have to be dismissed. But no one must ever connect the theft to that former associate professor who had risen through the ranks to become Rathburn's new president.

He opened the glass doors and was about to place *Fungoids* on the bookstand that had awaited its return for over a decade, when he suddenly realized the stand was not there. He glanced quickly at the other cabinets. This *was* the center-most cabinet, the one reserved for the missing book. But instead of the bookstand, there was only a gaping black space on the middle shelf.

What had she done with the damned thing? She said herself that it was a stipulation of the bequest.

He ran his hand around the shelf, feeling for it in the shadows of the cabinet. No matter, he thought, as he laid the book on the shelf. At that moment a line from *Negations* popped into his head: "Lean near to death. Lean very near...." But he knew that wasn't quite how the line went.

He was about to close the glass doors when two cadaverous arms lunged at him from the cabinet. Leeman screamed as the rotting limbs reached for him, the bony fingers swiping at his face, at his clothes. He tried to back away but his legs no longer worked, his feet glued to the floor by fear.

Out of the shadowy recess of the shelf emerged Simon Bray's blanched, moldering face, its lipless mouth displaying two rows of decayed teeth tightly clenched in a fit of rage; its piercing dead eyes burning with the purest hate. And then, the rotting hole that had been Bray's mouth parted wide in a silent shriek that shattered Leeman's soul.

Leeman jerked back to avoid the dead man's grasp, but the bony fingers caught his jacket. The ashen arms pulled him toward the decomposing skull writhing in the shadows. In an effort to be free, Leeman threw himself backward.

He only succeeded in pulling the thing down on top of him.

§

The sight of police cars in front of Cole Library sent Veronica charging up the steps. Bob Serviss was waiting for her at the door. He looked like he had not slept much.

"What's going on?" she asked.

"There was an accident," Serviss said.

The word *fire* leapt to her mind. "The books!" she said, hurrying for the door.

"The books are fine," he said. "I guess." He felt ill-equipped to handle the situation. "It's Dr. Leeman."

"Ohmigod, is he okay?"

Serviss shook his head. "The late watch found the doors unlocked a little after four this morning. Dr. Leeman was inside. He'd—"

A police officer stepped outside and interrupted: "Excuse me, ma'am, are you Ms. St. Clare? We were hoping you could give us some information. Would you mind stepping inside?"

Veronica glanced nervously at Serviss. "Is Dr. Leeman all right? I hope you don't want me to—"

"No," Serviss said in a reassuring voice. "They brought him out about an hour ago."

The police officer led Veronica to the Rare Books room where a man in a dark blue suit was leaning casually against Bray's tomb, sipping coffee. He placed the Styrofoam cup on top of the tomb and stepped forward. "Quite an unusual place," he said, smiling. "I'm Detective Harris. Would you mind answering a few questions?"

Veronica noticed one of the metal cabinets lying on its side in the corner. The glass doors were missing. "What happened in here?" she asked, hurrying back to where the Bray Collection was displayed. Detective Harris followed her.

The other cabinets appeared to be undisturbed. Stacked neatly in front of one unit were several books, the contents of the mangled cabinet she had just seen. Nearby, the carpet was matted with a dark auburn stain.

"Do you know of any reason why Dr. Leeman would come here in the middle of the night?" Harris asked.

Ignoring the question, Veronica knelt beside the pile of books and started to examine each one closely. "Those were scattered around the body," Harris said. "I'm assuming they fell out when the cabinet tipped over."

The detective read the startled look on Veronica's face when she found *Fungoids* at the bottom of the pile. "Is there something missing?" he asked. Veronica shook her head numbly. She slowly got to her feet, hugging the Soames book to her breast. "Any of these old books of particular value?" Harris asked.

"Yes," she replied hoarsely.

"I know how hard this must be for you," Harris said, "you knowing Dr. Leeman so well."

"I'm beginning to think I didn't know him at all," she said.

"Do you have any idea why Dr. Leeman would come here at two in the morning?"

"He was concerned about security," she said hesitantly.

"I see," Harris said. "Any reason why he would use a flashlight instead of just switching on the lights?" Veronica only shrugged. "Ms. St. Clare, forgetting for a moment that Dr. Leeman was the head of the university, do you think it's possible he came here last night to steal one of these valuable books?"

Veronica started to say something, then checked herself. "No, I don't."

Harris nodded slowly. "You know," he said, "something like this was bound to happen sooner or later. These cabinets were never designed for public use. They're too unstable. Public Safety will be sending an inspector out to make a ruling, but I'm pretty sure they're not to code. You'll probably need to replace them before students can have access to this room."

"That's exactly what Dr. Leeman had been saying," Veronica said softly. "And then, to be crushed under one."

"Actually, he wasn't crushed at all. These cabinets aren't that heavy. That's the problem," he said, shaking one of the units, "not enough weight in these flimsy sheet-metal walls to give stability."

"Then what happened to him?" Veronica demanded.

"The glass," Harris explained. "When the cabinet fell over a piece of the door sheared off and caught him in the throat."

Harris shook his head. "If you ask me," he added, before walking away, "this was an entirely avoidable accident."

Bob Serviss had been listening from a few feet away. He moved closer and quietly asked Veronica, "Just what was Dr. Leeman doing here after hours?"

Veronica St. Clare regarded the marble tomb set off to one side of the library. "I think he simply wanted to return a book he had borrowed," she said. "A book that was long overdue."

The Haunted Patrol Car
Jody Lynn Nye

Why did they laugh when the sergeant handed you the keys to 0230?" Officer Carmela Sandoz asked her new partner.

"Pay no attention," said Sergeant David Barker, a large-boned African-American with a pot-belly and a few threads of gray in his dark brown hair. "It was Conlon's car. Get in."

Eyeing him warily, Carmela levered her 150 pounds into the passenger seat. She had thick, dark hair in a bun at the back of her head. Her strong features had always prompted her mother to say she was built for work, not for beauty, but she had handsome dark eyes and a wry, bow-shaped mouth, which at the moment was pursed apprehensively. "Conlon? The cop who was killed? Right in his…oh."

"Yeah," Barker said, finishing her sentence for her. "Right in his patrol car. This one. He still hangs around it, but you don't have to worry about him. He'd never do anything to hurt you. He'd always help his fellow officers."

"Uh-huh," Sandoz said, wondering if she ought to get out of the car now or wait until the end of shift. She hesitated. "Look, Barker, I don't want to hurt your feelings, but I don't believe in ghosts."

Barker shook his head. "It doesn't matter. He's in here, whether you can handle that or not."

Sandoz took what she hoped was a surreptitious glance around the gray-upholstered interior of the vehicle. She glanced up. Barker was staring out the windshield, but he had a little grin on his face. He'd been watching her. This was the frat-boy initiation, to see if the new kid was gullible or not.

"Let's get out there," she blurted. Barker's grin grew wider.

The streets were quiet on a Tuesday morning. From her experience as a four-year beat cop, Sandoz had a theory that when people got crazy on the weekends they didn't tear the city up during the week. Looking back on a pretty wild Fourth of July Saturday, she didn't expect to see a lot of street crime. It was too damned hot to mug people. She rested her elbow on the door frame, grateful for the wind caused by the car's movement. They rolled along Palmer Boulevard, a main street bordering the shopping district. They could usually count on someone raising hell along here somewhere, but under the blazing hot sun it was as dead as…well, Conlon.

"So," she asked, a little too casually, "what was he like?"

"The man was an Irish cliché," Barker said, with a real grin this time. "Big and burly, red-faced, reddish-brown hair going thin on top. I liked him. He had the 'gift of the gab.' Could bullshit anybody into doing about anything. Liked to sing. Drank a lot, but never on duty. A little on the hard side."

"You mean he was violent."

"Maybe a little," Barker admitted. "But a good cop. The accident was regrettable. He single-handedly took down a guy who was holding eight hostages in a bank. Kevin was a great talker. He managed to convince the guy to come out and talk to him, then jumped and disabled him while his guard was down. Got him all the way back to the car, which is where he made his only mistake. He stopped looking at the guy while reaching for the door handle. The felon spun around and rammed into his belly, back first. Trouble was, he had a shank in his hand that he had hidden in the lining of the back of his belt. Kevin lost his grip, and the guy took off while Conlon bled to death. Kevin never saw it coming. It's a shame. He didn't get the recognition he deserved, because the guy was pretty roughed up by the time they cornered him. You know the stories about how a spirit sometimes hovers around where the body died. Kevin never seemed to leave this car. A few of the cops say they can feel cold on the back of their necks or hear someone say something out loud. We told his wife about it. She thinks it's funny."

"Funny!"

"Yeah," Barker said. "His job was his life. He'd never really be happy anywhere else. I don't mind. It's like having company."

He steered the big car through the streets, cruising up and down along the streets and alleys in a methodical manner. They were following a routine patrol, nothing special. Carmela looked at the neighborhood closely, memorizing the ins and outs of the buildings. That hanging fire ladder was too easy a grab from ground level. She listened with half an ear to the radio chatter, the dispatcher talking with officers throughout the precinct. Carmela scanned the store fronts, looking for anyone with 'perp' behavior showing. She didn't know exactly how she knew what that meant, only that she could trust her instincts. If somebody was acting in a furtive manner, it was worth checking out. Most of the time she was right.

"So, why'd you leave the Fourteenth?" Barker asked, bringing Sandoz's attention around to him.

"My husband, Domingo, got transferred on his job," she said. "He was a book-keeper in the main office. He got promoted to manager, and they put him into a new branch they opened up. It was too much of a commute for both of us. I don't mind. We don't have no kids. You married?"

"Yeah. Ain't got no kids, either. Well, welcome aboard, in case I didn't say before," Barker said heartily. "Let's get a snack to celebrate. Dispatch, this is 0230. We're going 10-7 for ten minutes."

"Roger," said the female dispatcher's voice through the usual static, her voice coming out of the console radio and the units riding both officer's left shoulders. Barker pulled the patrol car into the parking lot of a Dunkin' Donuts on the right side of the street.

"Keep an eye out," he said, leaning back in the window. "Won't be long."

Through the window Carmela saw Barker laughing and joking with the pretty, young African-American girl behind the counter. He paid, she was glad to see, and was handed a box in the familiar orange and white. He came back to the car and got in.

The scent made Carmela's mouth water. "Mmm-mm, fresh!" she said, reaching under the flap. Barker swept the box out of her reach. "Hey, what's the deal?"

"These are for Kevin," Barker said, setting the box on the back seat. Carmela looked at him as if he was insane.

"Yeah, right."

"No, I'm serious," the older cop said, getting in and buckling up. "By the end of shift they'll be gone. You'll see."

"Bull." She reached over the seat. Barker smacked her hand and shook a finger in her face. He met her gaze with serious black eyes.

"Do *not* touch the doughnuts. You're supposed to trust your partner. Do you trust me?"

"Yeah. I suppose…." Carmela began, uncertainly.

"Then, trust me. Do not touch the doughnuts." Barker squeezed his radio mike. "Dispatch, this is 0230, 10-8."

"Roger."

"This is for you," Barker said, handing her a squashy, fist-sized package wrapped in waxed paper. "You like jelly doughnuts?"

"Oh, yeah," Carmela said, flipping the paper down. She took a bite with gusto, feeling the rough sugar on her teeth and the rush of tart, sweet jelly filling her mouth. Bliss. "I've got this sweet tooth that won't stop. Otherwise, I'd be a supermodel."

"Me, too!" Barker laughed.

The radio broke in. "0230, we've got an 18 near you at Commerce and Grand. Three-car pileup."

"10-4, 0230 responding," Carmela said, grabbing for her mike.

"Pretty early in the morning for a fender bender," Barker said, turning his lights on and rolling.

The day dropped into the pace that Carmela had come to expect as a beat officer. Once they'd taken reports from the drivers and witnesses, they got a call to investigate an alarm ringing in an empty warehouse. Turned out to be a bunch of kids looking for a place to hang out out of the heat. They gave her a lot of lip. Barker stood back to let her handle it. She was relieved to know he wasn't the kind of guy who treated female police officers like little glass statues, to be protected. He was a good guy.

When they returned to the car, she eyed the box on the back seat, but didn't try for it again. Barker had looked so sincere when he talked about the dead officer's ghost, she got a funny feeling that he really believed it. One thing she'd learned about growing up in the neighborhoods: you didn't step on someone else's superstitions. God would get you for it, sooner or later. The back of her neck prickled. She wasn't afraid—not exactly—but the whole crazy idea made her nervous.

She went back to scanning the scene. Okay, so far. A couple of kids ducked into a doorway when they saw the blue and white Buick pass them. She glanced at Barker, who shook his head. If they were doing a drug deal it was small potatoes, and they'd get rid of the evidence before he and Carmela could get out of the car. *Don't sweat the small stuff.*

"Look up!"

Carmela did. Sure enough, clinging to the fire escape ladder she'd seen earlier was a skinny, young guy in a hooded sweatshirt and sweat pants. He wasn't going to his own place, that was certain, not looking guilty like that.

"I see him," she told Barker. "Pull over."

"See who?" Barker asked.

"The guy up there," she said. "You just said 'look up.'"

"I didn't say anything." Carmela turned to glare at him. "It had to be Conlon."

Carmela sputtered. "Don't start that crap with me, man! We've got a situation going on." She pointed up. "I just saw a guy go into that third-floor window."

Barker radioed it in and asked for backup. They pulled over.

He swarmed up the ladder while Sandoz went to ring all the security doorbells to get someone to let her in. The second patrol car came along within three minutes.

Four of them cornered the perp in apartment 306, where he was rummaging through a drawer in the tidy, chintz-curtained master bedroom. The 20-year-old African-American male was just a junkie looking for something to sell for a fix. The second Sandoz leveled her weapon on him he assumed the position. Barker cuffed him and they hauled him downstairs, reading him his rights, all before the superintendent came upstairs from the basement.

"Man, doughnuts!" the kid said avidly, as they shoved him into the rear seat. "Can I have one?"

"Don't touch the doughnuts!" Barker ordered.

The kid dropped right back against the seat, his eyes wide. "Okay, okay, man. Chill."

Carmela was perturbed. Coming down from the adrenaline surge of a pursuit and capture her temper was frayed. "They're just frickin' doughnuts, Barker."

"They're Kevin's." He turned his head slightly to shout into the back seat. "You don't touch them, right?"

"Right, officer-man."

"There's nothing in this car besides the three of us," Carmela argued.

Barker shook his head. "Conlon talked to you, didn't he?"

"I'm still sure it was you. Don't shine me on."

"Hey, you calling me a liar?"

Carmela wasn't willing to go that far. "…No…" But she had nothing else to say. If the guy was convinced his patrol car was haunted, she wasn't going to change his mind, but he wasn't about to convince her, either.

The air between them was tense when they brought the burglar into the station and processed him. Carmela realized that it was up to her to break the ice. She was the newcomer, challenging the traditions of the precinct. If he wanted to think he had a ghost riding shotgun, well, it didn't matter, really.

"Want to get some lunch?" she asked, casually, without looking up from the eternal mass of paperwork that every cop had to deal with over a single incident. "I know a really good barbecue on the edge of the district."

Barker took the extended olive branch and her report, stacking the latter with his. "Sure."

Carmela swallowed a bite of pulled-pork sandwich and sighed. The car sat in the carryout restaurant's parking lot, facing outward toward the street so they could watch traffic. "This is hot as hell, but the smell always makes me think of family reunions." She shifted the messy sandwich to her right hand and licked red sauce off her hand. She reached for some of the thin, yellow fries lying on the car seat between her and Barker. They were just right, too: hot, salty and crisp at the ends.

"Same here. My daddy used to make the best barbeque in the world. His granddaddy brought the recipe up here from Alabama." He eyed her. "You and Domingo ought to come around next time I'm cooking on a weekend."

Carmela nodded. "We'd love it." She crumpled the sandwich wrappings into a ball and shoved them into the paper bag. While she was wiping the sticky sauce off her hands, the radio erupted.

"0230, are you 10-8 yet?"

"Just about," Barker said, activating his radio with the side of his hand.

"10-32, a man with a gun reported in the building at Singer Mall. Security is evacuating the rest of the building. Possible 405."

"Hostages? Shit," Barker said, thrusting the rest of his second sandwich into the trash bag. "We're on it. We're only a block from there. We'll need backup."

"Oh, God," Carmela said, buckling her seat belt as the big car leaped forward. "It's going to be a zoo over there."

Not only a zoo, but a media circus. By the time they arrived at the shopping center, somebody had called in a tip to the television stations. Barker had to put on his siren to get through the crowds and the reporters.

"Come on, people!" he shouted out the window. A female reporter in a flowered sundress came towards them with her microphone outstretched. Her cameraman tailed her like a dutiful dog, lens pointing into the car. Carmela grabbed the lens and shoved it away.

"Hey!" the cameraman protested.

Didn't these people ever think that their actions had consequences? People could be dying in there!

The mall was a long, red brick structure anchored at either end by major department stores. The main entrance lay in the center, flanked on either side by restaurants. The corridor led into a central atrium that went up to a dome lit by little star-shaped lights. An identical passageway led to the rear parking lot past two more restaurants. The customers had been ushered out of the building by the security guards, but they hadn't gone away. Hundreds of onlookers hung close to the doorway. The first thing that Barker did was order guards to put up sawhorses and keep the crowds behind them. Another patrol car rolled into the parking lot and parked tail-to-tail with Barker's unit. Dispatch was busy reporting over the radio which units were on their way to assist. A SWAT team was being scrambled, and a command center would be put together as soon as Barker and Sandoz reported back.

"Thank, God," said a narrow-faced man wearing a gray suit who met them as they came in the door of the mall. An armed security guard stood by with his hand on his holstered weapon. "The guy's in the Frederick's near the other entrance. He's been shouting out demands, but we're afraid to get close enough to understand him."

"How many people has he got in there?" Barker asked, all business. "Are there any rear shop doors we can stake out?"

The manager, Lee Trimble, had nothing but bad news. He thought there were four hostages. The mall was old, but it had been constructed during the 40's on a WPA contract, so there were no weak places they could ram through the walls and surprise the guy, nor were there fire doors in every unit. The mall had been grandfathered on a lot of safety issues. Regrettable, but nothing anybody could do about that now. They had to get those people out of there.

"Show us," Barker told Trimble.

Carmela trotted behind her partner, glancing into the empty stores, seeing if anyone remained behind: thrill-seekers or any other kind of idiot who wanted to be a hero. Her, she was grateful for the Kevlar vest buckled on over her summer-weight uniform shirt.

Without people, the mall was dim and spooky. Carmela caught a glimpse of movement out of the corner of her eye and jumped. They were passing a beauty parlor. She had seen her own reflection in the big mirror that stretched all the way across the back wall. For a moment she thought she counted five figures, but when she looked again, there were only the four that ought to be there: Barker, the manager, the guard and herself.

Don't you go seeing ghosts, she admonished herself.

"He's in there." The manager flattened himself against the wall and pointed down the hall at the lingerie shop. It looked like every ladies' underwear store in the universe: peignoirs lined with fluffy marabou on dummies in the window, gondola racks filled with little nothings on hangers, very chic toiletries on shelves. Bags scattered on the floor dropped by customers running away from the start of trouble. And somewhere inside, five scared people. The officers got between Trimble and the store, also with their backs against the wall to minimize their presence as targets. The store had two windows, one on either side of the door, but no movement was visible behind either one. The perp and his prisoners must be farther back. That made the store dangerous to approach any closer.

"You get out of here," Barker said. The manager needed no further urging. He strode away, lifting his elbows high at every pace like a power walker.

Carmela almost laughed at him out of sheer nerves.

The security guard hesitated.

"You, too. This is a police matter now. You'd be very helpful keeping anyone else from getting in here. I'd be obliged if you'd mind the doors. Go on."

The guard nodded and hurried after Trimble.

Barker glanced at Carmela. "A hell of a first day for you, Sandoz."
She nodded. "What do we do now?"

"Let's make sure we can't just handle this without the big boys," Barker said, and took a deep breath. "Hey, in the store! Why don't you just let those people come out? What do you want?"

A voice, muffled but still understandable, shrieked out, "Go away!"

"Come on, mister!" Barker continued. "You know that there's a thousand people outside there right now. They all want you. You hurt anybody, and you don't walk away from here. You don't want that, do you? What do you need to make this peaceful?"

"Nobody cares what I want!" the voice yelled. "You'll shoot me if I show my face!"

"That's not true. You've got to leave sometime," Barker said, sounding very reasonable at the top of his lungs. "You're going to need to eat, sleep, take a leak, and you can't do that if you've got to look after other people. Help me get you what you want, and let's let those innocent people out of there."

The crackle of the radio surprised them both. Barker flipped his off. Carmela touched Barker on the shoulder and ran away on tiptoe toward the far entrance.

She was surprised at how much the crowd had grown in the few moments since they'd gone inside. Not two but five news vans were now pulled up as close as they could get to the mall entrance. A ring of police cars was mustered, keeping an area open outside the doors. To her relief she saw the civilians had been moved back about thirty feet. It was still too dangerous if someone started shooting. She hoped it wouldn't come to that.

"Barker's got the perp talking," Carmela told the officers that clustered around her behind the shield of 0230. The site commander, Captain Watson, a big guy with graying hair at the temples, nodded.

"We'll let him be the contact. Let's see if we can get the suspect to talk on the phone." He turned to Trimble, who was standing by, fretting. "What's the store's number?"

Accompanied by two sharpshooters, a team of negotiators and Watson, Carmela returned to the interior. Barker was still shouting at the empty storefront, but now it sounded like a conversation.

"Yeah, man, but if they gave you a pony, where would you put it? Where I grew up there wasn't room for a hamster!" Barker glanced back when he heard the sound of footsteps on the tile floor. Carmela handed him a portable telephone. It was an extension of a control unit the commander carried. Everybody would be listening. The sharpshooters scurried to points of vantage where they had the store front covered. "Look, yelling wears me out. I've got a phone. Yours is going to ring. Pick it up. Let's talk. Okay?"

There was a brief pause. "…Okay…."

Beside Carmela, Watson's shoulders relaxed a little. Barker had established a rapport with the suspect. They might all get out of this in one piece.

"I'm dialing the phone now," Barker called. Under his breath he whispered to Watson. "The guy's a real loony-tune. He doesn't sound like he's high, more like he went to pieces. Keeps yelling at the prisoners."

Through both microphones Carmela heard the phone ringing. She held her breath counting the rings. Five. Six. Seven. Her heart was pounding like a drum by the time the voice came. "Yeah?"

"My name's Dave," said Barker, sounding as genial as a bartender on a Friday night. "What's yours?"

The guy's name was Scott Hamlin. Barker didn't have to encourage him to talk. He raved. He rambled. Barker led him on gently, eliciting information a thread at a time. Soon, they had a home town and an age, which Carmela radioed in whispers so Dispatch could look for a record.

It rolled up on the portable computer within minutes. Scott Hamlin, age 32, college graduate, drifter, had been in mental institutions for at least two extended periods, both times as the sentence when he had been found guilty, but insane. He had a temper. Little things set him off. The second conviction was for beating a man in Georgia half to death because the guy's poodle barked at Hamlin. The record didn't say what had happened to the dog.

Watson and the professional negotiators gave Barker instruction on where to lead the conversation, but he let the officer take it from there. The team waited in the dim corridor lit only by neon in the store windows. It was eerie.

"He's a natural," the leader, a thin man with a mustache, said in a low voice. "I ought to get him into the hostage negotiation program. I haven't heard anyone with verbal skills like this in years. Not since…"

He stopped and sucked in his upper lip. Carmela wanted to ask him if he was going to finish the sentence, "Not since Conlon died," but she didn't dare. She didn't want to know. It did almost sound like Barker was channeling somebody else. His voice took on a soothing, lilting, nearly hypnotic quality. She was relaxing just listening to him. She brought herself up with a start. This was a dangerous situation. She could not get comfortable and let down her guard. She started thinking about the poor people trapped inside a lingerie store with a certifiable nut case. They must be scared out of their wits wondering what the guy was going to do.

Barker got Hamlin to talk about his prisoners. Two older women customers, a teenaged female store clerk, and the manager, fiftyish, blond and attractive.

"I don't want to hurt anyone," Hamlin said.

"Tell us what you want," Barker said. "We want to help you. We *all* want to help you."

"I want a ride to the airport," Hamlin said, his voice growing dreamy. "I want a jet waiting there for me. I want to go to Cuba. Fidel knows me. He's got a hotel room for me. I've got to be there for the Cinco de Mayo." All the cops looked at one another. Definitely a nut case.

"But you're armed," Barker said. "They won't let you on a plane if you've got a gun. You know about metal detectors, right?"

Hamlin sounded uncertain. "…Yeah…"

"And we're only gonna buy one ticket to Havana. You've got to let those other people go. How about it? Throw out your weapons and let the women leave, and we'll go right to the airport. Okay?"

Silence fell. It lengthened until Carmela felt herself leaning inward toward the speaker.

"No!" Scott Hamlin shrieked. She jumped back, shocked by the fear in his voice. "I don't want to be alone!"

Barker looked back at the team, uncertain what to do next. They huddled for a conference. Carmela itched to spring into action. If she could get in there, she'd drag the guy out, and teach him what it meant when you kidnapped a pair of grandmothers who had come down here to buy brassieres and ended up being held at gunpoint by a cuckoo.

"Let me go in there," Barker said, interrupting the negotiators' whispers. He held out the phone, his thumb over the mike. "He trusts me. I can bring him out."

"Not until he surrenders the hostages," the leader said. "If you go in without concessions, he has all the cards."

"I'll offer him a trade. Me for them."

"No," Carmela protested, but everyone ignored her. "Captain Watson, I don't like this. I don't trust this guy. He sounded way off the wall. Even if we get him to trade, he's likely to go nuts."

Barker shook his head. "He trusts me. If I tell him we can't go until he's unarmed, I might get him to let his guard down long enough to take his gun away. But it'd be easier if I did it face to face."

"All right," the leader said, but not happily. "This is the part I like least, sergeant. If you really want to do it."

Barker's face was expressionless. "That's why they pay me the big bucks, sir."

"Okay."

Barker lifted the telephone. "Scott, it's Dave. You don't have to go alone. If you let the ladies out, I'll go with you to Cuba. Okay? I like the music. We'll go to the Copacabana, okay? You like rum?"

"...Yeah...No! I'm not letting them go. One of them just looked at me. Don't look at me! I'll kill you!" They heard a loud clatter. Hamlin must have dropped the phone to scream at a hostage.

"Scott! Scott! Pick up the phone, Scott!" Barker shouted. "Scott, pick up the phone!"

Bang! The explosion was twice as loud, coming from the shop and the police microphones. The SWAT team surged forward a foot, and looked back at Watson for orders. He patted the air with a hand, listening to the speaker.

"Scott!" Barker kept yelling.

An endless interval passed before the whining voice returned. "The Copa is real? I thought that guy, Barry Manilow, made it up."

"What happened to the woman, Scott?" Barker asked. Carmela stared at him anxiously, willing the poor woman to be all right.

"Who?"

"You fired a shot, Scott. We all heard it."

"I killed her," the man said simply. "She was looking at me."

Carmela sagged. "Oh, my God."

"That's bad, Scott. Is she bleeding?"

"Nah. That kind don't bleed. She's a vampire."

Barker covered the phone. "I've *got* to get in there. Scott, there isn't enough room in the store for me if those women are in there. I'm shy. I want them out of there before I come in. Will you let them out? I'll come and stand in front. When you see me, you let them all out, and I'll come in. All right?"

Another long pause. "…Yeah…."

Barker checked the straps on his vest, then unholstered his weapon and handed it to Carmela. He switched on the radio on his shoulder, nodded once at Watson, then walked out in front of the store.

"Okay, Scott, I'm here."

They exploded out from behind a rack of pink and black negligees like a bunch of rabbits. Two plump Hispanic ladies about 70 years old, a pretty Asian girl in a black smock, and a blond woman in a suit dress ran out the door, almost bowling Barker over. They were all alive.

"You've got to come in now!" Hamlin yelled into the phone.

The women saw the police and headed straight for them. Carmela helped grab the hostages and hustle them outside. The solid heat of a July evening was a shock after the air-conditioned cold of the mall. She didn't see any blood. None of them was clutching herself anywhere.

"Which one of you's hurt?" she asked over and over. All four of them were crying. The blond lady was having hysterics.

The Asian girl finally answered, in hiccupping gasps.

"He. Shot. The. Mannequin," she panted. Paramedics hurried over to help her. One of them put a blanket around her shoulders and helped her toward an ambulance. She looked back toward Carmela. The mascara around her almond-shaped eyes was smeared and running. "He's. Crazy."

Hamlin was insane. Carmela left the hostages with the other officers and ran back inside. Her partner must not go in there!

When she returned, Watson and the others were bent over the speaker, listening to both sides of the conversation going on in the store. Watson shook his head.

"He's good."

"He's damned good," the lead negotiator said. "But it doesn't mean a thing if he can't get results."

"The perp shot one of the mannequins," Carmela blurted out.

"What?"

"The hostages are all okay. He shot a dummy. He thinks they're alive. Barker's gonna die."

But Barker's lucky streak seemed to be holding. As the force listened, he persuaded Hamlin to come out with him.

"Why wait? I've got a car at the curb. We'll go right to the airport. We can eat some peanuts and have a beer until the flight time."

"…Okay…"

Watson spoke into his radio. "He's on the move."

Barker's deep voice boomed out from the interior of the store. "We're coming out!"

The silken clothes on the racks shivered, then parted. The dark bulk of her uniformed partner contrasted bizarrely with the man on his right. Scott Hamlin was basketball-player tall and so skinny that the bright red sweatshirt he wore flapped on his ribs like a tent. His pants were bright red, too, and he had long, narrow track shoes. His skin was pale, and his long, bleached hair hung lank to his shoulders.

"God, all he needs is the round red nose," one of the other officers commented.

"Too scary," said Carmela. But Hamlin did look like a sad clown, all except his eyes. Those seemed to have their own mad light inside. Thank God Barker had the guy's weapon. An assault rifle, of course. Those damned things were everywhere. It was like you got one free with a car wash these days.

"Steady," said Watson. The sharpshooters leveled on the doorway.

The second they reached the atrium, Hamlin seemed to realize that he and Barker were not alone. He started freaking out, flapping his hands and yelling. Barker had a solid hold on his shoulder. The other officers moved in to surround him and hold him still. He fought with the strength of a snake. Carmela clapped her own handcuffs on the guy's wrists.

The moment his wrists were bound Hamlin seemed to stop fighting. He went as limp as his hair. The others pulled back a pace, but the experts kept their weapons trained on him. Barker kept a good hold of him as they ushered him down the corridor toward the main entrance.

"You lied to me," he whined.

"Sorry, man," Barker said. Carmela fell in beside them.

"Nice job, Barker."

Her partner sent her a weary grin.

The word had gone out that the situation was over. Spotlights hit the group as soon as they emerged from the building. People started cheering, and she heard the inevitable commentators as television stations all over the city went to live broadcasts from the scene. Hamlin shuffled down the curb. Carmela opened the rear seat of the patrol car as Barker and two of the backup officers shoved him toward it.

"Get in," Barker said.

Suddenly, Hamlin twisted his long body almost in a loop, ducking under the arms of the men holding him. He did one of those jumps you only saw in the movies, leaping through the circle of his arms so that his cuffed hands were in front of him. He tripped Dave to the ground and sat on his neck, rummaging in his pockets for the handcuff key. The other officers grabbed him, trying to subdue him. The freak's eyes lit up with red fire as he easily tossed them aside. Carmela leaped onto his back with her nightstick across his throat and brought him to the ground. His hair flapped in her face as she struggled to hold him. He was screaming. A loudspeaker ordered him to hit the ground and surrender. Carmela knew a dozen guns were trained on them at that moment, but she was in between them and the perp. If she could just…reach…his right hand….

She'd heard the insane had the strength of ten men. Scott Hamlin clambered up to his knees and flexed, flipping her off him. Carmela went flying as if she weighed nothing. She landed on her back and sprang up only to find herself looking down the barrel of her own gun. Hamlin's hands were free. God, he moved fast. He brandished it at the other two officers, who froze, watching his eyes.

"Come on, Scott, drop the gun," Barker said, standing up behind them.

Hamlin turned and shot him. Barker fell, clutching his arm. "You lied to me!" he screamed. He brandished the gun in Carmela's face, then in Barker's. "Take me to the airport. Castro's waiting!"

You didn't argue with a madman. Carmela climbed into the driver's seat. Barker took the passenger side. His hand was wet where he clutched it to his upper arm. His eyes were hazy. He must have been in a lot of pain.

Carmela felt fear. What were they supposed to do next? Why didn't the sharpshooters take the guy out? There was enough light out there to do surgery. Hamlin got into the back seat and slammed the door.

"Let's go," Hamlin said, leaning forward with the gun on her.

"We can't go," she said. "Look at all those people. We can't move."

Hamlin smacked her in the side of the head with the pistol. She sagged, furious at how much it hurt. She took a couple of deep breaths and glared at Hamlin.

"No more arguments!" he shouted. "Drive!"

"You're not doing yourself any favors, man," Barker said. His voice was thin with pain but adamant. "Give the gun back, nice and slow."

"No way." Hamlin gestured with the weapon. "Come on, hurry up."

"I can't," Carmela said. "Look, Dave's bleeding. I've got to bandage him up."

Hamlin's clown face went blank. There was a big fat bruise starting on the side of his face, probably from where she'd rammed his head against the pavement. She must have had one to match from being pistol-whipped. She hated him, but couldn't let him see it. "...I guess..."

The car was abruptly lit up from outside by a dozen spotlights. Not all of them were police. She could see shapes moving around outside. It was the media. The officers in charge were trying to get them back behind the barricades. Carmela exchanged glances with Barker. The media must be loving this, a hostage situation with a twist. Every move they made was being filmed and dissected by the commentators. Now, she knew how a fish in an aquarium felt.

"Come on," Carmela said, determined to keep his attention on them and not what was going on around them. She was afraid more stimuli would set him off again. "See? He's got a first aid kit."

"Give me that!" Hamlin took it away. He searched through it, emptying the supplies out and feeling the sides of the box. Carmela and Barker exchanged glances. He was looking to make sure there were no weapons hidden in it. Just what they needed, a crazy but smart crook. "Okay," he said, handing it back to her. Barker stuck out his arm. She cut through the thick sleeve and examined the wound. A red gash had been opened in Dave's dark flesh. The bullet must have skimmed it. Dave was lucky.

"Just a surface wound," she said. She staunched the bleeding and bound it up with gauze and sticky tape. This was not the way she wanted to start out in a new department. She had not covered her partner. They were both in danger, and it was her fault. A feeling of guilt overwhelmed her, as if the whole world shared the blame for her failure.

The radio on her shoulder crackled into life. "Hamlin," Captain Watson's voice said. "We want you to throw out the weapon and surrender."

"No!" Hamlin shouted, his spooky eyes going wide. "I want to go to the airport!"

"We'll talk only after you throw out the gun."

"No! Dave lied to me. I don't believe any of you. Just get me a jet, right now! I'm going to be late!"

Carmela felt sweat breaking on her upper lip and in her armpits. They were having to begin all over. The guy wasn't going to trust them again. He couldn't see Watson, so he cast about in every direction while he talked to the disembodied voice coming out of the radio. "You clear all of those cars out of the way! I'll let them go when I get my jet. They have to drive me, right now!"

"All right, all right," Watson said. "We need some time to clear the area."

"No time!" Hamlin said, his eyes wild. "Hurry!"

"We're trying, Hamlin. Hang on."

The perp bounced around the back seat looking out at what was going on around them. Headlights flared as Watson ordered cars moved out of the way of 0230. Carmela's heart sank. If he got his way, he had no need to keep them alive at the other end of the trip.

"I'm hungry," Hamlin said, suddenly. "You got any food?"

"No," Barker said. "You give yourself up, and they'll feed you dinner."

Hamlin wrinkled his long nose, sniffed. He finally seemed to see the box he'd been jumping over every time he shifted from one end of the seat to the other. He pulled it open.

"Hey, doughnuts!" He started pawing through the box. Carmela saw chocolate-iced cake, French crullers, and her favorites, powdered sugar doughnuts.

"Man," Barker said, holding out a hand to caution him, "do not touch the doughnuts."

"Screw you." Hamlin shoved the gun in Dave's face. "You want another one of these up your nose?" Barker recoiled, his hands up, empty.

"Man, I'm telling you for your own good."

Hamlin laughed bitterly. "What, am I going to die of clogged arteries?"

Barker was halfway frantic trying to stop him. "Don't do it! Don't touch them!"

Carmela felt sudden relief overwhelm her, as though it was not her own emotion she was sensing. She knew it was the right thing to do. She reached out and grabbed Dave's hand.

"No, go ahead," she said to Hamlin. "Help yourself. Have as many as you want."

"Hey, thanks!"

Dave just shook his head as the perp took a cruller coated in melted sugar out of the box. Carmela's mouth watered. The guy took a bite.

"Ggghhh!" Hamlin sputtered.

When she was a kid Carmela had seen the movie *The Exorcist*. She felt like she was in the middle of the bed-spinning scene, with the crazy music rolling around her. Hamlin flailed around in his seat, choking. Pieces of doughnut went flying in every direction, spattering the interior of the car with crumbs. Hamlin goggled like a fish. His tongue hung out of his mouth, covered with slimy pieces of unchewed doughnut. He clawed at his throat as if trying to pull invisible hands away from him. His face turned red and turned redder as he struggled. His long legs kicked. Carmela ducked just in time to miss being struck by a flailing foot. The guy's head flung to the right, then left, then right. Bruises bloomed on his cheeks. Red welts appeared on his wrists.

"Come on," she said to Dave in an undertone. "Let's get out of here."

Unnoticed by their captor, they flung open the doors and crawled out of the car. Carmela scrambled around to help Barker to his feet. The two of them rose to a crouch and ran, keeping low, toward the nearest car. Their fellow officers who stood beckoning grabbed them and brought them around the back.

"He's having a fit!" Barker exclaimed. A paramedic knelt beside him, unwrapping his arm. Another medic started swabbing at the side of Carmela's face. Her cheek stung. She batted at the young man, wanting to see what was going on.

Inside the back seat of 0230, Hamlin flung himself from side to side. Occasionally he rose up, slinging himself around or twisting one of his arms around behind his back. They could hear him yelling incomprehensible gibberish, muffled by the car's insulation.

Watson strode over to them. "We thought you were beating the guy up! The reporters have been driving me crazy screaming police brutality, but he's doing it to himself."

"Uh-uh," Barker said firmly. "It's Kevin."

"Kevin Conlon?" Watson asked. He stared at the patrol car. "Is that 0230?"

"You're nuts," said the lead negotiator. "Conlon is dead."

"I think he's right," Carmela said, wonderingly. "Hamlin touched the doughnuts."

"Dammit, I told him those damned doughnuts would be the death of him," Watson said.

"Well, they saved our life," Carmela said.

As they watched, the perp slumped down, disappearing from view. Police in riot armor slunk up to the car. They dragged Hamlin out. He was unconscious. His clothes were ripped. His long hair was tied in knots. He had a cut lip. One eye was swollen shut, and he was bleeding from his left ear. They slapped him into restraints and got him onto a gurney. Detectives swarmed around Carmela and Barker, taking statements. No one brought up what they had seen before their very eyes. Nobody could put into an official report that a ghost had roughed up a suspect in plain sight of five television reporters and a thousand bystanders.

The parking lot cleared out. It was long past closing time. The security guards locked the mall entrance and drove away. Barker sat on the bumper of 0230, nursing his wounded arm. He looked up as Carmela came over to him, jingling the car keys.

"C'mon, I'll drop you at home."

"So, what do you think?" Barker said. "You believe me now?"

"We owe him," Carmela said positively.

"French crullers are his favorite," Barker said.

She nodded, gesturing for him to get into the passenger seat. "Tomorrow, I'll buy."

Glitter
Jacqueline Seewald

*L*inda *Cleary blinked as she studied the blue gemstone* glowing with a deep purple inner light. There was a hypnotic quality about the light it generated, as if it had the capability of putting her into a trance. There was also a sinister darkness emanating from its core that caused her to shudder. It was something of a natural contradiction, she mused. The gem glowed with light yet, paradoxically, at its essential core was stygian darkness.

"Tanzanite," Krug said, holding the gem out in his beefy palm. "That's what this is all about." He made an inclusive gesture that figuratively encompassed Tanzania and perhaps all of East Africa. Then he abruptly pocketed the sparkling stone.

Linda shook her head as if to dispel the image of evil that had momentarily seized her mind. Surely, her thoughts had become too fanciful. This strange gem had somehow overstimulated her senses and imagination. That in itself was so unlike her. She prided herself on being a realist, not some foolish dreamer.

Linda followed Krug out into the bright afternoon. The atmosphere around them was alive with noise and bustle. Mererani was a boisterous, lawless community not unlike a California settlement of the gold rush era. It was hard to believe this armpit of humanity was so near the natural splendor of Kilimanjaro. *What would Hemingway have thought of this place,* she wondered. *Would it have fit his macho view of Africa?* Certainly, Mererani was dangerous and adventurous enough for his tastes. Krug with his great physical height and powerful build would likely have intrigued the famous author.

Linda studied the Dutchman thoughtfully, wondering how she would portray him in her article for the magazine, if she decided to mention him at all. His blond hair was cropped in a military style crewcut and he dressed in no-nonsense khakis. Perhaps some women would have found him attractive, but she did not. She was not some foolish romantic who liked to fantasize about macho men. There was a hardness about him; his eyes glittered coldly like the gemstones he sought to acquire. He reminded her too much of her father, a man who also had an authoritarian streak, who bullied her until she moved out of their family home in open rebellion. He had crushed her mother's fragile spirit with constant criticism and degrading demands. Her mother died young, like a flower stabbed by frost. Linda went off to college, vowing never to return. She'd kept that promise.

Krug cocked one butter-colored brow in a gesture of patronizing appraisal. "I cannot imagine why you were given this assignment."

Linda was accustomed to male chauvinism and unaffected by it. "I go where I'm sent, where I'm needed," she responded. "My editor felt there was a story here, maybe several."

"Your editor is a fool."

"That could very well be," she agreed.

"What you do not understand is that this is not a safe place for a woman." His tone insinuated a threat—or so it seemed.

Of course, this was not a safe place for anyone, man, woman or child. A series of violent clashes between the South African mining interests. that Krug represented, and local miners had already led to bloodshed. That was what had drawn her editor's interest initially. However, Linda was known as a reporter who didn't back off on stories. It was a reputation she'd earned through hard experience.

"I'd like to go down into your mine, see the conditions the miners face each day."

Krug frowned. "That will not be possible." He did not bother with explanations or apologies. Somehow, she hadn't expected that he would.

"Maybe you could fill me in on the some of the background here?" she asked politely. She was trying to keep up with him as he walked through the mine site, no small feat considering the difference in the size of their stride. Krug was easily six foot five while she was a diminutive five foot five.

"Very well, I will tell you a little about the history of tanzanite. It is found in only one place on this earth, right here in the hills near the base of Mount Kilimanjaro. It is a semi-precious gemstone discovered by Masai herders in 1967 after the heat from a grasslands fire turned some brown crystals into the remarkable indigo stone I showed you. Tiffany saw the potential and introduced it to the world polished and flawlessly cut calling it 'the most beautiful stone discovered in over 2,000 years.' I understand it is selling very well in your country. Americans love it. I predict they will be buying even more of it in the future."

"And what does it take to bring these beautiful stones to my country?" she prodded.

He looked at her out of the corner of one indigo-colored eye, as bright and multi-faceted as a polished tanzanite gemstone. "You of course wish to write an article condemning our mining company."

She shrugged. "There have been some rumors. You could attempt to put them to rest. My magazine only reports the news. I pride myself on gathering facts, not trying to slant them."

He gave her an irritating smile of condescension. "That remains to be seen. The media is always slanting the news. Your press is ultra-liberal and antagonistic to conservative interests. You don't mind if I reserve judgment and remain cynical, do you?"

She shrugged. "Right now, I'm just trying to collect information."

"All right. I will accept your word and explain the situation here. The regime in power was eager to attract foreign investors. The government sold our mining firm a license for mining rights. The officials of our company believe that there are approximately 50 million carats of tanzanite in our mine."

She let out a small gasp. "You stand to earn a fortune."

"So does Tanzania, many millions in taxes and royalties, if the market holds."

"Then, why the violence?" She met his eyes directly.

"We are blameless. There are many illegal independent mines. There are unscrupulous individuals hired to destroy our reputation. Rival companies will use any means to gain control of the mines."

"Didn't one of your security men kill a teenage miner recently?"

Krug's face turned darkly menacing. "That young boy tried to kill me. I barely survived his assassination attempt. But I wouldn't expect your press to present our side fairly. I saw an article on the boy's death accusing our company of recruiting men from the forces of the old South African racist regime."

"Perhaps there's some truth to it?"

Krug gave her a hard look, his eyes narrowing. "I am general manager of this mine, and I can assure you that we have a strong social sense of responsibility here." He spoke in clipped, guttural tones. "Our workers are well paid. They receive three times the minimum wage. But they are expected to earn it. And now, I'm afraid I have no more time for you, Miss Cleary."

"That's perfectly all right. May I have your permission to interview some of the miners working for your company?"

"Not possible."

"Some cooperation might make a good deal of difference in the story that I eventually write, Mr. Krug."

He seemed momentarily pensive, and she decided this was a good sign. "Upon further reflection, I will let you speak with our workers. Hans will take you and stay with you while you tour the settlement."

"That won't be necessary," she said.

"I think it will. For your own safety." He gave her a smile that chilled her right down to the marrow of her bones.

"If it's all the same to you, I would rather select my own subjects for interviews."

"Very well. You are obviously a strong-willed woman. My time and energy are needed elsewhere. Some things we must learn for ourselves." He gave her a considering look, and then walked briskly away.

Hans was a shorter but burlier version of his boss. She followed him wordlessly to a dusty spot where trees had been slaughtered leaving only a barren wasteland.

"Here are workers," he said in a brusque manner.

She walked among the men who sat sprawled out haphazardly consuming their mid-day lunch. A few glanced at her curiously.

"Who here speaks English?"

They ignored her as if she hadn't spoken. Linda turned to Hanks. "Surely someone here must speak English."

He shrugged. "They are mostly ignorant. They speak their own dialects. Of European languages, they learn only what they must to survive here." Hans spat on the ground in disgust. "If you want to speak with educated people, go to the university."

Linda was determined to at least interview one worker without benefit of an interpreter who would most likely distort or completely change the nature of what was being communicated. She knew of one way for certain that would insure her some success, if any of the workers could actually communicate in English.

"I am prepared to offer generous pay for just a few minutes of talk." She removed a wad of bills from her pants pocket and held it up, looking from one man to the other, satisfied that at last she had gotten their full attention.

Hans tried to grab her arm but she pulled away. "What are you doing? Don't you understand you could start a riot? These men would kill for that much money."

"Sorry," she said, although she was not the least bit sorry.

"I speak some English." The words were spoken haltingly in a tentative manner. The boy eyed Hans uneasily.

Linda observed this particular miner who sat alone was eating a meager meal. He was little more than a child, that was clear, although he had already attained a good height. He was probably part Masai. His body was gaunt, skeletal, his face skull-like. He appeared cadaverous. She introduced herself and he told her that he was called Nyoka. His smile revealed crooked teeth of sickly yellow.

"I have been to missionary school," he said proudly.

"Why are you working here?" she asked.

His visage saddened. "I had to leave to help support my family.

They are very poor. My father died in the mines. So, we older children must do our part to support our mother and the younger ones. My oldest sister came here to work but she had to go back home." His eyes lowered to the ground. Linda had the feeling that he was leaving out a good deal; however, she was not about to press him. "I am the oldest son and must now do my duty to my family. It is a matter of pride."

"What's it like working in the mines?"

Nyoka glanced nervously at Hans.

Linda turned to the security man. "I require some privacy. Could we please talk alone?"

Hans gave her a grunt and walked a short distance from them.

"Nyoka means snake in Swahili. It is not my real name; it is what I do in the mine," the boy said. "I slither into a mining shaft and place explosives to blast open new tunnels."

Linda was appalled. "That's terribly dangerous work for a boy your age."

Nyoka shrugged. "I am a fast runner. I manage to hurry up the ladder before the dynamite blows. God has protected me—so far."

"And others have not been so fortunate?"

Nyoka did not reply, but his liquid, dark eyes spoke volumes. Linda found herself shuddering.

"I would like to go underground with you, just to see what it's like."

Nyoka shook his head vehemently. "No, too dangerous! It is cruel there. A place of death. The air is hot, so hot you can hardly breathe, and sometimes there are flash floods that kill without warning. The mine tunnels, they could collapse at any time."

"I don't have to go down very far or for very long," she said. With care, when Hans wasn't watching, she folded money into Nyoka's hand. "You can use this for your family."

He examined the bills surreptitiously. "This is three-month's salary for me. But still not a good idea, and the man that watches will not let you go with me. Also, they will fire me if they find out I take you down."

"I'll meet you here this evening," she said. "But only if I can get rid of my escort. I'll be careful. They won't know."

"You would do best staying with the man," Nyoka said, indicating Hans. "This is bad place for a lady. Most of the women and children here are prostitutes. They do not remain long. They do not live long. My sister worked in a bar; she was raped by miners one night. Then she got sick with AIDS virus. Now, she is home with my mother. She is dying. Be very careful, Missus. There are some bad people here, evil spirits."

Linda could have told him she was always careful. She'd been on a number of difficult assignments and wore a holstered revolver beneath her jacket and a knife sheathed in her boot. She was also proficient in self-defense.

Human life was cheap here. The independent miners lived a minimal existence, sleeping out in the open for the most part, with no running water and poor sanitary facilities. Those who could not afford bottled water took it from shallow wells sometimes contracting illnesses like typhoid and cholera. She had no illusions at all.

However, she did feel sorry for this boy who wasn't trying to get rich quick but simply provide some decency and dignity for his family. How many others like him worked in the mines? Perhaps her story should be a human-interest piece on him, if he would allow it. She would discuss the idea with him tonight after they had a cursory look at the mine. She also wanted to know if Krug was being honest with her. Somehow, she doubted it. People always lied to reporters. It was human nature.

Hans stopped her as she started to leave.

"Not that one," he said. "Choose another."

"He appears to be the only one who speaks English."

"Big mistake. I will find you someone else."

"Why?"

Hans narrowed his small gray eyes, screwing them into silver bullets. "That boy is Umboli."

"What is Umboli?"

"A tribe to stay away from. The other natives fear them."

"Why is it that?"

"They are different."

Linda was becoming irritated. She was certain he was taking her for a naive fool.

"In what way are the Umboli different?"

"They are dangerous, not like the rest."

"Head hunters, cannibals?" Her voice dripped sarcasm.

"I tell you for your own good. Don't believe me. I don't care. I tell you only because Krug says to watch out for you."

Arriving at what passed for a hotel, mostly filled by foreign visitors like herself, Linda made it clear to Hans that she did not intend to go out again that day. "Thank you for watching out for me," she said sweetly. "I'm going to rest and take a bath. The heat took a lot out of me. No point you waiting around here. I'll look for you tomorrow."

She watched to make certain that he left. Once inside, she relaxed in the coolness of the building. Ceiling fans circulated rapidly reducing the afternoon heat. She did plan to do as she said she would. She watched the sunset from her window. The sun was an angry blood-red, promising another scorching day to come. She sipped a cold drink thoughtfully and ate lightly from the tray summoned through room service. When it grew dark, she was ready to meet Nyoka.

She was startled when Hans reappeared. "Krug wants to see you," he said without any preliminaries.

"When?"

"Right now."

"Tomorrow will be soon enough."

"He says he must see you now. It is important."

With a sigh, she followed Hans to a waiting jeep. He drove her to Krug's quarters without uttering another word. Krug's living quarters were spartan but tidy. Just what she would have expected from this man.

"Hans told me you spoke with one of the Umboli workers today."

"That's right. What of it?"

"It would be best if you chose some other worker for your interview."

"One who needs an interpreter?"

"You do not trust me?" He gave her an amused smile.

"Why should I?

"You are an attractive woman but your mind is closed. That is not so attractive. And it is not a good quality in a journalist."

"Let's just say I'm skeptical by nature. Is there some logical reason why I should avoid the Umboli?"

"They are not like other people."

"So Hans said."

He offered her a drink, which she declined.

"The other natives would tell you much the same story."

She was becoming perplexed. "Forgive me, Mr. Krug, but you and Hans are talking in riddles. Give me some straightforward information."

"You would not believe me if I told you."

"Try me. My mind just might be more open than you think."

He tossed back a shot of whiskey. "Very well. According to local legend, the Umboli are not native to East Africa. In fact, nobody knows where they came from. Their tongue is unfamiliar. They also did not look as they do now when they arrived here. Some say their form was not human, that they are shape-changers."

"That sounds like a lot of superstitious nonsense."

"Perhaps, but there are frightening stories about these people. The other workers keep away from them, because they fear the supernatural powers of the Umboli. They say the Umboli are capable of casting spells and curses on their enemies."

"What garbage! I'm glad you haven't seen fit to discriminate against them."

"I would prefer that they not work in the mines, but they are finders."

She raised her eyebrows. "Finders? I don't understand."

"They have an uncanny ability to locate things that others cannot."

Then, it dawned on her. "Like tanzanite?"

"Exactly."

"You think they are unnatural in some way? Like aliens?"

Krug shrugged. "Who can say? Shakespeare put it well when he said there are more things in heaven and earth than are ever dreamed of. Who or what the Umboli tribe are I cannot say. I merely warn you to have a care in dealing with them."

Hans returned her to the lodging. The night was overcast with wispy clouds hazed across the crescent moon. Linda was nervous; a sense of foreboding made her shiver. But she was determined to keep her rendezvous. As she hurriedly made her way back to the mine site stealthily on foot, several men leered at her and called out. But no one actually tried to molest her. She breathed a sigh of relief when Nyoka signaled her.

"You were not followed?" His voice was barely a whisper.

"I got rid of my escort."

"All right, then I will take you down." He handed her a miner's hat and showed her how to work the lamp on it. "Be very careful," he warned.

The area he took her to was deserted. She wondered about that but decided to talk as little as possible for the present. She noticed that the boy's clothes fit him poorly, pants and shirt too large, hanging around his thin body like a shroud.

She soon found herself underground and had trouble breathing. The air was thick as pea soup and terribly hot. But he had warned her.

"We are not likely to be discovered here," he said.

"Why is that?"

"Everyone is afraid to come here. This is a haunted place. The dead weep here. Sometimes they cry out for vengeance. They are angry."

Linda's uneasiness increased. "Who are you speaking of?"

"My father and twenty other Umboli miners. There was a cave-in and they were buried alive. The mining company would not try to dig them out."

For the first time, Linda heard bitterness in the boy's voice. "That's a serious accusation. Are you certain?"

"I am certain. I come here and speak with my father and the others often. Their spirits are not at rest. Because they did not receive proper burial, they are tortured. They cannot repose in unhallowed ground. There will be no peace until there is justice for their deaths. Their suffering spirits cry out to me." The boy's voice had taken on an oddly ethereal quality.

Linda felt an awareness here, as if someone or something were overhearing their conversation. She found herself trembling. Get a grip, she told herself. She didn't believe in ghosts. People created the things they feared. She was just suffering the effects of an overactive imagination. She ought to get back to the surface. Lack of oxygen was splattering her gray matter.

"Was it Krug who refused to dig them out?" She edged away from the wall, moving back to where they had come from.

"He was in charge then, as he is now."

"Why do your people work in the mines?"

"We have lost ourselves. We are no longer true Umboli."

"You lost your individual identity, your self-worth?"

"We wished to become like the others. It was a mistake. We sold ourselves for money."

The sound of footsteps coming toward them reached her ears. Nyoka turned to her with an accusing look and quickly put out their lights, placing his hand over her mouth.

"Miss Cleary, I know you're down here!"

A bright searchlight shone around the chamber and finally focused on her.

"Hans shadowed you. Please follow me up." Krug turned reproachfully toward Nyoka. "How could you bring her down here? This shaft is off limits. It's unstable; it could collapse at any time."

"Maybe it should."

Krug's metallic eyes darkened ominously. "You're fired."

The youth seized Linda by the waist and snatched the revolver from her holster.

She let out a cry. "Nyoka, what are you doing?"

"It is time to redress injustice. My father calls to me. He tells me we must have justice."

"Think of what you will be doing to your family! They need you."

But the boy's eyes were unfocused. "My father says to avenge his death, to bring honor to him and the others who died here."

"Give me that gun, boy!" Krug demanded.

Nyoka ignored him. "Can you hear them? They wish to punish you for your crimes. Their voices grow strong in outrage."

"He's gone mad," Krug said angrily.

"You hear them, don't you, Miss?' Nyoka said to her, his voice strangled with emotion.

Yes, she could hear them. At first there was only mumbling, but the volume grew until the very stones reverberated and rumbled. The sounds were like furious screams, agonized wails of anguish. She had never heard human voices create such a cacophony. Now she could envision their deaths, their desperation, their fear and terror. The trapped Umboli miners' final moments had to be unbearable.

Linda put her hands over her ears; the screams were deafening, high pitched and terrifying. The sound shocked and horrified Nyoka as well; he trembled and sobbed. The weapon shook in his hand and gave Krug an opportunity to lunge forward and wrestle the boy for the gun.

"Run for help!" Krug shouted as they struggled.

Linda did run and she didn't stop moving even when she heard the revolver explode, not until she finally reached the surface. She was breathless, light-headed, ready to black out. It was then that an enormous cataclysm rocked the ground hurling her forward on the quaking earth and into the rising dust. Although there was a ringing in her ears, in her mind, she could still hear the screams of the dying miners, and her blood chilled icy cold. The cave-in had entombed Krug and Nyoka with them.

The bodies of Nyoka and Krug were not found. But there was probably nothing left to find. They were crushed under too much debris. Linda Cleary contemplated the fragility of mortal existence as her plane left Africa. She realized that she was partly responsible for what had happened. Her mind had been closed, set in its groove. She had seen things narrowly in black or white. The force of her will, her determination never to compromise, had brought on the confrontation between Krug and Nyoka. She hadn't meant for either of them to die, but the reality of the situation was they were both as dead as if she had intended it. She would bear the burden of that guilt for the rest of her life. As she closed her eyes, she had a final vision of Nyoka smiling grimly at her, his head nothing more than a skull. Deep underground the tanzanite remained, waiting for more finders.

Dark August Rain

Nicole Givens Kurtz

*A*gnes Gray clutched her oak bookshelf for strength. She knew a killer, a good, efficient murderer. He swarmed upon the unsuspecting victim and—without mercy—pounced. With thick, ruddy hands, the brightness of life left in horrible gasps and frantic clawing, desperate to remain. In its wake, blue-faced, eyes bulging and dotted with petechial hemorrhaging, the woman—it was always a woman—met her tragic end.

And Agnes had witnessed every single one of his crimes.

She had, in fact, known him the crux of her entire life.

Because, well, she had *created* the bastard.

Kent Mulberry's latest dark deeds lay sprawled across the hardwood floor on white, 8x11 sheets of paper. Stained with black printer ink and Agnes' sweat, the remnants of his misdeeds frolicked with dust bunnies and cat hair. At the clap of thunder, she jumped. Heart hammering, she let go of the shelf and the breath she was holding.

"It's done," she whispered, and turned to face him.

"It is," came the response, echoing through the study. The cold air that slipped down between the fabric of her sweater and her cotton blouse gave her a chill. Agnes offered her best grin, wide with a pinch of flirtation to disarm Kent's disappointment.

Several short feet away, Kent Mulberry, he of her imagination, gave her the usual joyless smirk. Dressed in his customary charcoal gray three-piece suit and ebony wing tips, he placed his hands in his pockets while striking the pose commonly found on her book covers.

"I'm a shadow of my former shadow," he announced.

"The fans still adore you." Agnes crooned, and brushed a hand over her outfit. She always felt so inadequate around him, under-dressed next to his flawless English outfit.

"We only meet over a dead body." Kent grimaced, and then sighed.

"This is our last, and you've made it good."

Kent quirked an eyebrow, but did not reply. She liked that about him. Silent. Strong. Dangerous. He'd made her wealthy, popular, and adorned. Despite that truth, she needed to move on to other projects.

"You in here?" Questioned a lyrical voice from the doorway.

Agnes shooed Kent out of her writing office. He vanished in a smoky swirl that smelled of expensive cologne. Just in time for Sasha Thorne to poke her head in. Long wavy braids spilled down to her shoulders. Square, black-rimmed glasses on her face made her appear smart and savvy. She smiled when she saw Agnes and came into the study.

"Evening, Sasha." Agnes glanced behind her to make sure Kent had left before putting her full attention back on the literary agent.

The literary agent, and lover of all Kent Mulberry stories, had come down from Chicago to usher the close of the series personally. Sasha discovered Agnes Gray's little anti-hero nearly a decade ago, and had helped bring Kent Mulberry to life. Like some literature godmother, Sasha had been the architect of making Agnes's writing dreams come true, so it was fitting she'd come to see it end.

No older than thirty, Sasha was all lush curves and perfection. Her flawless looks could've been airbrushed if she wasn't standing in front of Agnes. Smooth, dark skin, bee-stung lips, and bright, intelligent eyes set in a heart-shaped face. Sasha's outward beauty took a backseat to the woman's cunning and her ability to sell her clients' manuscripts. They weren't friends, but Agnes respected her.

"I thought you were talking to someone in here." Sasha came all the way inside, searching the room as she did so.

Agnes blanched. "Um, no, just brainstorming out loud. So, let's get ready to go."

Sasha shook her head. "Not so fast, Aggie. I want to see it."

Agnes froze. Sasha always wanted to see *it*. "Now?"

Sasha nodded. "It's done, right?"

Sighing, Agnes squatted down and began to collect the sheets from the floor.

"Right?"

"Yes. We finished it only a few minutes ago."

Sasha laughed. "Love how you talk about Kent like he's alive."

Agnes forced a grin. "Writers' characters *are* alive."

"I'm going to have to take your word for it." Sasha bent down to help collect the papers.

"Don't step on the rug!" Agnes flung out her hand to stop Sasha from stepping forward.

Sasha swallowed hard and cleared her throat. "Those are some strange markings on that area rug. It's not Oriental."

"No, uh, it isn't an Oriental rug, nor Persian…"

The rug, Agnes glanced down at its dark markings, and then quickly away, unable to complete the thought. Agnes' mouth had gone dry. With trembling hands, she shuffled up the papers with those stacked on her desk. That was close.

"Well, Indian then?" Sasha bent down to look closer at the rug, but she didn't try to touch it again.

A deep, rumbling of cackles erupted as the lights flickered. The thunder rumbled so violently, the walls seemed to shake.

Kent.

His voice roared all around her. *Foolish woman! The rug's not Indian. She's supposed to be the smart one?*

"Hush up!" Agnes whispered.

Sasha froze. "Pardon?"

The sooner they left, the better. Kent didn't like visitors, and despite how much Sasha's assistance had helped Agnes's career, he didn't like Sasha. So, she hurried to the study door, grabbing her purse in the process. She waved to Sasha, frantically.

"Let's go. I think there's a break in the storm." Agnes forced her voice to be calm.

Sasha straightened. "Are you all right? What about the book?"

"Yes. Right as rain." Agnes forced a smile she didn't feel. "If we go now, we'll avoid needing a boat. The book will be here."

Sasha hesitated and then walked over to give her a one-armed hug. "This new book is going to blast right up to the top. I can feel it."

Agnes swallowed the hard lump of emotion there. "Yes. Me, too."

They left the study and walked to the door. Agnes paused to pull on her slicker and boots while Sasha tightened the belt of her trench coat and picked up her umbrella. Agnes knew Kent was watching, listening.

"Don't you get lonely in this big, empty house?"

Agnes hadn't ever been alone. Kent had always been there. "No. Not at all."

Overhead rumbling continued. It sounded like Kent's grumbling when displeased. She shuddered and hunched back into her coat. She never liked Kent when displeased. His tantrums never ended well.

§

The anger burned inside. Quiet now, but still riotous in its fury, it beat in fast pumps through him. He longed to punch that Sasha right in the center of her self-righteous smugness. The respect for his creator, his *birth mother*, stayed his hand, but the itch kept insisting. His hands became tight fists, one around his cane, the other around the cool office air. She'd nearly stepped on him with her expensive Jimmy Choos. The *nerve*.

Outside the storm raged in concert with his fury.

Maybe it had everything to do with the hypocrisy that remained a constant and consistent button of annoyance. Yet, to pretend that Kent didn't exist, was to invite denial. To deny oneself is to court insanity. He wouldn't tempt that darkness, nor should Agnes. They'd been together for a long time.

So, Kent's fury fed his growing dislike for Agnes' so-called attempts to banish him from existence. In the past, he'd managed to talk her into keeping him, think of the fans, those dedicated readers who bombarded her social media with protests. She'd agreed. But now, Sasha had talked her into ending him for good. Of course, he protested, cajoled, and even, dare he say it—begged.

The End had been a great source of accomplishment for him, but now that it would be his final ending, Kent felt the need to sever their partnership, too. Agnes' veiled strokes to what she believed was his fragile ego had done nothing for him except breed contempt for her. As if he needed public appreciation to feel whole. Kent breathed. Perhaps, he did. She manipulated the other characters like all were action-figures just so she would be lifted up—praised and acknowledged. Agnes Gray—great mystery writer. But readers clamored for *him*.

And it was time he struck out on his own.

As the rain drummed out his thoughts, Kent swirled above the carpet, an angry cloud readying to rain on Agnes' parade.

§

"This is a dark August." Agnes placed the cloth napkin across her lap.

The heavy summer squall seemed less threatening now that she'd left the house. Seated at the Writers of Mystery Awards banquet, Agnes finally relaxed. Kent had settled down or gone to sleep. The ending of his books had hit him hard.

"Why?" Sasha fingered the restaurant's attempt at silverware with an amused look on her face. When she glanced up to meet Agnes' eyes, she asked, "What makes it dark?"

Agnes shifted uncomfortably as others at the table turned to face her. With a deep, steadying breath, she told her fellow diners and writers seated among her the truth. They leaned in with their curiosity ignited by Sasha's frankness.

"In this area, the rains come in August, every August. A monsoon type of rain. Every day. It rains so much, the skies are black, dark. Hence, a dark August. But the darkness isn't just in the absence of sunlight, but also in the vile and evil acts people perform as a result." Agnes reached for her water glass and sipped.

Sasha sat to her right, and kicked her under the table. Out of the corner of her mouth remarked, "Really! Good hook for the new book."

"There's an ache to the evening when the rains come, as if the swollen sky's outpour had become too great." Agnes fingered the fork.

"Are you all right?" Sasha whispered. She leaned over to Agnes and touched her hand.

Agnes opened her mouth to speak, but a thin pain filtered into her forehead. Kent's voice spoke, clear and loud, his tone undeniable— rage. *Silence! Stop rambling on like some lost hippie high on medical marijuana. Is this the future you have so quickly embraced?*

Each word was an ice pick slash through her mind, as if he meant to punch her until she did indeed become silent—perhaps permanently. She winced, her eyes shutting to the agony. When Kent got angry, he knew just how to make her pay for his fury.

"Yes. Yes!" Agnes whispered through the pain. *Stop Kent! Stop!* She clutched her napkin, twisting in her hands to keep from screaming outright.

When she opened her eyes, she saw Sasha sitting back in her chair with an expression of concern and horror. Her hand remained extended toward her, but didn't touch her, just like in the study, Sasha seemed frozen with indecision.

"Aggie? Aggie!" Sasha inched up in her chair.

"I'm fine. It's just a headache." Agnes forced a smile, and nodded at the others at the table glaring at her with a mixture of concern and amusement. "Must be the wine."

Sasha frowned, but didn't contradict her.

"Then hold off on the champagne. Mixing them will only compound your headache," another writer chimed in.

The others murmured agreements, and to Agnes' relief, turned their attention to the speaker.

Except Sasha.

Always watching with a shrewdness that Agnes enjoyed, Sasha folded her arms in her lap. Agnes pushed her fear and the rippling pain from Kent's mental assault aside. There wasn't any doubt that Sasha had seen enough to be suspicious. Agnes took solace in the notion that she and Kent Mulberry would be no more after tonight. Once the manuscript goes to Chicago with Sasha, she'd take that rug outside and burn it—as soon as the squall ceased.

$

"Thank you for coming down here and for accompanying me to the banquet." Agnes climbed into the driver's side of the car with fear creeping up her neck. "I'll see you back to the hotel."

Sasha got in on the passenger side, her clutch in her hand. "Oh, no, you don't. I left my rental at your place, and you're not getting out of handing over that manuscript. I want to read it on the plane."

"I can drop it off tomorrow morning before breakfast." Agnes gripped the steering wheel and tried to come up with rebuttals to Sasha's claims. Normally, she let her come in and the two would spend hours in the study or out on the patio enjoying a bottle of wine, cheese, and crackers, or cake, as Sasha talked royalties, rights, and promotions.

"And the rental?" Sasha shook her head and giggled, giving Agnes' concern the disdain she didn't expect.

"I will return it to the rental car company after I drop you off at the airport." Agnes felt the first beads of sweat appear on her brow. She wanted to run, to shove Sasha out of the car if only to keep her safe.

Safe? From what? Nothing had occurred to indicate Sasha had been in any danger, but Agnes had a sick feeling in the pit of her stomach. As the rain drummed down on the car's roof, Agnes felt like they beat out their warnings across her back.

"That's nonsense! I'm going to that big, dark house of yours, and get my hands on your latest masterpiece. What's wrong with you, anyway?" Sasha buckled her seatbelt. "You've been acting strange all night."

Agnes struggled to keep from lashing out at the literary agent, to scream that she should run out into the falling rain. Although it sounded preposterous on its face, Agnes couldn't explain why she felt the pressure of fear fondling her emotional strings, but she did.

"Listen, Sasha…"

"No, don't tell me. You don't have to explain," Sasha said with her finger to Agnes' lips. "I know the idea to end the Kent Mulberry series was mine, and I know I sort of strong-armed you into it. It still must be hard to do it."

Agnes removed Sasha's hand with a squeeze. "I agreed to do it. It was time. It's just, well, there's a lot going on. Kent had been my security blanket, and now that's over. I'm already thinking about a new character and series."

Sasha relaxed. "Great. Then let me pick up Kent, and take him on back to Chi-town."

Agnes nodded and started the car. With her heart in her throat, she gave Sasha what she thought was a reassuring nod and pointed the car in the direction of home. Perhaps she could fish it out of the study and get it back to Sasha before the woman came into the house. Yes. She didn't want Sasha in the house.

The drive home took her along darkened streets shiny from the rain and punctuated by the claps of thunder and flashes of lightening. Sasha drifted off to sleep, but the closer Agnes came to her home, the heavier the pit in her stomach became.

All too soon she pulled into the garage. The downpour continued uninterrupted and with complete indifference. The overhead light flickered as if winking at their arrival. Agnes swallowed and got out slowly. Sasha already had escaped the car and was fishing around in her purse.

"I know I put the car keys in here." Sasha mumbled.

"Stay here, and I'll go get the manuscript." Agnes hurried to the door, unlocked it and entered her house before Sasha could reply. The pressure folded on her the closer she came to the study. Kent. Once she switched on the study's light, the rug's unique patterns illuminated.

Black wingtips materialized dead center in the rug's oval markings. Slowly, Kent arrived until top of his head finished and he breathed. He put those angry gray eyes on Agnes and she came to a halt. He flexed his body as he filled in from Agnes' imagination.

As he'd done for the last ten years. Thunder rumbled overhead as if announcing his arrival.

"Good evening." Kent bowed briefly before righting himself.

Agnes nodded, but headed over to her desk. She collected the papers to her chest, and then secured them quickly with a rubber band. She kept her back to Kent and avoided stepping on the rug itself.

"What are you doing, Aggie?" Kent asked, but despite the question, his voice held all hints of amusement.

She didn't answer him as she turned to walk out of the study. Just as she looked up, the thunder roared and as it tapered off, a panic-stricken cry rose.

"Who are you?" Sasha questioned from the doorway. Her face looked like she'd been sucking on a lemon, her cell phone clutched in one hand, her purse in the other. Her eyes were the size of saucers.

"I'm Kent Mulberry, and I'm tired of hiding from you, pathetic woman. "

Agnes went to stand beside Sasha. "Kent!"

"You're real?" Sasha stumbled backward.

"Not only am I real, I'm fear itself." Kent stepped toward them, a broad grin across his face.

"No! Sasha, Kent's a piece of my imagination." Agnes reached for her, but Sasha recoiled.

With brooding interest, Kent jerked his head around as lightening rippled through the darkness outside. "A piece of your imagination? People enjoy violence and death as long as they can't really smell the blood, bile, and hear the wretched screams. From the distance of their sofa safety, I give them that rush of Neanderthal that resides buried in their DNA. I pacify their fear and they love it!"

Agnes could hardly believe it. For as long as she could remember Kent had remained anchored in her imagination, but now she watched in absolute terror as he stepped off the rug and headed directly for them.

She had purchased the rug in India—some dusty little tourist shop. The owner had been all too happy to get rid of it. But she had loved it, been *enchanted* with it. Then, Kent became more—but not this *real*.

"Stop it!" Agnes launched herself in front of Sasha only moments before Kent leapt, his hands outstretched toward the agent's throat. She thought to banish him with the mere thought of telling him to go home, but even as she did this, Kent remained.

He wouldn't leave.

Kent sniggered and stepped back from them. Agnes' heart galloped in her chest at the sound. She thought of all the women Kent had murdered in the novels she wrote.

"Trying to banish me, Aggie? I hear you, in here." He tapped his temple with a gloved finger, and he still wore a big, cold grin. "It isn't working."

No, it wasn't, but that didn't stop him from enjoying it. His joy and absolute lack of moral compass were the traits that readers loved about him. Modern readers enjoyed the fact that Kent remained true to himself, and honest about his intentions and thirst for bloodshed. "Get out of my way, Aggie," Kent said calmly.

The roaring of the storm outside fell to the hushed shower. Behind her, Sasha struggled to stand, fear made her knees knock, and her heels didn't help steady her.

Agnes turned to Sasha and shoved the manuscript into her hands. "Take this!"

Sasha took it with confusion marring her features. Agnes grabbed Sasha by the shoulders, spun her around, and pushed her toward the door. "RUN!"

"No!" Kent shoved Agnes out of his way.

Stunned, Sasha gaped at Kent before her fight-or-flight instinct kicked in. Kent punched her, but unlike the characters in Agnes' novels, Sasha, who hailed from the south side of Chicago, didn't fall like a sack of potatoes, but took the hit like she'd been hit before. Clutching the manuscript to her chest, Sasha seemed to wake up.

"Aggie, run! Come on!" Sasha screamed as she kicked off her shoes.

Agnes got to her feet and watched as Kent swung at Sasha again. The agent avoided his punch, but only just. No longer a phantom, Kent learned how to manipulate his body faster and faster as he manifested into flesh. Soon, he'd get the hang of it, and then, he'd be just as deadly in real life as he was on the page.

"Run! Just go! I'm fine!" Agnes picked up the Navajo vase on her desk and smashed it over Kent's head. It didn't break as cleanly as they did in the movies, and it didn't stop him. But it made him pause, and as he did, Sasha scrambled out of the study.

Kent's cold gray eyes looked like the angry storm clouds as they hovered over her. His mouth a slash, his gloved hands now fists, he growled. When he turned on her, Agnes didn't bother to run. She heard the garage door open, and the interior door slam.

Sasha had escaped! The manuscript would live on.

"I'm going to kill you for that. We've never let one escape. Never!" Kent closed the distance between them, a fast approaching force.

"No, we never have." Agnes swallowed and conjured a calm she hadn't felt until she heard Sasha's car leaving.

He grinned, and Agnes met his gaze with a smile of her own. She wouldn't scream or close her eyes like the female victims she wrote about because, she wasn't one of those. Not a victim. A sacrifice. She walked willing into the storm that was Kent Mulberry with her eyes wide open.

Kent's grin faltered, her behavior disturbed him, no doubt.

He stroked her cheek with a gloved hand. "It's rare for one to kill their god."

Before she could reply, Kent grabbed her throat with both hands, and squeezed, but just as fast a shriek of pain erupted from him as he staggered back from her, releasing her throat. Gasping for air, Agnes staggered back to her desk, the bloodied letter opener in her hand. She'd removed it earlier from her desk. Her slicker's long sleeves had hidden the weapon from Kent.

"What have you done? It hurts!" Kent roared as the rain faded in its intensity. He clamored at his shirt, the inky spot blossomed as he began to pool in the center of the floor.

"What I've always done. Banished you!" Agnes croaked, rubbing her throat.

"Why? Why would you? I *made* you!" Kent looked at the blood on his hands with a strange mix of confusion and fascination. It had a dark, nearly black color, like ink.

"You didn't make me, but I will end you." She went to her desk, drug in the drawer, and pulled out her matches. Aromatherapy helped shepherd her through writer's block, so she had matches for her candles. She scurried over to the rug, and as Kent collapsed to his knees squealing about his injury, she lit the matches and tossed them onto the rug. The flames caught and soon burned.

A short distance away, Kent screamed. He howled with agony, and Agnes clapped her hands over her ears. Her creation, her invention, dissolved into nothing but a puddle of water and what looked like ink. It pooled where Kent had been, and the rug rendered to cinders, leaving only burnt stains on the floor.

Outside, the clouds parted and the moon came into view.

A dark August no more.

Finders Keepers
A Charm City Darkness Story

Kelly A. Harmon

*A*ssumpta skirted the narrow, built-in bookcase at the end of the hallway and bounced down the stairs in search of another packing box. The slender shelving unit her father had built and stained a deep cherry always gave her the willies. There was nothing sinister about it, but for some reason the bookcase just seemed wrong to her. Maybe there was something to all that *feng shui* business.

Though it won't matter after today, she thought, since she and her parents were moving out. They were leaving the house her father grew up in—the one *she* grew up in—the one her grandfather had helped to build a half a century ago. All because her parents could no longer afford the mortgage payments.

What a grand way to spend your sixteenth birthday.

The doorbell rang.

"I'll get it," she shouted, abandoning her search to see who was visiting.

She turned the old steel key in the inside wooden door of the Baltimore row home, and gave it a good pull. It always stuck in the summer heat. Sixteen panes of glass rattled in the frame as it popped free of the jamb and opened.

Assumpta stepped down into the row home's tiny foyer, as big as a phone booth, and pulled the curtain aside on the outside door to see who called.

"Grandma!" Assumpta shouted, unlocking the second door and pushing it open. Her grandmother was short and plump, and the door barely swung past her on the stoop. Grandma's green eyes twinkled and a bright smile lit her face.

"Happy Birthday, *a stór*! How are you doing today?" Her grandmother spoke in the dulcet tones of an Irish woman whose brogue had softened after many years in America.

"Better, now that you're here!" Assumpta leaned down and gave her a tight squeeze. "But what are you doing here? Mom won't like it!"

Grandma's eyes twinkled. "Well, she can barely throw her own mother out, can she? And if things get really bad, we'll both leave. I wouldn't miss your birthday for anything. Especially this one."

"You don't know how much I've missed you," Assumpta said, stepping back and opening the door wide. "We don't get to see each other enough as it is."

"I know, I know," Grandma said quietly. She stooped and picked up her two large, paper shopping bags. "And us living down the road from each other. Well, you're sixteen today and a pretty grown woman, and I'd say you can make your own choices about things now."

"You don't know Mom all that well if you believe that."

Grandma's voice got hard. "Oh, I know her better than you think. Come. Let's get this confrontation over. Your Mom's not going to keep me away from any more birthdays—or other visits, for that matter."

Assumpta pasted on a smile. "Mom! Dad! Look who's here!"

Her father nodded and drank his coffee, leaning lazily against the sideboard in the dining room. *At least he hasn't gotten into the booze yet,* Assumpta thought.

"You're not welcome here today," Assumpta's mother said, barring Grandma from moving farther into the house.

"Let it be, Moira," Grandma said. "She's sixteen. She gets to choose."

"Not in my house she doesn't."

Choose? What are they talking about? Assumpta looked from mother to grandmother; both wore determined looks on their faces. *And could they please* not *ruin the one day of the year that's supposed to be fun?*

Her grandmother nodded and picked up her bags. "If you don't want us to do this here, Moira, we'll leave. But either way it's getting done. And it has to be done today."

"What needs to be done today?" Assumpta asked. It sounded ominous. A sweat broke out on her brow, and she felt a little faint. She didn't know what…but something was going on between her mother and grandmother, and although there always seemed to be some tension between them, it had never been this bad.

Her mother seemed to come to a decision. "No witchcraft. Not in my house."

Witchcraft? Her grandmother wasn't a witch!

"It's not witchcraft!" Grandma said. "It never has been, and it never will be. But keep as tight a leash on her as you have been, and she'll go exploring. There's no telling what she'll bring home after that." She sniffed. "Not that witchcraft is bad… It all depends on the intent—"

"Don't even," her mother said. "You'll have her believing that it's true—"

"*It is true*, Moira," Grandma said softly. "You've just never opened your eyes—or your heart—to understanding that there is more than the grace of the Lord out there. There is a power older than He—"

A power older than Christ? Assumpta thought. *How can that be?*

"It's not welcome here."

Of course it's not, thought Assumpta. Not when she had the most Catholic mother in the world. Who else would name their daughter Assumpta, just because she was born on the Feast of the Assumption—the day that Mary is supposed to have been lifted bodily into heaven? That kind of faith didn't leave room for anything else.

Grandma tried again. "They can co-exist."

"Blasphemy."

The thunk of a beer bottle hitting the counter top drew Assumpta's attention.

And there goes the day, Assumpta thought, glancing at the clock. *Nine in the morning, and Dad is already on the sauce. It's going to be a good one.*

Her father pulled the magnetic bottle opener off the fridge and broke the seal on the beer.

"Help me out here, Kieron," her grandmother said to her father.

He shook his head. "You won't win, Ma," he said, staring for a moment at his wife's face. "She's set in her ways."

Her mother stared at her dad in disbelief. Assumpta understood. Things between her parents were getting worse lately. They used to argue in private, but now her father didn't seem to care what he said in front of her.

Her mom's expression turned suddenly weary, and she nodded tightly. "You win. We'll do it here."

"We'll do what here?" Assumpta asked.

Her grandmother raised her eyebrows, looking at Moira. Moira swallowed, but nodded again.

"We'll see if you have *the sight*," Grandma said.

"There's no test for the sight," said Moira.

"Of course not, love." Grandma moved her shopping bags to the side of the table. Pulling out a dark green tablecloth, she snapped it over the small, oval table in the dining room, letting it float down to hang over the edges of the worn pine. "It either reveals itself or it doesn't. But I have a suspicion you've not even mentioned it to our girl. Perhaps you've even squashed some glimpses of it before Assumpta would recognize it."

"I'm right here, you know," Assumpta said. "I'm hearing everything you're saying." She'd gone from happy, to exasperated, to angry all between the opening of a bottle and the unfolding of a tablecloth. And now they were talking like she wasn't even here. Could the day get any worse?

"Right you are." Grandma gave her hand a pat. She took a seat at one end of the oval. "Sit beside me, dear," she said to Assumpta, patting the chair beside her. "Let's start with some easy questions."

Assumpta slid into the chair and nodded. "What kind of questions?"

"The usual sort." Grandma reached into her bag again. "Do you have vivid dreams? Do they sometimes come true?"

Assumpta nodded. "Well, that's normal, isn't it? Like when I dreamed I would ace my chem test, and then I did?"

"For certain," her grandmother said, laying a small spiral notepad on the table, but Assumpta heard a smile in her grandmother's voice. What was so funny about what she'd said? Her grandmother continued, "Have you ever thought something might happen just before it did? Or have you ever lost something, and found it later in a place where you know you didn't leave it?"

Assumpta nodded. "Everybody does that."

Her grandmother was nodding again, and the smile was on her face instead of just in her words. "How about this: have you ever heard strange noises? A warm breeze in a cold house, or vice-versa? Have you ever had the feeling that someone was watching you, but you were all alone?"

As her grandmother listed the possibilities, Assumpta felt herself grow cold. Every one of those things had happened to her. And more. A single event by itself meant nothing. But consider them all together like her Grandmother had asked, and they seemed to signify something much more...surely a person can lose things and find them, and dream, and hear noises...but if you do *all* of those things... *frequently*...then there had to be something more to it.

Assumpta turned to her mother, watching her slowly settle into a chair across the table from her grandmother, and her words came out more harshly than she'd intended. "Grandma is talking about all those little things you couldn't explain away by saying it was my imagination...or the house settling...or by me being forgetful...isn't she? What were you trying to hide?"

As Assumpta spoke, the blood drained out of her mother's face, and her mother seemed to sink even further into herself. Assumpta let out a deep breath and turned back to her grandmother. "I think you might be right about something, Grandma."

Her grandmother smiled at Assumpta. "Let's see how strong it is with you, dearie."

She took the pad of paper and flipped it open to the first page. In felt tip marker, she wrote the alphabet on it in a semi-circle: A at the bottom left, Z at the bottom right—M and N at the center top—and all the other letters in between, arcing gracefully across the page. She placed the pad in front of Assumpta then reached deep into her bag for something else.

The brown-paper bags were large and deep, the identity of much of their contents lost in shadow. But Assumpta recognized a blue silk scarf she'd given to her grandmother last Christmas mixed in with a few other things: some short white candles tied with raffia, some dried herbs or flowers sealed in a plastic bag, and some long sticks of incense. Her grandmother's rifling wafted up the scents of mint and rosemary from the bag.

"Here it is," her grandmother said, drawing a blue velvet drawstring bag from the bottom. She set it in front of Assumpta. "Open it."

"My birthday present?" Assumpta asked.

"An *idea* for a birthday present," Grandma said, eyes twinkling. "If it works for you, I'll take you to a shop where you can pick out whichever one tickles your fancy."

Assumpta smiled and worked open the laces of the bag, then dumped the contents onto the table. Attached to a thin silver chain was a dark, round stone, cool to the touch, with a red bead hanging from the bottom.

"A pendulum," Grandma said.

"I won't let her—"

"Not now, Moira," Grandma said gently, showing Assumpta how to hold the chain and suspend it over the lettered paper. "We need to do a bit of tuning," Grandma said. "Ask aloud any question you know the answer to is *yes*."

Assumpta held the pendulum like her grandmother had demonstrated and said, "Is today my sixteenth birthday?"

The stone began to sway at the end of the fine chain, tiny hitches back and forth—barely millimeters—until it formed enough momentum to begin a clockwise circle. As Assumpta held the chain, the circle grew wider and wider.

"Now we know that for you, a clockwise motion means *yes*," Grandma said. "Ask it a *no* question."

Assumpta nodded. She thought for a moment while the pendulum continued its clockwise spin, and then smiled. Wrinkling her nose, she said, "Do I like liver and onions?"

Her father chuckled.

The pendulum jerked on the chain, swung wildly for a few repetitions, then started circling counterclockwise.

Assumpta smiled. She glanced at her mother who clearly didn't look happy. But she didn't care. *I really like this*, she thought.

"That was neat. What is the lettered sheet for?"

Grandma grinned back at her and rubbed her hands together. "Now, the real fun begins." She grasped Assumpta's hand and held it over the lettered paper so that the pendulum hung directly over the middle of the page. "We know there are spirits in the area who are talking to you through the pendulum," Grandma said. "If none were willing to talk with you—or if they didn't have an answer—you wouldn't have gotten a reply to the *yes* or *no* questions you asked. So, now you have an option, ask them a question you don't know the answer to, or just start a conversation. If the spirits are willing to talk, they'll spell their reply by pushing the pendulum over the letters."

"Start a conversation...?"

Assumpta's grandmother nodded, releasing Assumpta's hand.

It felt awkward to have a conversation with someone you couldn't see, Assumpta thought, but the way of it was so exciting. She had to give it a try.

She took a deep breath. "Hello," she said to the room, her hand beginning to shake over the paper. It struck her that she was opening a door here that she might not be able to close. *Ever.* She looked at her grandmother who smiled and nodded encouragingly.

"I'm Assumpta," she said. "It's a pleasure to meet you. What would you like to talk about?" The pendulum started to move, a gentle swing at first and then back and forth over the letters on the left side of the page

"What letter do you think it is?" Grandma asked in a hushed tone. "F?"

The pendulum continued to move. "Guess again," Grandma said. "H."

The pendulum jumped on its string and changed direction slightly.

"H it is. What next?" Grandmother asked.

"I think it's got to be a vowel..." Assumpta said, watching the pendulum. "It's swinging too high to be an A, too low to be an I." She licked her lips. "E."

The pendulum jumped again and changed trajectory. If she were looking at a clock, it might be going back and forth over twelve noon. "L," Assumpta said, and the pendulum jumped again and changed only slightly.

"H...E...L...M?" Assumpta said the letters aloud. "No, P. Help." She looked at her grandmother. "Help? Who do we need to help?"

Grandma shrugged. "We need to keep reading the letters."

Her mother leaned forward and pushed Assumpta's hand to the table, halting the pendulum's motion. "This stops now. We don't need to do anything of the sort. We don't know what's asking for help."

An empty pie tin suddenly fell off the sideboard and clattered to the floor. There was silence as they all stared in that direction. Her mother crossed herself and stood, her fingers clenched into fists. Her face drained of color.

"I'd say someone really needs our help," Grandma said. "They don't want us to stop. Let's keep going."

"No!" Moira shouted. "It could be a demon. And you've welcomed it into my home with this witchery."

"It's not witchery!"

Assumpta's nose itched. "Does anyone smell that?" Sweet and cloying. Fruity, but she couldn't quite identify it.

"Pears," Moira whispered. "I smell pears."

Assumpta's father was nodding his head. "Dad grew pears."

The scent got stronger.

"Who did that pie tin belong to?" Grandmother asked Moira.

Moira looked away, silent. After a moment, Kieran picked up the tin and laid it back on the sideboard. "This pie tin belonged to my father. He loved pear pie."

Grandmother smiled. "I do believe your father is here with us."

Assumpta looked around the room, suddenly fearful. A ghost? "Grandfather O'Conner?" She'd never met her father's father. He'd died before she was born.

"Has he been here all along?" Assumpta asked, her voice quavering. She felt distinctly shaky. "Or is he just visiting?" It would be kind of weird if he were here all the time. Did he watch what they did in the house?

Her mind strayed to the stack of steamy romance novels she kept under her bed. Did he know she read them?

Assumpta felt her face grow warm and tried to calm herself. Maybe he was simply visiting. Like for her birthday. She liked that idea better.

Assumpta's father went to the fridge and grabbed another beer. He freed the cap, took several deep swallows, and patted his chest pockets.

"You don't smoke any more, dear," her mother said.

"Well, I really need a cigarette right about now with learning my poor, deceased father is still in the house."

Moira crossed herself again. "That's not possible. If he were haunting this house, we would have known."

"Not if Seamus had no way to communicate," Grandma said. "I'd say he's finally found a voice."

So much for just visiting, Assumpta thought.

"Well, why should he want one?" Moira asked. "He's been dead nearly twenty years. Why isn't he in Heaven?"

Assumpta let them argue. They obviously didn't care that their words might be freaking her out or that this all seemed too unreal. But could it be true? *Could her dead grandfather be talking to her through the pendulum?*

If he could talk to her through it, could others? People died all the time. Lots of people were already dead. There were probably tons of spirits she could talk to.

She would have liked to have met Grandpa O' Conner. He had grown pears in the garden out back. One of his trees was gone, hit by lightning when she was five. It died shortly after that. The other tree was the largest on the block. It had only produced pears once or twice since her grandfather died, but Dad refused to chop it down and put something else there. Now, she knew why.

She raised the pendulum off the table and let it still at the end of the chain, then whispered, "Is it really you, Grandfather?"

The pendulum didn't move, but she smelled the pears again. "I'll take that as a yes," she said. "Wish I could have known you." The scent of pears grew stronger. She smiled, liking this ability to commune with the dead.

"How can I help you?"

The pendulum started its to-and-fro swinging.

"D," she said, then, "F," when it continued the same path. It jumped. "I," she guessed from the direction it took. "M?" It didn't waver. "N, then," she said. "Fin...fine...find–" The pendulum jumped again. And she was much more certain now that the little jump meant that she'd guessed right. "Find," she said. "Find what?"

She watched the pendulum and whispered the letters aloud—confiscating her grandmother's felt tip when they became too many to remember—as her mother and grandmother argued. "We don't even know if this spirit is Seamus!" her mother yelled. "It's probably some demon pretending to be him, lulling you into trusting him. It's not him. I won't believe that. I can't believe you've brought this evil into my house!" Moira shouted at her mother.

"It's not evil," Grandmother said.

"The Church says it is," Moira said.

"The church doesn't know the old ways, Moira." Grandma frowned. "I knew letting you into those after-school church programs would be a problem—"

"I learned to sew and cook in those programs! And we hiked on the weekends, and collected for the poor!"

"You learned to turn your back on your heritage!"

"Because it's wrong."

"*You're* wrong."

"And that's why you're not welcome here anymore, Mom. I don't want you exposing Assumpta to any evil."

"It's not evil."

"You don't know what it is—" Moira stood, turning her back on her mother and walked to the sideboard. She adjusted the pie tin Kieren had retrieved, centering it back on the sideboard.

"Then, let's let *the finder* determine what's going on," Grandma said.

Moira whirled around, eyes blazing.

"The finder?" Assumpta's father looked up from the junk drawer he was rooting through. He pulled a crumpled soft-pack from the rear of the drawer and flicked his wrist a few times to liberate a cigarette. He put it to his lips. "What's a goddamned finder?"

"Language!" Moira said to her husband, and then to her mother, "Assumpta is no finder. She has no power."

"I know you'd like to believe that, Moira, dear, but the fact is, she does. She can speak with the dead, and this one—Kieron's father—knows that Assumpta can find things."

"He doesn't know anything," Moira insisted. "How can he? He's never even met her."

"Oh, spirits sense things, Moira. You know this. Have you really forgotten everything I've taught you?"

"That priest knocked it out of her head, Ma," her father said. He struck a match and lit the crooked cigarette, inhaling deeply. "All she knows is the church these days." He shook out the match and tossed it into the sink, muttering, "Doesn't even know her own marriage anymore."

"He'd lost Lochlan O'Neill's pocket watch," Assumpta said loudly, staring at the letters she'd written down, and wondering who Lochlan O' Neill was. "But now he knows where it is."

The arguing ceased.

"I'll be damned," her father said, setting his beer on the counter. "I haven't thought about that in years." He whistled through his teeth. "Would be worth a pretty penny right now." He turned to his wife. "That kind of proves the ghost is Dad," he said. "Why would some random spirit waltz in and mention Lochlan O'Neill's pocket watch?" He put the cigarette to his lips again and took a deep pull.

Moira slammed the tin back down on the sideboard. "It could be Lochlan O'Neill himself!"

"Who's Lochlan O'Neill?" Assumpta asked.

"A loan shark and a cheat," Moira answered. "A sore loser. He would want that watch back, even in death."

Her father took a drink of beer and chuckled. "Not likely, Moira. We don't even know if he's dead, though he'd be fairly ancient about now. It's true he was loan shark—"

"And a cheat!"

He nodded. "Yes—and a cheat. But he was just as amused that Dad had won the watch off him as Dad was. Dad said old Lochlan had patted him on the back and bought him a drink. Told him even an old cheat couldn't win against such luck."

"What's so special about the watch?" Assumpta asked.

Her father answered. "It's made of gold, and the front cover has a ring of diamonds around the edge, surrounding a large ruby."

"I remember that watch," Grandma said. "I saw it at your wedding. Seamus pulled it out every chance he got. Quite flashy."

"How can we find it?" Assumpta asked.

"Use the pendulum," Grandma suggested.

"No," Moira insisted. "It's evil."

"It doesn't feel evil, Mom," Assumpta said. "It feels…*right*."

"That's the way evil is," Moira said. "It makes you think everything is all right."

"I believe it's Grandpop. It would be terrible not to try to help him out."

"But–"

"Let her try, Moira," her father said.

Assumpta held her breath, waiting for the answer. Grandma was nodding, as if urging her Mom to say yes. Would she argue some more if her Mom said no?

"Go ahead," Moira said, her voice low and resigned. "But you'll go to confession tomorrow and talk with Father Tony."

"I will." Assumpta smiled. Going to confession tomorrow was no hardship since she went every Saturday before Mass. At least this time she would have something more to say than that she lied, or cursed, or talked back to her mom.

"Go ahead, sweetie," her Grandmother urged. "Let's see what old Seamus has to say."

Assumpta held the pendulum over the alphabet paper and asked aloud. "Where is Lochlan O'Neill's pocket watch, Grandpop?"

The pendulum hung slack for a second, then starting swinging: tiny movements at first, but growing larger and larger as it arced over the first half of the alphabet.

"G," Assumpta guessed. The pendulum continued to swing.

"H." The pendulum gave its particular hop and changed trajectory. Grandma wrote H on the pad of paper, staring at the pendulum. It swung horizontal, moving nearly parallel to the bottom half of the paper.

"A," Assumpta guessed, thinking the next letter had to be a vowel. Grandma wrote again.

"Ha," said Moira. "It's laughing at us."

The pendulum changed direction again.

"Quiet, Moira" said her father. He'd put out the cigarette, and his beer sat forgotten on the counter. Assumpta smiled. Maybe these newfound abilities could be a good thing. It was cool that her dad was taking her side on this. Their relationship had been growing more and more rocky lately. Maybe, this was a signal that all would be well between them.

The pendulum's course turned almost vertical.

"M," said Assumpta, and when she detected no change, "L." The pendulum hiccupped, but didn't change course.

"It didn't change, Grandma."

Grandma was smiling. "L again, sweetie." She'd already written it on the pad.

"Hall?" her mother was saying. "How can it be in the hall? I vacuum through there regularly. I've never seen the watch fob, let alone the watch—it's not there—I'd have seen it."

"He's not finished," Assumpta said, watching the arc of the pendulum. The path had moved widely to swing over the second half of the alphabet.

"T," Assumpta guessed, but the glass bead stayed true.

"S." The pendulum jumped and swung wide again, changing back to the first half of the alphabet.

"I," Assumpta said. "H," she guessed again, and the pendulum hiccupped. "Sh—"

"Crap," said her father, turning away from the table and reaching for his beer. He took a deep swallow. "It's the bookshelf. We've got to rip out the goddamned shelf."

"Language, Kieron!" her mother yelled.

Assumpta asked her grandfather, "Is the watch behind the bookcase?"

The pendulum hiccupped on the string and twirled clockwise.

Her father tilted his head back and finished the beer, then set the bottle on the sideboard with a *thunk*. "I really don't want to rip out that bookshelf."

"Then don't," her mother said. "It's a trick. Something cooked up between my mother and Assumpta. Assumpta has always hated that bookshelf. Your father is *not* speaking to her through some stone dangled on a string."

"How can it be a trick when you almost never let Grandma visit?" Assumpta cried. "We haven't had the time to cook anything up." She took a deep breath, tamping down her anger. She turned to her father. "It is Grandpa; I know it is!" Assumpta felt her face grow hot. "And I don't hate that shelf, you know. It just gives me the willies. Have you considered that it makes me feel that way because I've always known—at least subconsciously—that something was wrong with it?"

"Don't talk back to me, young lady—" her mother said, "Or to your father—"

"Calm down, Moira. I'll go get my crowbar."

"You can't tear it out based on this," her mother said, following him though the galley kitchen and to the back door.

"Sure, I can." He paused to unlock the old door with a twist of the steel key. "I built it. I can tear it out. And I'll put it back again when I'm done." He pushed open the storm door and stepped through the doorway and out into the tiny cement yard.

Her mother drifted slowly back to the dining room.

"Are you okay, Mom?"

Her mother didn't answer.

"I'll go clear the shelf," Grandma said.

They heard the storm door slam and the twisting of the key in the back-door lock. Her father returned with his crowbar and his large metal toolbox full of carpentry tools. "Let's get this done," he said, leading the way up the stairs.

Grandma had finished stacking all the books a few feet from the shelf and was dusting it off with a soft cloth.

Her father set the heavy box down near the bookshelf, then ran his fingers across the hand-carved daisies on the front of the shelves. "I do some good work when I put my mind to it."

"You always do good work," said Assumpta's mother.

"Hm," was all he said. Then, her father leaned back on his heels, putting all his weight, as well as his strength, against the bar. "I not only nailed this thing in, I glued it. I wanted to make certain it wouldn't pull out the nails and fall forward on anyone."

With a loud crack, the glue on the back broke away from the wall. Her father put down the crow bar and grabbed the shelves with both hands. He forced the cabinet left and right, wiggling it as much as he was able. Then, he grabbed a claw hammer and started pulling the nails from the back of the shelf.

When he was done, he pulled the entire unit away from the wall.

A gaping hole ran nearly floor to ceiling around the wall joists. Bits of plaster fell to the floor.

"What a mess," her mother said.

Her father nodded. "Dad died before he could finish this up. He was removing all the plaster from the walls and hanging drywall. I couldn't bear to finish the job he couldn't, so I put up the bookshelf instead. I always did love carpentry."

"But where's the watch?" Assumpta asked.

Her father dug a flashlight out of his toolbox. "Well, I never saw the watch when I was putting up the shelf, so I can only imagine it's fallen behind one of these joists." He stepped closer to the wall and turned on the light. "Dad slipped here when he was ripping out the plaster. Nearly fell down the stairs. I'll bet the watch flew out of his pocket and dropped out of sight before he even realized it was gone."

He crouched, shining the light into the darkness between the walls.

"There it is!" Assumpta pointed to a cluster of wires where a tarnished chain played hide-and-seek with the dark, coated copper.

Her father carefully pulled the watch upward, tugging gently when it caught.

He rubbed the dusty piece on his pants leg and turned it over. Diamonds sparkled in the light.

"What will you do with it?" Assumpta asked.

Her father pushed the release and the cover popped open. "It's a fine watch. I'd love to keep it—"

"Of course you'll keep it," her mother said softly. "It's a family heirloom and belongs with us."

"Even though it came from a liar and a cheat?" Grandma asked with a grin. Assumpta knew that look. This was no innocent question. "Maybe one day Lochlan O'Neill will come back and ask for it."

Her mother gave her grandma a wry look. "Sometimes you have to take the good with the bad, Mom."

"Like Assumpta's talents, then?" Grandma said.

"Not at all!" her mother said, angry again. "Even if they're not evil, they—"

"Then you admit they're not evil —" said Grandma.

"Moira, Ma…can you both just agree to disagree?"

"No," her mother said adamantly. "I will not condone my daughter's descent into evil."

Grandma *tsked* but turned away to the hall closet, pulled out a broom and started sweeping up the plaster.

"Then let's table this discussion for another time," her father said, "I don't want to sully the memory of this find. Or Dad's visit."

Assumpta asked, "So, what are you going to do with the watch?"

Her father closed the lid and rubbed his thumb across the smooth, burnished gold of the back case. "It was Dad's fault we almost lost the mortgage on this house," he said. "He borrowed so much to tear out the walls and upgrade the electrical…and then all the other projects… Your mother and I inherited a pile of debt when he died."

Assumpta rolled her eyes. She was tired of hearing about their money problems. At least this explained why they never seemed to get ahead, no matter how much her father worked: he'd been paying off his father's debts—and probably some of his own—for all these years. "That's why you watch every penny around here," Assumpta said.

Her father nodded. "Things have always been tight." He let out a deep breath, shoulders stooping. "As much as I'd like to keep the old thing, I think we need to sell it and pay off the mortgage. We'd be able to stay here, and I'd say that's a bigger legacy than this timepiece."

"Kieron, you can't—"

"I can, and I will, Moira," he said. "I think perhaps this is Dad's way of putting things right."

The smell of pears grew stronger than Assumpta had smelled it all day, and then abruptly disappeared.

Her mother's eyes grew wide as she looked around the narrow hallway, searching. "I think he's gone."

Grandma nodded. "I'd say so; his work here is done. He's probably off to Heaven now."

"Good," Moira said. "And now you can leave and take your pendulum with you. Assumpta won't be needing it again."

"I'll pack up if you want me to go," Grandma said, "but don't fool yourself. Today was just the beginning for Assumpta."

"But Seamus is gone."

"He won't be the only spirit Assumpta connects with. She's got talent. And the cat's out of the bag now. She knows what she can do."

"I forbid it. The church forbids it."

"But why would you do that, Mom? How can it be such a bad thing if I can help people?" Assumpta gave her mother a pleading look. "Why doesn't the church allow you to think for yourself?"

Her mother's hand snaked out and slapped her on the face.

"Moira!" her grandmother shouted.

"Ow!" Assumpta tried to rub the sting away. She backed away from her mother, giving her a hard stare, but tamping down all the harsh words she wanted to toss at her. She needed to get out of here for a while. She turned to her grandmother. "Will you take me out to lunch now, Grandma?"

"For certain," she said, leaning the broom against the wall. "If we leave immediately, we'll have time for a leisurely afternoon."

"No lunch," Moira said. "Assumpta has things to do around here today."

"It's my sixteenth birthday," Assumpta said, voice hard. "I'll have lunch with Grandma, and then I'll come home and do what you want."

"Another time."

"Another time won't be as special," she said.

"But—"

"Let her go, Moira," her father said. "The only thing needing doing is *unpacking*. And Assumpta can do that when she's ready."

Assumpta's mother gave her father a hard look, and then something seemed to pass between them. Her mother nodded tightly, then went downstairs.

Assumpta went to her room and grabbed her purse, making certain she had a notebook and some pens inside. She planned to ask her grandmother every question she could think of. Grandma would be glad to tell her anything. Maybe after lunch, they'd visit the shop Grandma mentioned. She'd pick out a pendulum for herself. And maybe some other things.

When she came down the stairs, her Grandmother's shopping bags were packed and she was standing by the front door. Her mom and dad were talking heatedly in the kitchen. She didn't want to know what that was about.

"Bye, Mom! Bye, Dad! See you later!" She grinned at her grandmother, opening the door for her.

"Where are we going to lunch?" Assumpta asked.

"How about Chinese?"

"The White Rice Inn?"

"For certain," her Grandmother said, her Irish brogue a bit more pronounced. "The shop we can visit is a quick walk from there. And after lunch, we'll go shopping for my special gift to you—your very own pendulum."

When Crows Come Calling
John Wolf

*T*albert Beeman *once watched an old woman die sitting* perfectly still inside a burning tenement building. He saw a man walk a tightrope five stories off the ground. Once on a business trip to Ohio, he observed lightning bounce like a rubber ball through a cherry orchard. Being from Chicago, not much surprised Talbert Beeman anymore. But the sight before him beat all.

Crows, at least twenty, stared right through Beeman like he was just so much hot air. City birds scattered at the sight of any moving object, but not these crows. Stiff wind ruffled their feathers and almost toppled some clean over, but nothing spooked them. The idling Model T might as well have been as invisible as Beeman. A dead cat roasted in the dirt between the road and drainage ditch. Not one crow attempted making a meal of it. They only stared, still as gravestones.

Beeman thought about getting back into the car and rolling right over the unnerving birds. They would pop under the wheels like so much spoiled fruit. The car was an investment though, and Beeman couldn't argue with an investment. The family loaning it to him for a whole twenty dollars would not be happy if it returned covered in blood and feathers. Beeman wouldn't be happy about losing twenty dollars either. The trip out to the Hurley property was costing him an arm and a leg already.

The Hurley property. There it sat up the road, just waiting for him. The long, gravel drive mocked him. Of course, walking wasn't completely out of the question, but his undershirt and collar were already soaked clean-through with sweat. Beeman would be damned if a bunch of feathers made him trudge through the heat and show up at a client's door smelling to high heaven. He clenched his fists and walked back to the Model T, determined to scare the crows out of the way.

Before he could climb back into the front seat, they shuffled across the road towards the ditch. None open their beaks, but their scraggly talons scraped against the ground. With all of them moving as one, it sounded to Beeman like the low scratch of a phonograph needle just before the music started. The crows marched straight and neat as soldiers on parade. When they cleared the road, the crows went back to their vigil. Even with the way now open, Beeman couldn't help staring at them.

Is this your name here, Beeman?

Hart.

The day Mr. Hart called Beeman to his office had been one of the most frightening yet exhilarating days of Beeman's tenure at the firm. For office peons, Hart's office only served two functions: the chance to climb or the order to leave. In a rare moment, Hart had given Beeman his choice.

Says here, Beeman, your name right there on the papers. 'Sale Pending.' I don't like that word much, 'Pending.' What the hell's taking so long?

Hart's desk had separated the men into two worlds. Beeman had his back to the wall, awaiting the executioner's ax. Hart stood behind a desk nearly the width of the room, its surface glossy and immaculate. Beeman thought about that desk a lot. How much it might weigh, the cost of freight to order it, how the surface shone and reflected Hart's flabby jowls. The boss slammed his hands upon it when he wanted to make a point, defiling it.

When was the last time you visited the Hurleys? Since two of them kicked the bucket?

Beeman had sent flowers and condolences, both unanswered. He lied to Hart and said he couldn't remember.

We have two choices here.

Hart always used "we" as if the problems Beeman fought daily even existed for a man of Hart's wealth and position.

Push this Hurley deal through or not. Get more invested in this work, or get out. Is that a problem for you? It's your name on the sale, not mine. Can I trust you to give this your personal attention?

Yes, sir. Beeman knew what the man wanted to hear.

Then close the deal, Beeman.

Hart's pudgy thumbs twitched in anticipation. There was money to be made after all. Beeman recalled that moment in the office, where it seemed like the weight of Mr. Hart himself was crushing him to dust.

"Yes sir, Mister Hart." Beeman repeated his words to the rolling heat around him and got no answer. He could live with that. He had spent enough time thinking; now there could only be action. Beeman rolled the Model T past the envoy of crows. He didn't look over his shoulder going up the drive.

A single gable jutted out from the second story of the farmhouse, providing the only source of shade for miles. Beeman parked beneath it and stepped out, briefcase in hand, and lifted his pressed suit coat from the passenger seat. He set it upon his shoulders despite the oppressive summer humidity and ran thin fingers through his mousy hair. The simple practice was now ritual. Appearances were meant to be kept up, especially now. Somewhere, in that sprawling farmhouse behind darkened windows awaited the sole living member of the Hurley clan and Beeman's future.

No one at the firm even heard the name Hurley until Lyle and Beau came through the doors, dressed in frayed Sunday best with hats in hand. They looked nearly identical. Each one seemingly carved out of a single, square chunk of plain-faced granite. Hart always said farmers were strong stock, but apparently not strong enough to survive falling off a silo and smashing their skull open like Francis Hurley. Beau and Lyle didn't have much to contend with since their brother had no wife or son to pass anything onto. There was only his land,

Beau and Lyle's seventy-acre parcels, and everything rented out under Francis to various farmers in the area. When Beeman brought the deal to Hart, the thumbs had twitched.

Two weeks later, Lyle Hurley had met his own end on his own farm. The details stayed quiet and so had the office. Eventually the grisly details had come out. Lyle Hurley had fallen onto his own thresher, stuck through his neck and belly. As some of the more yellow papers put it, "Bleeding into his own soil, bleeding like his own butchered stock." Nearly all the women in the office had fainted, and some of the men as well. Almost all of them gossiped.

Beeman kept his head down on his work. He didn't have time for suspicion or loose talk of suicides or guilty minds. Lyle's death was the first happiness he could remember since coming to work for Hart. Less family meant a single party, and a single party meant a quicker end to the whole mess. A quicker end meant a brighter future of Beeman's own. Then Beau Hurley vanished. Letters and telegrams went unanswered. The local sheriff received no answer when he called; travelers reported seeing Beau Hurley walking through the fields at night, calling out to empty air.

Now, several days and a few dollars later Beeman had finally arrived. What he expected to find, he did not know.

"Mister Hurley," Beeman whispered to himself as he marched up the walkway to the front door. "I am truly sorry for your loss and am just stopping in to…" Beeman rethought his approach and practiced again.

"Mister Hurley, we have business to discuss." Short and sharp, that was the way to fix this Beeman decided.

A careless jumble of parcels and letters blocked the door. Beeman approached the pile and found a layer of sand upon every item. Not the dust of age, which Beeman grew accustomed to as a clerk in the bowels of an estate office, but an incredibly thick layer of sand. Further inspection revealed more sand winding through the grass, some of it rising in yellow hillocks amongst the green like boils on healthy skin. Lush corn waved to him in the breeze, silk glistened gold in the sun. It was hardly Death Valley.

An inky form hopped through the field. Beeman squinted in the sun. More crows waited among the corn. Their unwavering black eyes remained on the door of the house. He thought of that scratching, needling from their claws against the dirt. The wind rose and rattled the corn. It was hard not to hear human whispers in it. Beeman cleared his throat and turned his back to them. It did little good. He could feel their eyes stabbing into him.

"Mister Hurley," Beeman called and rapped on the door. An unseen layer of sand fell from atop the door and spilled onto Beeman's hand. He stepped back fearing a blemish upon his coat.

"Mister Hurley!"

"Who's there? Lyle?" Someone called from down the drive where Beeman had parked the car. Beeman fiddled with his hair, keeping his hand alongside his eyes and blocking the crows from view. He walked back to the Model T. The seat remained empty. The back half of the property gave him nothing. Nothing waited in the corn behind the farmhouse. There were only more fields, an endless stretch with not another soul in sight. Beeman's feet tried to swim out from beneath him.

"Mister Hurley! It's Tal—"

"I know who ya are Beeman. Ya the one whose been sendin' me all them telegrams." Beeman looked around the other end of the car and hoped the old farmer wasn't trying to play hide-and-seek.

"Up here, ya damned fool."

Beeman followed the voice up to the house's second story. Hurley leaned out the window, crouching there on the sill like a bird himself. Gone was the stout farmer, here now replaced by a bundle of sticks wrapped in human skin.

Beeman smiled and gave a reflexive, curt nod of the head. "Mister Hurley, if I may come in for a moment there is an important matter to discuss."

"I know ya 'important matter' and I don't feel too keen on lettin' ya in. I'm bein' watched day and night now." Hurley's beady eyes crinkled further into his withered face like chips of coal in a melting snowman.

Beeman stopped smiling and looked across the road. "Yes, I see that."

Hurley's frail body stirred upon the sill. "What? Ya see them crows, too?" Beeman's skin pricked with gooseflesh at Hurley's words. He had never seen a madman, but he wondered if he witnessed one now. With the skittish tone and the way he perched upon that sill, Hurley seemed ready for an advancing army.

"Well, yes," Beeman said. "They've been in the road since I got here. Any idea why they do that?"

Hurley gave no answer.

Beeman shrugged. "Strange things, they don't make a sound do they?" He looked back up at an empty window. Hurley shoved open the front door. A cloud of sand and packages flew away towards the fields.

"Get in here boy! They lookin' at ya, we're both in the same boat."

Was Hurley truly insane? Beeman wiped his sweaty palms against his suit coat and nearly lost the grip of his briefcase. An insane man would not be deemed fit to conduct business with the firm. The farmers booted off Francis Hurley's land would see to that.

"Yes, very well, Mister Hurley." Beeman ran up the walkway and put back on his best, neighborly smile. Hurley grabbed him by the shoulder and hauled him inside. Despite the rough welcome, Beeman felt better within the cool haven of the farmhouse. The smile broke away at the shotgun leaning against the door. The dull twin barrels looked big enough to fall into. Beeman jumped as Hurley snatched the weapon and rested it on one arm.

"Come on then," Hurley gestured further into the house. When Beeman tried to let the crazed farmer go first, Hurley grunted and pushed him along. Hurley followed close behind. Every thud of Hurley's boots, every time the wind rattled a pane of glass, Beeman jumped a little more, expecting each sound to be his last.

The narrow hall brought them to a cramped kitchen. A squat wood burning stove stood off to the side covered in grime. The floor needed a good scrubbing to even start stripping away the streaks of dirt. Stacks upon stacks of canning jars surrounded the two men. Nearly all of them were empty. Mostly empty. Scattered bits of dried food clung to the jars' insides. Some were full of a yellow liquid Beeman hoped was moonshine.

To Beeman's relief, the old farmer set the shotgun against the stove and sat down at the small table. Jars of stewed tomatoes lay topsy-turvy across it. Beeman joined him, back to the door and blocking Hurley's path to the shotgun.

"Um, Mister Hurley." Beeman ran a finger across the table's surface and instantly regretted it. "We have to discuss some uh, pending business."

"We're not discussin' business of any kind a'tall." Hurley chewed his lower lip and looked out a soaped window.

"I'm afraid you have to. My firm has gone into contract with you to sell," Beeman's voice wavered as he took stock of the room again, "all this."

"It ain't mine to give, and it ain't ya's to sell, boy."

Beeman scoffed. "Oh, yes, it is, sir." He withdrew the latest mark-ups from his briefcase and held them up against the sunlight. "Haven't you heard the news? You're a land baron now."

Hurley continued staring outside. "Didn't bring ya in here to discuss all that; I brought ya in here to unravel it."

"You can't just back out, man."

Hurley's head snapped back to face Beeman, a wild look flaring up in his old eyes. "Ya damn right I wanna back out!" Hurly snatched up a jar of tomatoes, the red insides sloshing.

"This ain't no deed gettin' sold here! This is my soul, and ya don't wanna take it! The mark will pass to ya!"

Beeman brought the briefcase up to shield his face from a possible attack, but Hurley only held the jar in his hands, pleading with his eyes. Something about those eyes made Beeman think for one ridiculous moment that Hurley made sense. Then Beeman thought of the future.

He tried a different tact. "Why don't you wish to sell the land, Hurley?" The old farmer looked back out the window. Beeman continued, "Scared of going it alone? I'm very sorry for your losses, but before Lyle's accident both of you were of the same mind. I promised you a fair price from my people. That's no different now, until I walk out that door."

Hurley waved him away with a weak hand and studied the water spots in the sagging ceiling. The farmer's defiance put a little starch into Beeman. He clicked open the case and slapped the deeds on the table.

"Sign, please."

Hurley sighed. "Lyle didn't die in no accident, and Francis didn't die in one neither."

Beeman struggled to swallow over his dry tongue blocking the way. He finally managed, "What do you mean?"

"Lyle and me wanted to sell the land for so long, we really did. The boom goin' on, we figured it was for the best. Our folks been farmin' all their lives, Lyle and me watched it work them down to the bone. Daddy died right out there in Lyle's fields. Just died at the plow. Mule still drug him a good ways afterward. Daddy had a mouthful of dirt when we found him."

Beeman shivered.

"Never wanted that for me or mine. Lyle and me never cared for this life. Thought all of us could move to somewhere better. But Francis—" Hurley got out of his chair and opened the jar of stewed tomatoes. He leaned against the stove and dug out dripping red gobs of mush with his fingers. Beeman couldn't help staring at the shotgun directly behind him.

"Francis was the choir boy of the three of us. I dunno, maybe 'cause he got named after a Saint or somethin'. Always took to church and the like, even if our folks didn't press it on us too hard. Maybe he thought God were the one to thank for all his good luck. Francis was just better for this life than Lyle and me. We come from what ya wouldn't exactly call 'good' Christians, Beeman. Francis didn't feel takin' the land, his own land, away from the squatters he let move in was right. 'Weren't Christian,' he always said. Wouldn't sell."

Hurley stuck more red mess in his mouth, bit down. He huffed air through his nostrils, chewed. Red stains spread across his hands.

"So, me and Lyle, well, I guess we did somethin' *not Christian* right back at him. Our own flesh and blood. Maybe we ought to have read the Bible better."

"What are you saying?" Beeman glanced over at the door which now seemed very far from the table and the crazed Hurley, red juice dribbling over his chin. "You killed Francis and Lyle?"

The words clung to the air alongside the stench of cow pies and silage.

"Nah, just Francis," Hurley finished Beeman's horrified thought, "but Lyle was no accident neither." Hurley's eyes went hooded. "Oh, no, very much intentional."

"The thresher…"

Hurley nodded and sniffed the air like something fouler had crept inside.

"Your brother, he," Beeman wanted to pull his question back into himself but out it came, "Suicide? The guilt?"

"More like escape, I reckon. Ever see a mouse caught in a trap Beeman? They'll rip off their own tail; paralyze themselves just to get away. I found my brother Lyle the next day. Found him dead in his own barn just like them papers say. But know what they don't say? Hmm?" Hurley's eyes sparkled with more life than Beeman had seen since coming here. It made his stomach twist.

"Papers don't say nothin' 'bout me needin' to break down the barn door to get in. Whole place were locked up tighter than a drum from the inside."

"You said it wasn't suicide—"

Hurley shook his head. "Somethin' been clawin' that door to pieces from the outside, night Lyle went to the thresher. The crows ya see? They come callin' and he didn't want to answer."

"They wanted Lyle; you see?" Hurley whispered, "All his transgressions, he couldn't get away scot-free. Tried takin' his own way out, but they got him even after all that. Must've gotten in through the empty silo. Crows are damned smart I understand."

"Crows? Now come to your senses, crows couldn't murder a man." The madness seemed to crawl through everything in the disgusting kitchen. Beeman's skin itched with it. That maddening urge to look out the window, to make sure the crows were still there, Beeman fought through it.

"Don't believe me all ya like," Hurley said, and Beeman wanted to scream at him to get out of his head, to stop reading his thoughts. But, like the urge to stare out the window, Beeman choked it down.

"I'd tell ya about the look in Lyle's eyes, Beeman. The horror in them, but I can't do that. My brother didn't have no more eyes when I found him. No tongue for that matter neither, or so Doc Newman tells me."

Beeman closed his eyes, breathed deep; let the reek of the horrible kitchen bring him back to his senses.

"We both got blood on our hands." Hurley sucked tomato juice off his chin stubble. "Lyle told me about crows camped outside his place down the road. Always in the same strip of road, always sittin' there watchin' him. Said how Francis was with 'em. Said Francis spoke through the crows. 'Course I told him he was a damn fool. Then…well I already told ya what happened."

Beeman let out a dry, bony chuckle. "Now the crows want you?"

"Not just me, they want ya, too, they want all who are gettin' rich off this while the land's raped and folks go hungry. The land's fightin' back, too. Ya seen how we sell off parcels, buy them back, sell them again, over-farm them. It's sick and tired of us, Beeman; it's lettin' famine creep up on us. Ya see what's been happenin' to my land. Bit by bit it's dyin' and chokin' on sand, and on that sandy wind come the crows. Crows always come when there's blood spilt, and damn it all to hell, they smell it strong on us, Beeman. Make no mistake about that."

Beeman gripped his hands into fists. "Really? Spook stories and hoodoo? This is just business, you stupid hayseed! Facts and numbers, it's what we built this whole country on!"

Hurley stepped up to Beeman's face. A cloud of canned tomatoes and pickled eggs came with him.

Hurley grinned with red-stained teeth. "Ya right, Beeman. Country thrives on it, devourin' folks whole. Gets us all some way or another. My brothers, them farmers ya snatched Francis' land from, there's a price for all of it. Just watch and see. This area's gonna suffer, the country's gonna be put down like a rabid dog."

Beeman threw his hands up in the air. "Oh! And the crows are going to punish us all, is that it? They're going to corner me and peck my eyes out simply for doing my job? Eat my lying tongue? Or maybe just make me go loony like in those dime horror novels?"

"Take ya pick, Beeman," Hurley murmured. "Ya gonna be punished just like me if ya do this."

Beeman forgot he was addressing a self-confessed, armed murderer. In that instant, Beeman was in his office behind a shiny, new desk staring down an ignorant wretch with a head full of superstitious nonsense.

"Hurley, if you're frightened of some birds on the road and a few wisps of dust on your farmland, then you're a disgrace of a man. You're also a fool. Sell this land, and you can do anything you damned well please; go anywhere you want. Miles upon miles away, out to the Napa Valley where crows aren't even allowed to roost." Beeman let that notion sink in with him.

"Sign these papers, and make us both very wealthy and very happy men. Can you do that?"

Hurley chewed his lower lip again. "Don't make me sign that, Beeman. Just forget the whole business. I can't."

Now, it was Beeman's turn to grin as the old man squirmed. Beeman produced a fountain pen from his briefcase. He wanted to ram it straight through Hurley's quivering, lower lip. Instead, he slapped it down onto the table next to the deeds.

"Sign them. This is happening. Now. Or you can rot out here in this pig sty."

Hurley nodded his weary head. "Suppose I can sign those. Ain't the worst that'll happen to me."

The old man etched his name upon the signature line with gnarled, shaking hands. Beeman licked his lips and quickly scribbled his own signature alongside. Before Beeman could give Hurley the usual pat on the back and laugh he gave all his clients, the man slumped back down into his chair. Hurley opened another jar of tomatoes, chewed them up in his cragged maw, and wept. Beeman sighed in disgust at the man's face encased in dribbling tears and tomato juice. The usual customs could be ignored. Beeman decided just about everything inside the horrid place could be ignored. He stalked back out the door, briefcase in hand.

Beeman stepped over the jumble of parcels and sand. He would need to act fast after getting back to Chicago. In another year, the wind could scour the topsoil away like a knife. No one would buy up a patch of sand and dirt. He never thought of the crows till halfway to the car. Beeman licked his lips again and focused on putting away some documents, but he finally looked up.

The road beyond the rusted fence lay empty. With that fear gone, others rushed in to replace it. If anyone found out about Francis' murder, it would mean the end. Hart's reputation might be crippled, but Beeman's whole life would be utterly ruined. He gripped his briefcase tighter and continued towards the car. The farmhouse window screeched open behind him, and Beeman met it with a screech of his own. He finally lost the grip of the briefcase. The latch came undone and spilled nearly all the papers across the drive.

"What?" He called out to Hurley. The farmer waited in the window again. Tomato juice dried to a bloody crust on his chin like he'd bitten off his tongue.

"What?" Beeman repeated as he struggled with the briefcase. One hand rose towards the Model T's door.

"Got us both," Hurley rasped. "Why couldn't ya'll just let me be?"

Beeman rolled his eyes, "Goodbye, Mister Hurley."

Hurley leveled the shotgun below his chin.

"God damn ya, God damn us both," Hurley moaned and blew his head off.

Red splinters of glass sailed through the sunny day. Hurley seemed to hang in the air, floating like a feather on a breeze. Then his body slammed onto the hood of the Model T. Beeman gaped. His late business partner's head was sheared away into a gristly mess. Steam billowed from the crumpled hood and covered the corpse like a shroud. Crimson stained the cracked earth of the drive, but the dried soil sucked it down leaving bare dirt. Then the sunny sky turned to midnight.

Crows swooped over the gable in the same path as Hurley and dove upon his body. Their screeches conquered the summer air. They set about consuming the body piece-by-piece, pale flesh dangled from their black beaks. The entire murder feasted. Beeman screamed.

Two crows lifted their heads from Hurley's mangled corpse and resumed their blank, prophetic stare at Beeman. The wind whipped coarse sand across his face and tore the remaining deeds out of his hand. The papers drifted across the drive past the crows' feet. Talbert Beeman's name, written clearly and legibly on the surface, looked back up at them. Then the wind roared and buried the papers beneath the sand. He had the attention of the whole murder now.

Beeman backed away from the shattered car, away from Hurley's body, and away from the crows. The edge of the briefcase caught the back of his feet and Beeman slammed against the ground. His teeth clattered down and caught the tip of his tongue. Hot blood greased his mouth. When he screamed, more of it ran to the ground and disappeared.

The crows, silent again, leapt off and began their scratchy march towards him. The phonograph record ran again and again under that phantom needle. Beeman squirmed to his feet and hurried out the drive back the way he came. The crows came, too. The wind whistled, shaking the corn again. The dead cat shivered in the wind like it was performing a final, gruesome jig. Beeman tried to guess how long a walk it was back towards town, but the sun was too hot and fierce for him to think.

Someone would pass by, Beeman told himself. Then, he remembered there were no more farmers in this area, every single parcel now owned by Mr. Hart. Beeman swallowed blood and nearly fainted.

"Just birds." He spat blood at the crows. "Just birds!"

They opened their beaks and human screams issued forth. The noise cut Beeman's mind, it shattered inside his ears, and in that terrible instant he wanted nothing more than release. He did not need Hart's desk; he did not need the money, or a future. He only wanted free from that awful noise. Yet, it did not retreat, it only increased with the march of the crows.

Beeman threw a rock at them. They flapped their wings and scattered out of the way. They parted like an oil slick and regrouped in an instant. He drew his pen, weeping at the weak hope it might save him. The crows stared. Beeman scuttled down the road, desperately trying to ignore the growing caws and cries following close behind.

The Scarecrow

G. Ranger Wormser

B^{en—"}

The woman stood in the doorway of the ramshackle, tumble-down shanty. Her hands were cupped at her mouth. The wind blew loose, whitish-blond wisps of hair around her face and slashed the faded blue dress into the uncorseted bulk of her body.

"Benny—oh, Benny—"

Her call echoed through the still evening.

Her eyes staring straight before her down the slope in front of the house caught sight of something blue and antiquatedly military standing waist-deep and rigid in the corn field.

"That ole scarecrow," she muttered to herself, "that there old scarecrow with that there ole uniform onto him, too!"

The sun was going slowly, just beyond the farthest hill. The unreal light of the sky's reflected colors held over the yellow, waving tips of the cornfield.

"Benny—" she called again. "Oh—Benny!"

And then she saw him coming toward her, trudging up the hill.

She waited until he stood in front of her.

"Supper, Ben," she said. "Was you down in the south meadow where you couldn't hear me call?"

"Naw."

He was young and slight. He had thick hair and a thin face. His features were small. There was nothing unusual about them. His eyes were deep-set and long, with lids that were heavily fringed.

"You heard me calling you?"

"Yes, Maw."

He stood there straight and still. His eyelids were lowered.

"Why ain't you come along then? What ails you, Benny, letting me shout and shout that way?"

"Nothing—Maw."

"Where was you?"

He hesitated a second before answering her.

"I was to the bottom of the hill."

"And what was you doing down there to the bottom of the hill? What was you doing down there, Benny?" Her voice had a hushed tenseness to it.

"I was watching, Maw."

"Watching, Benny?"

"That's what I was doing."

His tone held a guarded sullenness.

"'Tain't no such a pretty sunset, Benny."

"Warn't watching no sunset."

"Benny!"

"Well." He spoke quickly. "What d'you want to put it there for? What d'you want to do that for in the first place?"

"There was birds, Benny. You know there was birds."

"That ain't what I mean. What for d'you put on that there uniform?"

"I ain't had nothing else. There warn't nothing but your granddad's ole uniform. It's fair in rags, Benny. It's all I had to put on to it."

"Well, you done it yourself."

"Naw, Benny, naw! 'Tain't nothing but an ole uniform with a stick into it. Just to frighten off them birds. 'Tain't nothing else. Honest, 'tain't, Benny."

He looked up at her out of the corners of his eyes.

"It was waving its arms."

"That's the wind."

"Naw, Maw. Waving its arms before the wind it come up."

"Sush, Benny! 'Tain't likely. 'Tain't."

"I was watching, Maw. I seen it wave and wave. S'pose it should beckon—s'pose it should beckon to me? I'd be going, then, Maw."

"Sush, Benny."

"I'd fair have to go, Maw."

"Leave your mammy? Naw, Ben; naw. You couldn't never go off and leave your mammy. Even if you ain't able to bear this here farm, you couldn't go off from your mammy. You couldn't! Not—your—Maw—Benny!"

She could see his mouth twitch. She saw him catch his lower lip in under his teeth.

"Aw—"

"Say you couldn't leave, Benny; say it!"

"I—I fair hate this here farm!" He mumbled. "Morning and night—and morning and night. Nothing but chores and earth. And then, some more of them chores. And always that there way. So it is! Always! And the stillness! Nothing alive, nothing! Sometimes, I ain't able to stand it nohow. Sometimes—"

"You'll get to like it—later, mebbe—"

"Naw! Naw, Maw!"

"You will, Benny. Sure you will."

"I won't never. I ain't able to help fretting. It's all closed up tight inside of me. Eating and eating. It makes me feel sick."

She put out a hand and laid it heavily on his shoulder.

"Likely it's a touch of fever in the blood, Benny."

"Aw! I ain't got no fever!"

"You'll be feeling better in the morning, Ben."

"I'll be feeling the same, Maw. That's just it. Always the same. Nothing but the stillness. Nothing alive. And down there in the corn field—"

"That ain't alive, Benny!"

"Ain't it, Maw?"

"Don't say that, Benny. Don't!"

He shook her hand off of him.

"I was watching," he said doggedly. "I seen it wave and wave."

She led the way into the kitchen. The boy followed at her heels.

A lamp was lighted on the center table. The one window was uncurtained. Through the naked spot of it the evening glow poured shimmeringly into the room.

Inside the doorway they both paused.

"You set down, Benny."

He pulled a chair up to the table.

She took a steaming pot from the stove and, emptying it into a plate, placed the dish before him.

He fell to eating silently.

She came and sat opposite him. She watched him cautiously. She did not want him to know that she was watching him. Whenever he glanced up, she hurried her eyes away from his face. In the stillness, the only live things were those two pair of eyes darting away from each other.

"Benny!" She could not stand it any longer. "Benny—just—you—just—you—"

He gulped down a mouthful of food.

"Aw, Maw—don't you start nothing. Not no more tonight, Maw."

She half-rose from her chair. For a second, she leaned stiffly against the table. Then, she slipped back into her seat, her whole body limp and relaxed.

"I ain't going to start nothing, Benny. I ain't even going to talk about this here farm. Honest, I ain't."

"Aw—this—here—farm—!"

"I've gave the best years of my life to it." She spoke the words defiantly.

"You said that all afore, Maw."

"It's true," she murmured. "Terrible true. And I done it for you, Benny. I wanted to be giving you something. It's all I'd got to give you, Benny. There's many a man, Ben, that's glad of his farm. And grateful, too. There's many that makes it pay."

"And what'll I do if it does pay, Maw? What'll I do then?"

"I—I—don't know, Benny. It's only just beginning, now."

"But if it does pay, Maw? What'll I do? Go away from here?"

"Naw, Benny. Not away. What'd you go away for, when it pays? After all them years I gave to it?"

His spoon clattered noisily to his plate. He pushed his chair back from the table. The legs of it rasped loudly along the uncarpeted floor. He got to his feet.

"Let's go on outside," he said. "There ain't no sense to this here talking and talking."

She glanced up at him. Her eyes were narrow and hard.

"All right, Benny. I'll clear up. I'll be along in a minute. All right, Benny."

He slouched heavily out of the room.

She sat where she was, the set look pressed on her face. Automatically, her hands reached out among the dishes, pulling them toward her.

Outside the boy sank down on the step.

It was getting dark. There were shadows along the ground. Blue shadows. In the graying skies one star shone brilliantly. Beyond the mist-slurred summit of a hill the full moon grew yellow.

In front of him was the slope of wind-moved cornfield, and in the center of it the dim, military figure standing waist deep in the corn.

His eyes fixed themselves to it.

"Ole uniform with a stick into it." He whispered the words very low.

Still—standing there—still. The same wooden attitude of it. His same, cunning watching of it. There was a wind. He knew it was going over his face. He could feel the cool of the wind across his moistened lips.

He took a deep breath.

Down there in the shivering cornfield, standing in the dark, blue shadows, the dim figure had quivered.

An arm moved, swaying to and fro. The other arm began—swaying—swaying. A tremor ran through it. Once, it pivoted. The head shook slowly from side to side. The arms rose and fell—and rose again. The head came up and down and rocked a bit to either side.

"I'm here—" Benny muttered involuntarily. "Here."

The arms were tossing and stretching.

He thought the head faced in his direction.

The wind had died out.

The arms went down and came up and reached.

"Benny—"

The woman seated herself on the step at his side.

"Look!" He mumbled. "Look!"

He pointed his hand at the dim figure shifting restlessly in the quiet, shadow-saturated cornfield.

Her eyes followed after his.

"Oh, Benny—"

"Well—" His voice was hoarse. "It's moving, ain't it? You can see it moving for yourself, can't you? You ain't able to say you don't see it, are you?"

"The wind—" She stammered.

"Where's the wind?"

"Down there."

"D'you feel a wind? Say, d'you feel a wind?"

"Mebbe down there."

"There ain't no wind. Not now—there ain't! And it's moving, ain't it? Say, it's moving, ain't it?"

Maw said, "It looks like it was dancing. So it does. Like as if it was—making—itself—dance—" Benny's eyes were still riveted on those arms that came up and down—up and down—and reached. "It'll stop soon now." He stuttered it more to himself than to her. "Then, it'll be still. I've watched it mighty often. Mebbe it knows I watch it. Mebbe that's why it moves—"

"Aw, Benny—"

"Well, you see it, don't you? You thought there was something the matter with me when I come and told you how it waves and waves. But you seen it waving, ain't you?"

"It's nothing, Ben. Look, Benny. It's stopped!"

The two of them stared down the slope at the dim, military figure standing rigid and waist deep in the corn field.

The woman gave a quick sigh of relief.

For several moments they were silent.

From somewhere in the distance came the harsh, discordant sound of bullfrogs croaking. Out in the night a dog bayed at the golden, full moon climbing up over the hills. A bird circled between sky and earth hovering above the cornfield. They saw its slow descent, and then for a second, they caught the startled whir of its wings, as it flew blindly into the night.

"That ole scarecrow!" She muttered.

"S'pose," he whispered. "S'pose when it starts its moving like that—s'pose some day it walks out of that there cornfield! Just naturally walks out here to me. What then, if it walks out?"

"Benny!"

"That's what I'm thinking of, all the time. If it takes it into its head to just naturally walk out here. What's going to stop it, if it wants to walk out after me; once it starts moving that way? What?"

"Benny! It couldn't do that! It couldn't!"

"Mebbe, it won't. Mebbe, it'll just beckon first. Mebbe, it won't come after me. Not if I go when it beckons. I kind of figure it'll beckon when it wants me. I couldn't stand the other. I couldn't wait for it to come out here after me. I kind of feel it'll beckon. When it beckons, I'll be going."

"Benny, there's sickness coming on you."

"'Tain't no sickness."

The woman's hands were clinched together in her lap.

"I wish to Gawd—" she said, "I wish I ain't never seen the day when I put that there thing up in that there cornfield. But I ain't thought nothing like this could never happen. I wish to Gawd I ain't never seen the day—"

"'Tain't got nothing to do with you." His voice was very low.

"It's got everything to do with me. So, it has! You said that afore yourself; and you was right. Ain't I put it up? Ain't I looked high and low the house through? Ain't that ole uniform of your granddad's been the only rag I could lay my hands on? Was there anything else I could use? Was there?"

"Aw, Maw—!"

"Ain't we needed a scarecrow down there? With them birds so awful bad? Pecking away at the corn, pecking."

"'Tain't your fault, Maw."

"There warn't nothing else but that there ole uniform. I wouldn't have took it, otherwise. Poor ole Pa so desperate proud of it as he was. Him fighting for his country in it. Always saying that he was. He couldn't be doing enough for his country. And that there ole uniform meaning so much to him. Like a part of him I used to think it, and— You wanting to say something, Ben?"

"Naw—naw—!"

"He wouldn't even let us be burying him in it. 'Put my country's flag next my skin,' he told us. 'When I die keep the ole uniform.' Just like a part of him, he thought it. Wouldn't I have kept it, falling to pieces as it is, if there'd have been anything else to put up there in that there cornfield?"

She felt the boy stiffen suddenly.

"And with him a soldier—" He broke off abruptly.

She sensed what he was about to say.

"Aw, Benny— That was different. Honest, it was. He warn't the only one in his family. There was two brothers."

The boy got to his feet.

"Why won't you let me go?" He asked it passionately. "Why d'you keep me here? You know I ain't happy! You know all the men've gone from these here parts. You know I ain't happy! Ain't you going to see how much I want to go? Ain't you able to know that I want to fight for my country? The way he did his fighting?"

The boy jerked his head in the direction of the figure standing waist deep in the cornfield, standing rigidly and faintly outlined beneath the haunting flood of moonlight.

"Naw, Benny. You can't go. Naw!"

"Why, Maw? Why d'you keep saying that and saying it?"

"I'm all alone, Benny. I've gave all my best years to make the farm pay for you. You got to stay, Benny. You got to stay on here with me. You just plain got to! You'll be glad someday, Benny. Later on. You'll be right glad."

She saw him thrust his hands hastily into his trouser pockets.

"Glad?" His voice sounded tired. "I'll be shamed. That's what I'll be. Nothing, d'you hear, nothing but shamed!"

She started to her feet.

"Benny—" A note of fear shook through the words. "You wouldn't—wouldn't go?"

He waited a moment before he answered her. "If you ain't wanting me to go, I'll stay. Gawd! I guess I plain got to stay."

"That's a good boy, Benny. You won't never be sorry nohow. I promise you! I'll be making it up to you. Honest, I will! There's lots of ways. I'll—"

He interrupted her. "Only, Maw—I won't let it come after me. If it beckons, I got to go!"

She gave a sudden laugh that trailed off uncertainly. "'Tain't going to beckon, Benny."

"It if beckons, Maw—"

"'Tain't going to, Benny. 'Tain't nothing but the wind that moves it. It's just the wind, sure. Mebbe, you got a touch of fever. Mebbe, you better go on to bed. You'll be all right in the morning. Just you wait and see. You're a good boy, Benny. You'll never go off and leave your Maw and the farm. You're a fine lad, Benny."

"If it beckons—" He repeated in weary monotone.

"'Tain't, Benny!"

"I'll be going to bed," he said.

"That's it, Benny. Good night."

"Good night, Maw."

§

She stood there listening to his feet thudding up the stairs. She heard him knocking about in the room overhead. A door banged. She stood quite still. There were footsteps moving slowly. A window was thrown open.

She looked up to see him leaning far out over the sill.

Her eyes went down the slope of the moonlight-bathed cornfield.

Her right hand curled itself into a fist.

"Ole scarecrow!" Benny muttered.

She half laughed.

She waited there until she saw the boy draw away from the window. She went into the house and bolted the door behind her. Then she went up the narrow steps.

That night, she lay awake for a long time. The heat had grown intense. She found herself tossing from side to side of the small bed.

The window shade had stuck at the top of the window.

The moonlight trickled into the room. She could see the window-framed, star-specked patch of the skies. When she sat up, she saw the round, reddish-yellow ball of the moon.

She must have dozed, because she woke with a start. She felt that she had had a fearful, evil dream. The horror of it clung to her.

The room was like an oven. She thought the walls were coming together and the ceiling pressing down. Her body was covered with sweat.

She forced herself wide awake. She made herself get out of the bed. She stood for a second uncertain. Then she went to the window.

Not a breath of air stirring.

The moon was high in the sky.

She looked out across the hills.

Down there to the left, the acres of potatoes. Potatoes were paying. She counted on a big harvest. To the right, the wheat. Only the second year for those five fields. She knew that she had done well with them.

She thought, with a smile running over her lips, back to the time when less than half of the place had been under cultivation. She remembered her dream of getting the whole of her farm in work. She and the boy had made good. She thought of that with savage complacency. It had been a struggle; a bitter, hard fight from the beginning. But she had made good with her farm.

And there down the slope, just in front of the house, the cornfield. And in the center of it, standing waist deep in the corn, the antiquated, military figure.

The smile slid from her mouth.

The suffocating heat was terrific.

Not a breath of air.

Suddenly, she began to shake from head to foot.

Her eyes wide and staring, were fixed on the moonlight-whitened cornfield. Her eyes were held to the moonlight-streaked figure standing in the ghostly corn.

Moving—

An arm swayed—swayed to and fro. Backwards and forwards—backwards—The other arm swaying. A tremor ran through it. Once it pivoted. The head shook slowly from side to side. The arms rose and fell and rose again. The head came up and down, and rocked a bit to either side.

"Dancing," she whispered stupidly. "Dancing—"

She thought she could not breathe. She had never felt such oppressive heat.

The arms were tossing and stretching. She could not take her eyes from it.

And then she saw both arms reach out, and slowly, very slowly, she saw the hands of them, beckoning.

In the stillness of the room next to her she thought she heard a crash.

She listened intently, her eyes stuck to those reaching arms, and the hands of them that beckoned and beckoned.

"Benny," she murmured. "Benny!"

Silence.

She could not think.

It was his talk that had done this. Benny's talk. He had said something about it walking out. If it should come out— Moving all over like that. If its feet should start! If they should of a sudden begin to shuffle—shuffle out of the cornfield!

But Benny wasn't awake. He couldn't see it. Thank Gawd! If only something would hold it! If only it would stop. Gawd!

Nothing stirring out there in the haunting moon-lighted night. Nothing moving. Nothing but the figure standing waist deep in the corn field. And even as she looked, the rigid, military figure grew still. Still, now, but for those slow, beckoning hands.

A tremendous dizziness came over her.

She closed her eyes for a second, and then she stumbled back to her bed.

She lay there panting. She pulled the sheets up across her face, her shaking fingers working the tops of them into a hard ball. She stuffed it between her chattering teeth.

Whatever happened, Benny mustn't hear her. She mustn't waken Benny. Thank Heaven, Benny was asleep. Benny must never know, how out there in the whitened night, the hands of the figure slowly and unceasingly beckoned and beckoned.

The sight of those reaching arms stayed before her. When, hours later, she fell asleep, she still saw the slow-moving, motioning hands.

It was morning when she wakened. The sun streamed into the room. She went to the door and opened it.

"Benny," she called. "Oh, Benny."

There was no answer.

"Benny!" She called again. "Get on up. It's late, Benny!"

The house was quiet.

She half-dressed herself and went into his room.

The bed had been slept in. She saw that at a glance. But his clothes were not there. Down in the field because she'd forgotten to wake him...

In a sudden stunning flash, she remembered the crash she had heard.

It took her a long while to get to the little closet behind the bed. Before she opened it, she knew it would be empty.

The door creaked open. His one hat and coat were gone.

She had known that.

He had seen those two reaching arms! He had seen those two hands that had slowly, very slowly, beckoned!

She went to the window. Her eyes staring straight before her, down the slope in front of the house, caught sight of something blue and antiquatedly military standing waist deep and rigid in the cornfield.

"You ole scarecrow." she whimpered. "Why're you standing there?" She sobbed. "What're you standing still for now?"

Battlefields

Vonnie Winslow Crist

*D*riving home from our niece's confirmation in Staunton, my husband and I decide to visit New Market Battlefield. We tour the visitor's center, try the interactive Civil War computer programs, and watch the re-enactment movie. I dab my eyes with a tissue after viewing the part of the film about a Jewish boy who searched for his Christian friend, carried him to safety, then stayed with him until he died. It is just one of many tales of heroism and sacrifice.

When I blow my nose, Chuck shakes his head, drapes his arm across the back of my seat, and squeezes my right shoulder. Chuck clears his throat, stands, then stretches as the lights turn back on. Before we leave the visitor's center, I pick up a battlefield map from the smiling information desk worker.

"Have a nice day," she chirps as we walk outside and past a drooping American flag.

We cannot take our RV up the lane to the edge of the actual battlefield—the vehicle is too large and unwieldy, so we pull on our jackets and climb the hill on foot. While we walk, I read from the map a description of the fighting that took place at New Market.

As I unfold the map to read the information on the back, I stumble on some loose gravel.

Chuck grabs my elbow. "Careful," he says.

"Always," I answer, but know it to be a lie. Chuck holds onto my elbow for a few more seconds, then lets go. Though my palm aches for his, we do not hold hands.

I stand on the ridge above the Shenandoah, study the glossy strand of river that winds its way like a ribbon through the Virginia farmland. Chuck's arms are crossed. He is scowling. I am not sure if it is the battlefield or this morning's argument about taking his mother with us to the theater that brings his eyebrows together. I sigh. The way the corners of his mouth curve down reminds me of Freda.

Freda is what I call Chuck's mother. She would prefer I address her as *Mother*, but I already have one of those. At our first meeting thirty-five years ago, Freda had looked me up and down, waited until Chuck turned away, and said, "Well, his *last* girlfriend was prettier."

I could not think of a response then, and she had caught me off-guard again this week.

"I can't wait to see *Cabaret*," Freda had said.

"Oh, are you going with friends?" I had been surprised since I didn't think she had any friends who liked musical theater.

"Not with friends. I'm going with you and Chuck. He knows how much I enjoy music, so he invited me to go, too."

I had felt like screaming, "Leave us alone." Instead, I said, "Really?"

Freda's lips had smiled, but her eyes had narrowed as she added, "Chuck always thinks of his mother."

§

I reach the top of the battlefield incline and glance behind me. Unruly dandelions struggle up the hill proud and true as the schoolboys from the Virginia Military Academy, who when called upon to assist their Rebel brothers, parade-marched through deep mud into Union cannon fire. None of the Cadets were over nineteen. None of them had been shot at before. None of them had seen a comrade fall. I think of my nephews. Five of them are between fourteen and eighteen—the right age for the battle at New Market.

Chuck is silent—so I listen to the whir of insects giddy with spring and the background rumble of eighteen wheelers on the highway. A red-tailed hawk swoops down, grabs a rabbit from some tall grasses near the split-rail fence. The raptor, talons clutching a limp gray body, lifts into the window of sky.

I'd like to blame it on the angle of the sunlight, but I know the ghostly young men in uniform I see leaning on the fence railings are real.

"Ready to go," I say, and hurry down the slope. A cool breeze ruffles my hair, flaps it against my face like dark wings. Just before reaching the bottom of the hill, I spot a hawk's feather caught in some bindweed. I pluck the feather from the tangled vegetation, twirl it between my thumb and forefinger, thinking of the souls of soldiers rising to meet the wind. And of the ghosts by the fence.

Chuck follows. He starts our RV and pulls back onto the interstate. "We'll stay at the campground in Harpers Ferry tonight. Then, visit Antietam tomorrow."

I nod. We have always by-passed Antietam. There are plenty of signs calling in brown and gold for us to visit the battlefield and see Bloody Lane. We have just never chosen to take that exit before.

"Is the visitor's center like the one at Gettysburg?" I ask as I slide the hawk's feather between the pages of a book I have been reading.

I have been to Gettysburg five times. Every time I go, I envision young men full of faith and bravado marching, banners aflutter, into the Wheatfield and through the Peach Orchard. When I tour Little Roundtop, scan the miles of Pennsylvania countryside, the tar-and-chip walkways and man-made railings added to accommodate the modern visitor seem intrusive. I always place my hand on a boulder and close my eyes. The emptiness of the landscape, creaks of swaying trees, roughness of stone, and laments of the crows tell the tale. I always spot soldiers, translucent and slightly blurred, when I look close enough.

It was thundering the last time I visited Gettysburg and stood where Abraham Lincoln read his most famous address. Our children were with Chuck and me, so we made sure to see the Maryland statues. The sculpted soldiers and horses looked melancholy in the storm twilight—but not as melancholy as the wounded and dead sprawled at the base of the monuments. I, of course, said nothing about the apparitions. It was several years ago, but I still recall the pungent smell of wet leaves, soaked earth, and death.

"No," Chuck answers. "There is not much there except a movie, I think."

I know he went to Antietam years ago with his parents. Chuck's father is dead, his mother still angry decades later. I think that is why she dislikes me—I still have a husband and hers abandoned her, though I'm sure he would have preferred to live long enough to meet all of his grandchildren. Before he met Freda, Chuck's father had served in the US Army as a medic, but he wouldn't talk about the things he saw and did when he was over in Korea. "Some things aren't worth remembering," he had said.

I study Chuck as he continues to stare straight ahead. He resembles his father, especially around the eyes. "She can come with us to *Cabaret*," I say.

"No, I will tell her she can't come."

"What about the extra ticket? Can we get our money back?"

"Nope, that's a hundred bucks wasted." Chuck puts on his mother's frown. I bite my fingernails and think about wasting one hundred dollars because I want to spend my anniversary alone with my husband.

When we get to the RV Park, we ride the bus down to Harpers Ferry. Before Chuck and I find a restaurant for dinner, we trek up the path to Jefferson's Rock, past an old church, and to a cemetery. The view of the confluence of the Potomac and Shenandoah from the graveyard is spectacular. And the translucent residents wandering between tombstones don't seem to mind our presence.

"Now, there's a river." Chuck admires the Potomac—wide, powerful, surging past Washington, DC to the Atlantic.

"I love the Shenandoah," I respond.

We used to stop by Harpers Ferry every August with our children on the way to a family vacation in Mathias, West Virginia. Observed by the drowned perched on rocks in the middle of the Shenandoah, we would picnic below Bull Falls and watch wood ducks paddle in the shallows, crayfish scuttle from under limestone, and minnows swim in shadowed pools. Our children would try to scoop up the river-dwellers in paper cups. Most summers, they caught a few minnows, a crayfish or two, and dozens of water spiders. We would release them. "See you next year," we'd call as we pulled away in our minivan. The dead would nod and wave farewell.

Today, like so many days before, the sun strikes the Shenandoah and explodes into a million shards. I watch as my river merges with the Potomac and together they travel to the sea. Chuck and I hike down the hill to a small Italian café crowded with tables and glowing with candlelight.

I prop my chin on my hands and watch Chuck rearrange his place setting making sure the knife and spoon handles are parallel. He studies his salad fork, then polishes it with a napkin. Disliking straws, he wipes the rim of his water glass before taking a drink. When he looks at me, I grin.

"Want to check my silverware?" I ask after sipping my ice water through a straw.

"If you need me to."

Chuck manages a brief smile, then examines the menu and orders sweet sausage in marinara sauce. I have the vegetarian special. Our dinner is quiet.

§

Chuck goes to bed early. I stay up and read a book about lost country life. Hours later, I slip beneath the covers and lean against Chuck's back. I fall asleep to typical campground noises: the murmurs of muffled voices, the twang of a guitar, and the occasional bark of a dog.

The sound of someone screaming wakes me. I sit up in bed, allow my eyes to adjust to the moonless night. The scream comes again from a tree limb beside the RV.

"What *is* that?" asks Chuck.

"A screech owl."

"Thank God that's all it is. I thought I was going to have to run outside and play hero."

"In your flannel pajamas?" We both laugh as I lay back down. The owl screams again. "What time is it?"

Chuck flicks on a flashlight, looks at a watch that is dangling from a hook on the wall beside the bed. "Four-thirty."

I groan. The owl screams one last time then abandons the branch outside our window.

We fall back to sleep, and I dream of the flocks of pigeons, jackdaws, collared doves, sparrows, and rooks that line the window ledges, rooftops, and arches of Tintern Abbey, Caerphilly Castle, Raglan Castle, St. Andrew's Cathedral Inverness, the High Kirk of St. Giles, and the ruined church in Coventry, whose name I have forgotten, that fell victim to German bombs in World War II. There is a tale of sacrifice attached to the village of Coventry. The tour guide tells me again that the townsfolk allowed themselves to be bombed by the Germans rather than tip off the enemy that the English had broken their communication codes.

In the dream, Chuck and I stand with the other chaperons in cathedral after castle after courtyard listening to an *a capella* choir. I see the angels in the architecture and the carved gargoyles peering down at us with their toadish smiles as the young choristers sing *A Song of Peace*. While the harmonious voices float above the rooftops, I notice the skies over Coventry *are* the same brilliant blue as the skies over Culloden, Antietam, Gettysburg, and New Market, Virginia.

Then, I am holding Chuck's hand and we are soaring with the terns and gannets and ghosts through the sky and over the sea to Skye to have sheep-cheese sandwiches with cups of Darjeeling tea in a tiny shop with two crossed swords on the north wall.

Though I never mention it to anyone, in Skye and all of the other towns, villages, and battlefields we visit, I see the departed. And they see me.

I wish that part was only a dream.

§

On Tuesday morning, the skies are not blue. As we turn onto the Antietam exit, oppressively low clouds move in from the west. We rattle down the Sharpsburg roads until we reach the visitors' center, park the RV, and hurry out of the cold into the low brick building. Chuck and I study the displayed artifacts, wander the gift shop, and after watching a well-done reenactment film, listen to a ranger tell us about the battle.

A group of soldiers is part of the audience. They are wearing camouflage pants, jackets, and caps. The park ranger sets the stage for the battle then directs everyone outside. As he continues his lecture about the pivotal Civil War battle, I study the servicemen. Most are young with soft skin. Some have acne. I shiver as it begins to sprinkle. Though the air is biting, I refuse to press against my husband and share his warmth. He pretends not to notice my discomfort like he pretends not to notice his mother's sly comments.

The soldiers are about the same age as Chuck was when we first met. I note a clearness in their eyes as they survey the terrain. The ranger babbles on. The soldiers nod at the generals' strategies, listen intently to the available armaments, shake their heads at the bad communications that caused the battle's outcome.

To my left, an American flag snaps in the wind. I wonder if a park ranger will remove it if the rain continues or worsens. The soldier nearest to me looks at the flag, too. My throat tightens as he gives a quick salute.

Chuck's number never came up in the Vietnam draft. We had discussed the possibility—I wanted to go to Canada, he was non-committal. I think he didn't want to leave his mother.

The presentation ends. Chuck and I eat lunch in the RV as the rain drums a tattoo on the roof of the motor home. We watch the other tourists scamper from cars to the visitor's center then back to their cars. After eating some chocolate chip cookies, we begin the driving tour.

The bus with the servicemen is ahead of us. They stop and study each marker, each noteworthy site. We pass them and go to Bloody Lane. I read the appropriate excerpt from the driving tour brochure.

"Rain's stopped, want to walk it?" Chuck asks.

"Sure."

Chuck pulls our vehicle into a parking space. He enjoys history when it is factual and well-documented. I love the personal tales, quirky details, and mythy half-truths. I climb out of the RV and lock my door. Chuck is waiting for me in front of the motor home.

Walking along the sunken roadway that the history books claim ran red with Confederate blood, Chuck and I find nothing to say. Sure, I will see blood gushing across the ground if I glance about, I keep my eyes focused on the path ahead of us.

We climb the memorial tower that howls like the dead as the May blusters intensify. From the tower's height, we view acres and acres of rolling battlefield. I see the soldiers' bus approaching and hurry down the tower's steps. I don't want to look into their eyes.

Next, Chuck and I drive to the rocky hillside that rises above Antietam Creek. We climb to an overlook. Burnside's Bridge still spans the Creek that turned scarlet with Union blood late in the battle. A group of Boy Scouts, costumed and carrying mock weapons, performs a play on the bridge. Their boy-man voices drift like a hymn to my ears as I peer down from the embankment where a small group of Georgian sharpshooters held on for hours against overwhelming odds. A nearby Confederate sharpshooter nods his misty head at me.

The soldiers arrive. It is time for us to leave. I rest my hand on a rock before heading back down the trail. The finality of death hangs like the scent of sweet violets in the air, and I avert my eyes from the dead which surround us. Chuck walks in front of me and I observe the slight stoop of his shoulders. We have both changed—thirty years of marriage does that to you.

As I near the parking lot, a serviceman passes me, taps his hat with his forefinger. "Ma'am," he says and looks at me with brave, brown eyes.

I can almost see through him, though I know he is still alive. This has happened before, and will happen again. The serviceman will not live to see his next birthday. It is unwanted knowledge, but I am certain of its validity. I have yet to have a false vision.

Once in our motor home, I think of our children, genetic continuations of the bloodlines that settled this country and fought in her wars. Though the draft is gone, my children are proud and strong. My youngest son volunteered to serve, and he now sleeps in a shipping container in Iraq.

I think of my father—drafted in 1944, he fought under Patton and eventually helped to liberate several concentration camps. He fills my children's heads with the glory of fighting for the right cause and he still has a military rifle stored in the attic, "Just in case."

I close my eyes, picture my father pressing the butt of that rifle against his shoulder, hear the metallic scraping as he moves the gun's bolt, and flinch when Chuck asks if I'd like to stop by the Antietam Cemetery. "Brochure says the Union dead are there."

As he speaks, I wonder where the Confederate boys are buried. I tell him, "No."

"Are you sure, Laurel?" He glances at me with eyebrows raised. He knows my fondness for graveyards and strange epitaphs.

I shake my head. "I think I have seen enough for one day."

The rain starts falling in torrents. When we cross Antietam Creek, I study the water. It bubbles dark with mud, and I consider how easily it could be bloody run-off from the battlefield if the date were different. Then, I look again, and see it *is* bloody run-off.

Chuck does not look at the water; his eyes are focused on the road. It takes us longer than usual to drive home. The headlights, water, and dark day erase the center line. The windshield wipers flip back and forth, squealing in protest, as the miles and minutes add up. I am glad Chuck is driving and not me.

We pick up our foxhound, retriever, and orange cat from the kennel and hurry to our house. Chuck unloads the food from the RV's refrigerator, while I make supper. A few minutes later, we sit at the table and have tomato soup and grilled cheese sandwiches.

The phone rings. It is Freda. She does not say hello to me. Instead, she says, "I need to talk to my son." I hand Chuck the phone.

Chuck's mother chatters at him for about ten minutes. I can hear him answer, "Yes. Okay. That so? No. Sorry." He sighs often. Finally, he says, "Good-bye," and hangs up the phone.

I pretend I wasn't listening. "Anything important?"

"No."

Chuck goes back to the bedroom to put on his pajamas. He is an early riser and I am a night person. He likes to arrive at family occasions ten minutes early, and I figure I will get there when I get there. He uses spreadsheets, diagrams, and charts, and never loses receipts. Sure to misplace it, I never take the checkbook with me. I am always estimating the amount I wrote a check for and consider myself lucky if I remember to whom the check was written. Chuck is not big on pets. We have two dogs and a cat. They are strays that I adopted, because I cannot live without animals. We are not really compatible. Some mornings when I wake before Chuck, I examine his face and wonder how we ended up together. I imagine he does the same thing.

But I believe in destiny, and know we were meant to find each other.

Chuck wanders back to the kitchen as I finish emptying the dishwasher. "Goodnight, Laurel." He leans in for a kiss. I kiss him like I'd kiss a cousin or a good friend. "I said I was sorry. What more can I do?" His voice is tired.

I shrug my shoulders. "I don't know why you invited her to go with us to see *Cabaret* in the first place. You know she hates me."

"I should have asked you, but she seemed so interested in the show when I mentioned we were going to get tickets. And she doesn't hate you."

"Tickets for *our* anniversary, and she certainly does *not* like me."

"I am just trying to consider both points-of-view. I want to make everyone happy." Chuck's voice has a pleading quality to it.

"You cannot please everyone. Once in a while, you have got to choose."

"I chose you when we got married," Chuck says.

I roll my eyes. "Then, act like it," I demand, knowing that this is a no-win skirmish. I feel myself sinking in mud, losing my footing like the Cadets at New Market. His mother is the baggage Chuck came with. Sometimes, I just wish he had left his baggage on the train when he got off at my station.

Chuck shakes his head, turns to go down the hall. "Goodnight," I say.

He glances at me, mumbles, "Goodnight."

"Wait!" I go to him, and really kiss him. "Let's call a truce."

He nods agreement and smiles.

What I don't say, though the image is as clear as the waters of the Shenandoah in my mind, is that the last time I saw Freda, I could almost see through her.

Though no one else knows, I am certain I will win this battle. Freda won't see her next birthday—and all I will have to deal with is her ghost.

Then, Chuck won't have to choose sides.

One More

Gregory L. Norris

*A*nother nickel. Just five more cents.
    Five more cents is enough for a loaf of bread. Bottles today are scarce at the beach. A late summer chill infuses the air. Few people come to the rides and arcades at the seaside amusement park when it's raining. For two days, huddled beneath the pier and reading a dog-eared novel someone left in a garbage can with three returnables, he's sat dreaming of bread. Soft bread, fresh bread, the kind that sticks to your teeth, his fantasies set to a baleful soundtrack of calliope music.

For days, it has rained. The boy, seventeen, is now past waiting for sunlight to return so, in the rain, he combs the purple sands of Hollings Head, Rhode Island, in search of one more bottle, one more lifeline. The tumbled, ground-down shells of mussels in the bay lend the sand its pale lavender color; the rain and hunger chill his fingertips to the verge of blue. Five more cents. Just one more nickel will silence his hunger and save his life.

With his hoodie up and his backpack slung around his shoulders, a plastic garbage bag filled with eleven cans and a handful of plastic liter bottles, he roams the beach. Hollings Head is fast becoming a place for the well-to-do—million-dollar condos replacing the tarpaper summer cottages and concession stands like a merciless, occupying army. Boys turned out to the streets by abusive hands and lamentable circumstances get swept under the pier, where no one sees them. For two months, this is how it has been. Every day, he looks for cans and bottles, turns them in at the little *groceria* nestled on Atlantic Avenue, across from the Tilt-a-Whirl. And if he collects enough, he eats. Every day, the same.

He used to love this beach, the boy remembers when he reaches the closest garbage barrel. Back then, he came here as a visitor, happy and well-fed, a boy with a name. At some point over the last few weeks, he either forgot his name or it was taken from him, like the remains of the tropical storm that had once been a named hurricane now soaking the coastline with its tears on its slow amble past.

Since nobody has come to the beach in two days except for a few adrenaline junkies eager to challenge the waves, the barrel is as empty as the last time he checked. The boy sets off to his next destination, farther up along the beach. Wet sand collapses awkwardly beneath his sneakers, which are soaked through. Since the start of the storm, the pain in his gut has dulled to an ever-present burning sensation. That scares him almost more than the looming specter of the changing season, summer cooling to autumn; the fear that he might somehow be surrendering to his hunger before the coldness can have a go at his marrow.

You're giving up, a voice in his head taunts as he trudges a hundred yards through driving rain to another barrel on the beach. It, too, is filled with a soup of rainwater and empty food wrappers. The beaches at Hollings Head are kept immaculate, because the condo owners have taken over. No candy wrappers or cigarette butts, no cans, no bottles. *No half-eaten burgers or funnel cakes. No food*, the voice adds.

Just five more cents.

The nameless boy plods on, shivering with every step as icy rain pelts him, a clear testament to the death of summer. The air stinks of ocean, churning and seething in the remnants of the storm. The rain falling before his eyes creates a gray veil, obscuring the way ahead, as if to telegraph the days to come will be turbulent.

He walks on.

The boy knows the routine well: barrels at every hundred yards, one beside the payphones, another near the dunes. He has walked this route every day, mostly in sunlight, but now in the rain. The music from the amusement park drags down, slows, warped by the downpour. All the barrels are empty. His journey ends at the base of the dunes, as do his hopes. There are no bottles. That means no bread. Without bread, the dull burn that was once a clawing pain might short out completely, signaling oblivion.

The boy stops and stands beside the barrel, his tears hidden in the rain. He has reached the end of the beach. Beyond this part of Hollings Head, the dunes give way to castles, expensive homes set behind a gate dominating stretches of private beach. Do not enter. It's no place for homeless boys. He can't go forward. In some ways, he can't go back to that place beneath the pier where he huddles and tries to steal sleep, his dreams populated by bells, whistles, and the calliope music from the merry-go-round.

He gazes across the ocean. Silver-capped swells crash against the shore, leaving fresh, purple bruises upon the sand. Behind him, the dunes rise up. Blankets of windblown marsh grass and sea roses obscure what lies beyond, though he knows what he will find on the other side: a house, tall and sinister, its gabled peak peering over the tops of the dunes.

Don't ever go near that house, he hears his mother warn, perhaps ten years ago when they sat on this same beach and when there was an abundance of food, warmth, dryness. The same hand that would force him from his home earlier in the summer adds in a whisper, *It's a dangerous place.*

Another voice, this from a fellow vagrant under the pier, joins in. "Whatever you do, stay clear of that place. He'll try to lure you inside. There ain't nothing good about it."

The nameless boy stands frozen in the rain, staring at the two visible windows of the house's gabled roof. The windows gaze back, like eyes made of glass. He hasn't thought about this place much until now, hasn't considered that twice in his young life, he has been warned away. What he can see of the house from the beach is framed by roiling storm clouds. Curiously, the big house on the beach is colored the same pale purple as the sand. He stares, unable to break his gaze until the wind gusts and, over its howl, he hears the hollow metallic clatter of a can dislodged by the gale, rolling somewhere up in those dunes.

Five more cents.

Before he can talk himself out of it or consider the implications, he tromps through the sand and into the tangle of reeds and thorns. Clumps of roots and sand give way and tumble; eventually, he finds firm footing. The perfume of the marsh roses is sweet, intoxicating, but the enormous clusters, washed ashore hundreds of years earlier from a wrecked Chinese merchant ship, block his path. He picks his way carefully around them, tracking the metal clatter. In his haste to find the can—and possibly save his life—he stumbles face-first into a tangle of thorns. Fresh agony ignites across his left cheek and forehead.

The boy picks himself up and looks down, realizing that he has tripped over the weathered planks of an old boardwalk. The boardwalk meanders, forming a thin channel through the roses. Wiping his face, he sets off along the path. Roses have grown over one another, a wild tangle, a modern Hydra. He ducks under the brambles, his backpack snagging on thorns. After an arduous near-crawl, he emerges again on a stretch of level sand, directly in front of the purple house.

The house was built here long ago, that much is clear. Instead of rising up from the beach like the McMansions behind the gate, he is given the impression that the three-story house with the gabled roof is either slowly sinking into the earth or was buried until the tropical depression exhumed it. No illusion created by the storm, the house matches the color of the sand. It evaporates before his wide-open eyes. He blinks. The house pulls back into cohesion, but barely.

White sheers hang in every window. One set of impressive French doors dominates the first floor, at eye level. The boy focuses on the doors, sees one is slightly ajar. A figure stands among the curtains, indistinct. Fear slithers over his flesh, only to break at the sound of an aluminum can, skipping across the sand. A flash of darker purple teases his eyes. An empty grape soda can rolls to a jarring stop right at his well-traveled left sneaker.

He scrambles for it before the wind can steal the can from him, falling to his knees on the ancient boardwalk. There, with the key to his survival clutched in both hands, he notices the latticework of additional planks leading from different directions through the dunes, all ending at the French doors of the purple house.

At staggered distances along each of the pathways, soda cans and bottles jut up from the sand, dozens of them. Some unaffected part of the boy's consciousness notes their labels—orange soda, strawberry soda, chocolate soda, grape. All sugary-sweet, anchored into the sand at intervals, along every stretch of time-eroded plank.

A jolt of fresh coldness trips down the boy's spine. He hastily stuffs the soda can in with his others, and races from the dunes.

§

As he savors the warm, moist heaven of fresh bread in the cloistered cold beneath the pier that night, he ponders the bottles and cans. In his memory, they take on an ominous pattern, becoming a trail of glass and aluminum crumbs scattered through the dunes. He knows but doesn't focus on the malevolent design behind the arrangement; he only sees his next meal. A dozen bottles or cans add up to sixty cents. Two dozen, enough for a cheeseburger at the corner grill in the amusement park—a fat, juicy cheeseburger pink in the middle, dripping with grease and smothered in mayonnaise and ketchup, with lettuce, tomato, pickles, and a slice of red onion. The bottles and cans are there for the taking. All he needs do is take them.

He thinks of the figure standing just inside that one open door, not much of a deterrent in the face of starvation. Still, the warnings nag at him, tease his dreams amid the echo of crashing waves.

Stay away from that house!

If it's sunny, he won't need those cans and bottles. He'll get more than enough for a cheeseburger picking through the barrels at the amusement park and on Hollings Head Beach.

But morning comes, gray and raw. Rain falls in thin curtains, little more than a steady drizzle but enough to keep the crowds away. There is no warmth to the day. Cold and hungry, the nameless boy clutches the empty garbage bag in one hand and slings the backpack containing the fragments of all he owns in the world onto the other's shoulder. He must return to that mysterious house in the dunes one more time.

Just once more.

§

The clouds are breaking. The day grows lighter. Rain lets up, but in its place a cold and numbing wind blows. Nobody comes to the beach at Hollings Head; nobody except a nameless, hungry boy, a thin figure, gray and ghostly, like a wisp of smoke, fading more with every second. Soon he'll be lost from sight.

He picks his way carefully through the marsh roses, finds another of the plank paths running between them. Coming back here isn't so much about survival as luxury—he's risking his life for something more than the basics. It would be so good to have a hot meal, and those empty cans are the ticket. He exits the dunes and falls beneath the gaze of the pale purple house once more. Broken sunlight spills through a lapse in the clouds, illuminating the weathered exterior. The boy's mind drifts, and he wonders about its age. Like a relic born of the same ocean that stained the sands purple, how long has this house brooded over the beach? Did it wash ashore as an ancient shipwreck that transformed itself into a house, adapting to the land like the roses from China? Or is it actually the skull of some primeval sea monster, its windows really empty eye sockets?

The brief flash of sunlight does little to warm his skin. The house possesses his eyes. Only the hunger in his belly breaks the trance.

Leaning down, he wrests the first soda can out of the sand, stuffs it into the garbage bag, and moves on to the next, a yard ahead of him. One yard closer to the purple house. The one after that lures him even nearer. The bag grows heavy. He can taste his next meal. He grabs cans, advancing up the boardwalk, unaware he's gotten almost to those French double doors until a shadow sweeps over the sand, engulfing him. The boy looks up. Something tall and dark blocks what little sun there is. He staggers away, trips.

"Don't be afraid," the man says, his voice deep but soothing. "I was hoping you'd return."

The nameless boy realizes that in his haste to collect cans, he hasn't kept an eye on the French doors or seen the man wander out of the house, a handsome man with short silver hair and a mustache, dressed in well-tailored clothes. The man leans down and extends his hand.

"It's all right, don't be frightened. Let me help you."

The boy freezes, his spine on the sand, at first too stunned to move. Yes, the silver-haired man is handsome, even fatherly. With the rise and fall of the boy's chest, he smells a trace of the man's cologne, robust and comforting. He doesn't take the offered hand right away. Clearly sensing the boy's distrust, the silver-haired man flashes a sad smile, showing a length of perfect white teeth.

"I understand, son, really I do," he continues, withdrawing his outstretched hand. "I just want to help you. I see you out here every day collecting cans and bottles and it breaks my heart. Don't you have a home to go to? Doesn't anybody miss you?"

"No," the boy says. It's been days since he's heard his own voice instead of all the voices in his head playing their verbal tug of war in counterpoint against the calliope music, and it sounds alien to him.

The silver-haired man slowly shakes his head. "No one at all? What a shame. I'd like to help you. That's why I left you the cans. Are you hungry?"

The aching pain in the nameless boy's stomach seems to double by addressing it. Yes, he is hungry, almost starving. Bread just isn't enough. Yes, he wants to eat and be warm and not live this miserable transient existence.

"Let me help you," the silver-haired man says, again extending his hand.

The boy looks up, sees the trustworthy smile and, not sure why for he stopped trusting anyone weeks ago, he reaches his frail fingers out. Hands touch. At the instant of contact, something icy-hot ignites across the boy's skin. He faces the man and sees the sun has vanished from sight behind a veil of storm clouds, and a shadow has fallen over his benefactor, lending his skin an unsettling pale purple tinge.

Then thunder crashes, not from the dying storm but a door slamming in place. The boy blinks. When his vision focuses, he is no longer outside, sitting on the dunes, but inside the house, standing.

How did I get in here? a voice in his head demands. Another answers, *He pulled you inside.* But as shocking as that concession may be, it pales against the vision that greets him in the vast open space of the house's first floor, which captures all of his attention. He has never seen anything like it.

A pale, purple carpet covers the little of the floor that is visible. Elegant furniture fills the living area—overstuffed Victorian velvet settees and mahogany tables carved with wings, claws, and lion heads. Some pieces look ready to take flight or run away or lunge for his throat under their own power. Bronze statues and torchieres crowd between the furniture, but there are no lights on, and an oppressive stagnancy barely broken by the glow seeping in from the windows hangs over the open space.

More curious are the stacks of books, thousands of them, their spines piled on the floor, all around the edges. In some places, the books rise to three times a man's height. They're old books, hardcover editions; big books heavy with weight and age. Strung across those books is the most unexpected of all the strange sights inside the house: a series of tracks, like the tracks of toy trains, only bigger, more complex. The metal tracks wind and dip around the edges of the room, rising in some spots where the books are piled highest and plunging down to loop over the lower stacks.

"You must be hungry," the silver-haired man says. The boy whips around to face the shadow at his back, an action that stirs a column of dust. "Would you like to eat?"

The man aims his hand and the boy follows it. Unseen until that moment, he faces a banquet table. A light snaps on, illuminating trays of cream-filled pastries, cakes and cookies, fresh fruit, hamburgers, whole piles of them, three high on a serving platter. Cans and bottles of soda line the table.

Like a rabid animal, the boy lunges for the spread, grabbing and biting until his mouth is caked with a mess of half-eaten food. Barely chewing, he rips into the meat and chokes down finger pastries. He has become a primitive, notions of civilization lost to hunger. Lost, forever.

The weight of all that food in so fragile a stomach alters his pain. A sour sensation shudders through him. The boy reaches for a soda can. Grape. The can is purple. He looks and all the cans, like the ones left for him on the beach, are sugary-sweet concoctions. He hesitates.

"Is something wrong?" the voice over his shoulder says, not as a question, more an acknowledgment.

Slowly, the boy turns, and a second shiver wracks his body. In the bald glow of the lamp beside the banquet table, the silver-haired man's features come clearly to him now. His skin has absorbed the dusty pallor of the surrounding room. Purple veins rise in spider webs along his neck, and his perfect white teeth, the boy notices, appear unusually sharp.

"You've eaten too much, too fast," the man says.

The words wash over the boy without a name, sour and repulsive. It isn't cologne he's smelled, but an odor of decay, covered up.

"You need to slow down, enjoy yourself," the man continues. "Everybody who visits loves to take a ride in my roller coaster."

The man smiles, and as the *clunk-clunk* noise of movement along the tracks forming a necklace around the vast room reaches his ears, a jolt of terror unlike anything he's ever experienced cramps his guts. *The doors*, both voices in his head shriek in unison. *Where are those French doors?*

The nameless boy looks behind him, sees the doors and something else. From the shadows along those tracks comes a collection of wagons, strewn together like a makeshift roller coaster. In the moody gray glow, it's difficult to be sure, but he sees other people, seated in the wagons.

Escape, now! the voices urge.

Yes, run back to the dunes, run and keep running, as far away from this house as possible.

He attempts to run.

And finds that he cannot move.

§

Paralyzed, the boy sits behind the silver-haired man, propped into one of the wagons. Tears stream from his eyes, which stare straight ahead, unable to do more than water.

"They wouldn't let me ride the one in the park after the rumors started, so I built my own. You'll love this—it's so much fun!" the silver-haired monster chuckles, a boy in some ways himself.

The ride begins and the wagons clunk along the tracks, building momentum each time the roller coaster plunges downward. At the corners of the room, the wagons take wide, sweeping arcs, nearly jumping the tracks before breaking with a jolt, resuming the climb upward for another terrifying plunge down. Each pass around the room dislodges more books from the stacks, gives the boy with no name a better look at the house, his eyes unable to blink.

There are no white curtains in the windows, as he earlier thought. Only cobwebs.

Apart from the purple-skinned monster with silver hair, there are no people in the ride with him, only skeletons wearing the rags of old clothes.

But there also isn't any pain. He isn't hungry any more. In fact, he doesn't feel anything. The poison he has eaten has freed him from his hunger.

§

The ride coasts to a stop, and the boy is dead.

The silver-haired man feels sated, gorged on what he has done, but also horrified. He wants the killing to stop, but knows his hunger to feed in the days and weeks ahead will again grow all consuming.

He'll tell himself it will be for the last time. That he'll stop after one more.

Just one more.

Red Leaves
Marc Sorondo

*A**rt itself was a mystery to Julian. This piece in particular* was especially enigmatic.

Julian's obsession with art was fueled by his inability to create it. He'd tried many times, spent desperate years trying to fulfill the creative urge, to bring something powerful and beautiful into the world. His mind could envision things, but his body lacked the gift required to give his ideas form. He'd painted and sculpted, dabbled in carving and drawing, but his hands distorted his vision.

Now, his many failures had broken that part of him that hoped his genius remained hidden waiting for him to stumble onto the proper medium. Now, hopeless, he replaced the need to create with one to collect. He'd spent years and millions of dollars, he'd cashed in favors and made enemies, and it had all been worth it. Julian possessed one of the most impressive private collections in the world.

His newest acquisition was, in Julian's opinion, the crowning jewel of the entire collection. It was beautiful and ominous, and it was an artifact that perfectly represented the mystery that was art.

It was titled *Red Leaves*, though there was not a single leaf in the entire piece. Painted nearly one hundred years ago, it was not done in any style common at that time. It was realistic, so much so that it could be confused for a blown-up photograph from even a short distance away.

Red Leaves was painted almost entirely in shades of grey. It depicted a medieval Italian piazza, all dirty cobblestones below and sooty bricks behind. The square was empty aside from a central fountain, one lorded over by a stone angel frozen at its center. The angel's wings were spread behind her; her hands reached forward, as if to embrace the painting's observer.

It was so simple…and yet it wasn't. It had that quality that separated real art from everything else, the indescribable essence that only a gifted hand could capture. The face of the angel, serene, regal, perfect, drew the eye. It alone was enough to classify the painting as the work of a master.

And then, much to Julian's delight, there was the mystery that had surrounded the piece from the very beginning.

The artist was a man named Calen Scratch. Nothing was known of his biography. No other works had ever turned up that could be attributed to him or tied to him in any way. The painting stood as the only record of Scratch's existence.

The painting's first owner was a man named Edminster who had grown wealthy selling lumber in New England. He'd owned the painting for just under six months when he disappeared. It happened during a particularly vicious blizzard. One moment his family had left him in his study, sitting beneath the outstretched arms of the painted angel; the next, he was gone, the wind and snow of the storm obscuring any trail he may have left. Edminster was never seen again.

Edminster's widow sold the painting to a man named Blum, who had initially intended to donate it to his alma mater to adorn its great hall. He'd decided, shortly after acquiring it, to keep it for himself. It hung on the wall opposite Blum's desk for three months. It was there, the angel staring out at him, as Blum rigged up a noose over his desk and hung himself. He dangled there, bulging eyes locked on the painting, over a note he'd left on his desk. The note was brief, written in a hurried hand, as if Blum had believed he had very little time in which to kill himself. He no longer wanted to live, he'd explained, because there was so much evil in the world, so much blood…so much blood.

Blum's widow didn't touch that room aside from having the noose removed. She'd left it for him as if he'd come back some day and have more work to do.

Two years later someone robbed Blum's home. Only *Red Leaves* was stolen.

It was lost for a very long time after that. It may have been lost forever, except for the painting's seemingly magnetic attraction for tragedy. It was found in the home of a drug smuggler nearly seventy years after it had been stolen. The smuggler, one Antonio Vega, was presumed dead. All that was found of him was a puddle of blood and a series of bullet holes in the walls. The authorities chalked the killing up to a rival drug lord and spent little time actually searching for the body or the killer. Whatever had actually happened to Vega, that painting had seen it all, hung on the wall over the puddle of scarlet that was left behind.

The next owner was a man named Ronald Casey, a real estate mogul who'd purchased the painting as an investment and kept it hidden away in a climate-controlled warehouse, unappreciated like a coin in a piggy bank. Julian had begged Casey to sell the painting, offered outlandish amounts for it, but Casey always refused.

Julian smiled. Casey was dead, killed by a massive heart attack less than a month ago, and his money-hungry kids had already sold that painting to Julian. He knew they were selling other precious pieces as well, bloating the dollar amount of their inheritances so they could buy palatial homes, exotic cars, and generally squander their father's hard work.

Julian's butler, Winston, entered and found his employer just as he'd been when he'd left the room fifteen minutes earlier: arms limp at his sides, mouth opened slightly, eyes wide, standing before his newest acquisition.

"Still admiring it, sir?"

"I don't know that I'll ever stop admiring it, Winston. Isn't it beautiful?" Julian said without taking his eyes from it.

Winston looked at the painting. He found it drab, oppressively so. The statue at its center made him think of an adornment on an ornate tombstone. There was no life to the picture. Quite the opposite, Winston thought the painting was dead, soulless.

"I've a crude eye, sir. I'm not one to appreciate the finer points of a work of art." Winston waited a moment. "Sir, I hate to interrupt, but the museum gala begins in less than an hour."

Julian nodded. He took one last look at the angel's face and then turned away.

§

Julian had studied *Red Leaves* for a bit every day for nearly two months. Some days, when especially busy, he'd spend a very few minutes looking it over. Other days he'd become lost in it, walking in that piazza, viewing the fountain from different angles, only to discover that he'd spent hours standing before the painting.

He knew that piece, knew every bit of it so well he could close his eyes and recreate it exactly on the canvas of his mind. He knew that painting as if it were a part of him, so, when he noticed the single leaf blown against the bottom of the fountain by some Italian breeze not previously alluded to in the painting, Julian gasped.

He leaned in, examining it from inches away. It was crimson, like a spattered droplet of blood on the canvas. When he looked closely, however, Julian could see Scratch's photorealistic detail, the veining of the dead leaf, the way its dried edges curled.

It was, Julian realized with a sense of horror, something that belonged, something that must have always been there. He had somehow overlooked that striking, brilliant detail. He'd somehow been lost in those shades of grey, fallen so deep into them, that he couldn't even see that small splash of color.

Julian felt as if he'd been lying to himself, hiding something away from his own awareness. He stared at the painting, studied it, determined to know its every secret.

§

Julian summoned Winston to the gallery with the push of a button and a buzz sent through an intercom. He waited, standing before *Red Leaves*, a sheen of sweat on his forehead, a slight tremor in the hand that he'd brought to his mouth.

"Sir?" Winston said as he entered.

Julian waved him over without saying a word.

"Yes?" Winston said as he stopped beside his employer.

"Tell me, Winston," Julian said. He pointed to the base of the fountain. "What do you see?"

Winston looked at Julian and found him to be serious; more so, he found that Julian almost looked afraid. "Well, I see…leaves. Three red leaves."

"Exactly," Julian said. "Do you recall having seen those leaves before?"

Winston thought of his initial impression of the painting and recalled only that he'd thought there was so much grey. "I can't say I remember them, sir…but…isn't the painting called *Red Leaves*?"

"It is, Winston. It is." Julian leaned forward so that the tip of his nose nearly touched the canvas. "And I had never understood why before…" he whispered.

"Sir?" Winston said. "Can I do something for you?"

Julian shook his head as if rousing himself from a daze. "Yes, I'm sorry. I was a bit distracted. Would you make me an espresso, please? I'm feeling a bit drowsy."

Winston nodded. "Of course. Shall I bring it here or…"

"I'll have it in the library. I'll be heading there in just a minute."

Winston nodded again. Then he turned and left.

Julian looked at the painting. Either it was changing or he was. He couldn't tell which of those possibilities was more terrible. He thought that art itself was a mystery, but that this piece was so shrouded in the unknown and the unknowable, it was obscured by so many layers of uncertainty, it was like a question without an answer, a puzzle with no solution. Art was a wonder, doubly so because no one could really understand how it came into being. This painting though…Julian wanted to understand it, but he wasn't sure that was possible.

§

Winston came into the gallery and, as expected, found Julian standing before that damned painting again. He feared that Julian was slipping into madness, that his obsession with the painting was consuming him.

"Ah, Winston," Julian said with a smile that his butler didn't recognize. He waved Winston over to stand beside him. "You recall that I summoned you a few weeks ago and asked you to look at three leaves blown against the fountain in his painting?"

"I do." Winston wanted to grab Julian by the collar, to shake him and shout at him to sell the damned painting and never think of it again.

"Good. Tell me, when you looked upon the painting last, did you note these?" He motioned to a pair of leaves, frozen in time as they skittered over the cobblestones near the edge of the frame.

Winston looked from the two scarlet leaves to Julian's face. He thought, with a mixture of terror and pity, that Julian had begun drawing leaves in, taking time and care to make sure that they were perfect, that they blended in with the artist's style exactly. He thought that Julian's crushed dreams of artistic greatness were manifesting themselves in these subtle vandalizations. "I don't remember seeing them last time, sir, though I was focused only on those three."

"Indeed, as I had thought myself at first." Julian was quiet for a moment. "Please take a good look at it now, Winston. Take in its every detail. Be careful to note the number and positioning of the crimson leaves."

Winston nodded and looked at the painting. He tried to see where Julian's work differed from that of Calen Scratch. Instead he found that Julian's hand had mimicked the style of the painting perfectly. Winston wondered at the connection between genius and madness.

After a few moments, Winston looked at Julian and said, "I believe I've noted them, sir."

Julian considered this. "Thank you. That will be all."

§

Winston cringed as he entered the gallery. "You rang for me, sir?"

"Yes. I was hoping you'd take a look at something for me." Julian motioned to the painting.

Winston gasped. "Sir, I don't understand."

"And how could you…how could anyone hope to understand," Julian said.

The leaves were everywhere now. A pile had formed at the base of the fountain. Others were blown against the stone angel, pressed against her feet, curled around the fingers of her outstretched hand and held there by the breeze. Leaves numbering in the hundreds were scattered about the cobblestone of the piazza. Every leaf was the same shade of crimson, each one like a spot of blood flicked from the end of a saturated brush.

"It's terrible," Winston muttered.

"Yet somehow beautiful," Julian said.

They were quiet for a moment, both looking at the painting.

Then Winston said, "Sir, forgive me for asking, but…did you do this?"

Julian smiled. "You flatter me to suggest that I could make such masterful additions. I could not paint with such skill."

"Are you certain? Can you be sure?"

Julian's smile fell away. "What are you suggesting, Winston?"

"Sir, I mean no disrespect, but you've been…well, you haven't been yourself since you purchased this piece."

Julian sighed. He looked at the painting. "I can see why you would suspect some sort of insanity. I'm always alone in here. There's no way for you to know what's been going on."

"I'm worried for you," Winston said.

Julian nodded.

"Why not sell this piece, or you could donate it to the museum, or..."

Julian held up his hand, and Winston fell silent. "That is out of the question, Winston."

"I understand, sir, but..."

"That will be all, Winston," Julian interrupted.

Winston nodded. He looked down at his feet, turned, and walked out of the gallery.

Julian watched Winston's back as he walked away. Then he watched the door close. He felt his eyes itching to see the painting; the muscles in his neck almost seemed to twitch in anticipation of turning to face it. He forced his gaze to remain locked on that closed door.

The possibility that this was all some sort of madness, that he was adding those leaves, had never dawned on him. He sought within himself and found that he couldn't be sure, not really. How could he trust his memories when they defied reality? He wasn't sure if it was harder to accept that he was crazy or that an old painting was changing by itself.

Then a flash of motion caught the corner of Julian's eye. He turned and found a single red leaf moving across the canvas of the painting in jerky tumbles as if driven by an inconstant wind. He almost thought he could hear the faint scratching of the leaf's progress over the cobblestone.

Julian wasn't sure if he could trust his own eyes. He wondered, if he knew enough to question the reality of what he saw, did that mean he could trust his senses?

He looked down at his hands. They were trembling. He brought them to his face, covered his eyes, and said, "No more."

When he pulled his hands away, he found that the painting was a chaos of movement. Leaves shifted in the breeze, collecting into piles at the base of the fountain and the four corners of the piazza, swirling in the air currents in the open spaces.

Julian could hear it now, the wind passing through the narrow alleys between ancient buildings and forcing dry leaves to dance on the stone ground. He even found that he could smell it, that the air inside the gallery was crisp and cool and held the scent of turned foliage.

Julian shook his head as if denying the painting, as if he refused to accept what he saw, but he trusted, deep down he knew that his eyes did not lie to him. He knew that the mystery of *Red Leaves* went far beyond a few coincidental misfortunes and an obscure artist. This mystery went so much deeper than all that.

It terrified Julian, but he was also drawn to it. If his other pieces were art, what was *Red Leaves*? If masters had painted the other works that adorned the walls of his gallery, who or what had painted this scene? As if in answer to both those questions and a million others that he'd yet to think of, Julian's mind whispered *something more*.

He could feel the breeze now, cooling his face and tousling his hair. He looked down and found that he was ankle deep in a sea of scarlet leaves that shifted with the wind.

Julian could no longer tell where the painted world stopped and the real world began. He could no longer be sure there was any difference between the two.

He looked up at the face of the angel and exhaled all the air from his lungs in a rush when he saw her stone eyes looking back at him. Her outstretched hands seemed to be reaching out to embrace him. Her spread wings seemed ready to enfold him.

Julian inhaled and held the breath. It was so beautiful. He wanted to touch her, to feel her hands on his face and the downy grey softness of her wings wrapped around his body.

She reached for Julian and he stepped toward her. His hand touched her cheek; it was hard and cold. Her hands touched him and they were like the hands of death: cold, lifeless, unforgiving.

The angel's stone hands wrapped around Julian's throat.

He grabbed them, tried to pry them from his neck. In his struggle, he looked up at her serene face, into her unblinking eyes. She was horrible and beautiful. She was everything he loved and feared at once. She was truly a work of art.

He studied her face even as black spots formed in his vision and popped like bubbles. Even when his sight blurred and faded to black, he saw her face in his mind.

§

Winston knocked at the door, not wanting to barge in unannounced. "Sir?" he called when Julian did not answer.

He waited another moment. "Sir?" he called again.

Finally, he pushed the door open. The gallery was empty but the light was still on. He walked in, thinking he would turn it off before going to find Julian.

He reached the light switch and reached out but paused when his fingers touched it. He looked in the direction of the painting; he couldn't see it from that angle.

He'd never had the chance to examine it without Julian present. He didn't want to waste the opportunity to look at those leaves without anyone watching.

He walked over, part of him dreading the sight of all that crimson on the canvas.

Then he saw it was all stone in shades of grey. There was not a single leaf remaining. Winston wasn't sure how such a thing could be done, but he knew very little about art. He leaned in and sought some sign of the paint that had been added, but he found nothing.

A chill ran up Winston's spine.

He turned and rushed toward the light. He was pleased to leave the painting in darkness where no one could see it. For reasons he couldn't understand, it felt safer that way.

The Spirit of the Back Stairs

Darrell Schweitzer

***B**ut first, Sarah died.*
At the very end, impossibly huge tropical butterflies covered my wife's outstretched hands, materializing out of the air as I watched, as if she had called them into existence merely by thinking, by her last, confused thoughts in those final moments: iridescent blue Morphos from the Amazon, gleaming under the streetlights, and great swallowtails and something the color of twilight on the upper side, with the serene face of an owl underneath. This particular butterfly perched on the tip of her finger, its underside as inscrutable as Sarah was just then, as we both were, filled with wonder and dread and sadness, unable to find the right words.

But first she died.

And the butterflies swarmed, their greedy tongues flickering over what little remained of her decaying flesh; and she turned to me, as if trying to speak once more, and her face was only a mass of dark wings rippling across her skull, a thing of dream, impossible even for New York, but what is one more incongruous detail among so many?

"I'm back," she said.

But first she died, suddenly, *snap!* the jaws of the city closing impersonally over her. There I was, at home, committing literature, what my own mother had once called the next worst thing to Allen

Ginsberg, when a phone call told all: that Sarah had died on the subway not an hour before, in a freak accident as the press of a crowd of unruly teenagers just out from a rock concert had quite randomly, with no malice aforethought or even recognition, shoved her off the platform at the very moment the train arrived—which proceeded to cut her in half.

"I'm back," she said.

I went to the morgue to see her. I had to do that eventually. A policeman was waiting for me, and two morgue attendants, and they asked me lots of grim questions, but politely, as if they were trying to be supportive and didn't quite know how. No one accused me of anything.

Sarah had, once. We'd had our screaming fights. We were talking divorce half-seriously.

I had done my share of accusing, too, and things worthy of accusation. Neither of us could claim innocence. But that was over now. All the uncertainties resolved honorably, neatly.

"There's enough left for an open-casket ceremony," one of the attendants said softly.

How thoughtful.

Her face wasn't touched. Somehow, there on the slab, she lacked even the red, soaking waistline I had been expecting. Possibly they had wrapped plastic around her middle, to contain the mess.

How very tidy.

I was offered a ride home, but I walked, and it didn't even become real to me until I had gone quite a ways along the west side of Central Park, past one, two, three gaping mouths of the hungry subway; and I tried to think, not selfishly of myself, but of her, of the loss of her career, of the actress she would never become and the sets she would never design, and of the Off-Off Broadway production of something called *Macbeth, Moor of Mantua*, which would now look very different if it ever got as far as opening night. The script had sounded awful, pretentious and trivial—she had died for nothing, for less than nothing, for someone else's verbal garbage, and life went on, the city went on, thank you, its great, glaring heart never missing a beat.

I didn't feel anything at that. I was acting myself, forcing myself into the expected role of grieving husband.

The hurt came slowly, wordlessly, a fog of pain, and by the time I reached our building I was weeping softly.

"I'm back," she said.

I sat in the apartment, my apartment now, no *her* apartment—still littered with pieces of her life, her hairbrush by the sink, her unfinished set design sketches on her drawing board, her books on the shelves, her cat hiding under the bed, somehow vaguely aware that something was terribly wrong. I sat there on the bed staring at her things, only beginning to feel the loss, like a soldier who's shot in battle, and it's only like a punch at first, a hard tap that knocks the wind out of him for a second or two before his nervous system can sort out the astonishing discovery that half his guts have been blown away.

I think hours passed. After a while, it was dark. The phone didn't ring. No one, it occurred to me, no one who mattered anyway, was in on the secret yet. I hadn't called relatives. I hadn't made arrangements.

I could still pretend. I did something silly.

The black cat, Pazuzu, scratched my leg ever so gently, then hissed and scooted back under the bed. I looked down. Sarah's white slippers were at my feet.

I thought of the guy on *Soap* who could only talk through a dummy, and when the other characters hid that, he had to resort to half a grapefruit to voice the otherwise unspeakable.

I wasn't laughing as I put the slippers on either hand, working them like puppets.

It seemed the correct, even reverent thing to do.

"She really is dead," said the right slipper. "You saw."

"No," said the left. "If we deny it, if we tell a really huge lie long enough—who knows?"

"You do," said the right.

"Deny it. Moment by moment. That's all any of us have anyway, ever. Just the splinter of time we call *now*. We never know if we're going to live another minute, long enough to say that certain word, or even to exhale. So, deny it with every breath while you still can."

"You had a lot you still wanted to say. A lot you never got around to," said the right slipper.

"Yes, I did. I do," said the left.

"Never wait. If you love someone, if you hate them, if you want to be excused to go to the bathroom, say it *now*. Not later."

"It's easy enough to tell me that now."

"Words are easy," said the right slipper. "It's the timing that trips you up."

I dropped my hands into my lap.

"Oh God, I want her *back!*" I said. "I want her to come *back*. That's all."

"Dead people don't come back," said the right slipper.

"Just this once—"

"Wish it," said the left. "Wish it very hard. Lie to yourself. Dream it. Very hard. Day by day, second by second. Fool yourself. In the end it won't matter. Imagine how it might be—"

"Things like that don't happen in the real world," said the right.

"This is New York," said the left.

I was sobbing out loud then, and I heard something stirring in the apartment, behind things, under things; I thought it was the cat at first; pans clanged in the kitchen.

"Peter. *I'm back.*"

I bolted up, tripped, and fell flat on my face with a sound that was almost a scream; terrified, puzzled, unbelieving, convinced I was crazy all at once. I recognized her voice. I knew it. Her voice.

The apartment was empty, of course. A pan had fallen out of the cupboard.

It was only much later, as I had sobbed for what seemed like hours, rolling on the bed, tearing at the sheets, amazing myself with the depth and intensity of my own feelings, only then was it all true, really, really true that she was gone, not here, had not returned; only then that my outraged nervous system had figured out what all the signals meant.

Eventually I slept, and imagined, and dreamed, and lied to myself very hard—and Sarah was there, lying on her back beside me, tall and thin and pale, her blonde hair almost white. She still wore her street clothes and high heels, her purse clutched firmly in her immaculate hands. She looked more like an investment broker than a theater person, spotless, proper, ideal.

I leaned up on my elbow and whispered to her: fond little jokes, funny things we'd said to one another when we were both twenty, telephone pickup lines, including the ever popular *We can't go on meeting like this,* the perennial classic *Doctor Mbogo's office. Less-ay! Less-ay!* plus the inevitable *Spooch!* the word which is inherently funny on a syllabic level.

But she did not answer. She just lay there, perfectly still. Moonlight and city-light streamed in through Venetian blinds, making the bedroom a grillwork of bright and dark, the colors muted, and Sarah a statue of flawless marble.

A single black butterfly revealed itself on her chin, opening its wings suddenly, then darted off.

I reached out to touch her, in my dream, and my right hand went through her, cutting her in half, and came up warm and wet.

I drew back, disgusted. I felt the fear rising slowly within me, the helpless dread. I gagged myself with my other hand, to stifle a scream.

Then the image rippled and was gone, and I ran my hand over the bedspread and felt only dust and dirt and a few coarse hairs.

I was aware that I was dreaming then, unable to wake up, listening to traffic noises that surged outside the window like a restless sea.

It was the smell that woke me.

I rolled over, sat up, and choked. The apartment air was thick with a putrid stench I could almost *see* in the filthy air.

I brushed hair and dust off the bed beside me, looking around angrily for the cat, wondering just what decaying treasure the little dear had dragged in. But I saw nothing.

Sarah's workroom was a mess, papers scattered over the floor, the drawing table knocked over, ink smeared over the oddly Egyptian set-designs, as if some spastic infant had attempted finger painting.

The inky hand-prints were small and thin, but distinctly adult, distinctly feminine.

The smell was strongest there, around the drawing table and the toppled stool.

I spent the rest of the morning cleaning up, disinfecting, wiping, spraying. The phone rang again and again. I ignored it.

Then I sat for hours at my own typewriter, telling myself the big lie, conducting a continuation of the dialogue of the slippers.

How shall I my true love know from the other one...?

She is dead and gone—

No, she isn't.

I want her back.

You might not like it.

No?

Yes, the inherent shortcoming of living on lies is that you lose touch with the truth.

Holy platitudes, Batman. That's really profound.

Meaning, did you really love her as much as you now think you did?

Yes. Goddamnit. Yes.

Wanna find out?

The phone rang and rang. Finally, I rose, went into the bedroom, and answered it. Everyone had found out somehow, already. There were outpourings of sympathy from relatives I hardly knew existed. Level-headed uncles took over, made plans. The funeral was tomorrow. Should someone come and stay with me?

No, I told them. No. It isn't necessary, because she isn't really dead.

You're crazy with grief, they said.

No. I've never been more clear-headed. She is here, with me now.

We'll be right over, they said.

It was then, as I still spoke, that Sarah put her hand on my shoulder and said softly, "I'm back."

I dropped the phone. She turned me around gently. She was there, in the evening twilight, as I had seen her in my dream, immaculately dressed, her purse over one arm, her polished nails, glistening in the semi-darkness.

She didn't flinch when I turned on the lights, but raised her head slowly and said, "Hello, Peter."

"Hello, Sarah."

The stench was horrible. She drew me toward her, toward a kiss. I gulped, tried to find something to say, tried to pull away. "No, please, no—"

"What are you afraid of, Peter? That I want to eat you? It isn't like that."

She let go of me. I sat down in a stuffed chair. She sat on the edge of the bed.

I turned off the lights again.

"What are you thinking, right now?" she said.

"I don't know what to think. I can't deal with this."

"You wished it. You wished it very hard. You must have had a reason, a clear idea of what you were doing."

I thought I knew then. For a flickering instant I was *certain* that somehow our whole life together was summed up in this instant, the lines of our existence converging to this pinnacle, this incredible reprieve, in which I would give everything meaning, heal all the hurts, demand satisfaction, make good every bit of neglect, anger, selfishness each of us had ever inflicted on the other. It was as if I were drowning, and with everything flashing before me.

And I couldn't find the words. I only felt numb, empty.

"This is just too...strange. I'm afraid," I said at last, almost weeping for the feebleness of that excuse.

She smiled. I felt a twinge of hope just then. I tried to convince myself that she had actually returned to life, that we could go on as before and maybe do better; but, as I watched, her face seemed to crack slightly. The lines around her eyes were, ever so minimally, disturbingly, different.

"How do you think I feel?" she said. She laughed softly. It was real laughter, her real voice.

The phone rang again and kept on ringing. I turned out the light. The two of us sat there in the deepening gloom, staring at the phone. She nodded at last, and I reached over and picked it up.

The police sergeant I had met at the morgue spoke, his voice obviously straining for calm. He seemed in shock, unable to say what he had to say.

"Mister Riley...there has been a...*desecration*. I don't know how to put it any other way."

"A what?"

"Your wife's body has disappeared."

"But that's impossible," I said. "Body-snatchers in this day and age? Ghouls?"

"We don't know, Mister Riley. We haven't got much to go on."

"*Well how about this?* How about, she got up and walked away, and she's here in my apartment with me right now—"

"Please Sir. You're understandably upset. It is very hard, I know. If there is anything I can do—"

"She got up and walked!" I screamed, and threw the phone away.

"Walked," said Sarah softly. "I don't remember."

I sat back, staring at her. She was no more than an outline in the dark now. The stench was worse than ever.

Tell yourself the big lie.

No. Believe it.

"You're the *esprit de l'escalier*," I said.

"The what?"

"The French have an expression, *the spirit of the back-stairs*, meaning the right words that come to you after the situation is over. When you're leaving, going down the back stairs, you suddenly know what you should have said, what you should have done, only it's too late."

She reached over and took my hand in hers. Even after those few minutes, her touch had changed. Now it was cold and hard. The smell was overwhelming. It was all I could do not to strike out frantically, not to run screaming and choking out of the apartment.

Instead, I sat there, trembling, and she held me, and she said, "Don't leave me now. I think we have only a little time. This isn't a return. It's just a visit. Let's use it well. So, please, just for this little while, accept me as I am."

I couldn't bring myself to flick the light back on, but I could tell from the street glare coming in through the window that she was crying and her tears were black, streaking her fish-belly white cheeks. The skin seemed to be peeling away around her eyes.

She reached up with her other hand, a shriveled, old lady's hand, to brush her hair out of her eyes, and some of the hair came away at her touch.

"So soon," she said. It was a question mixed with a statement. "So soon?"

There was a huge, dark stain on the front of her blouse.

I remembered what they'd told me over the phone.

You're crazy with grief.

This can't be happening.

We're sending someone right over.

"I think we should go out," I said. "We can't stay here."

"Yes," she said.

"A last night on the town."

"Promise me one thing."

"One thing."

"You won't be afraid of me?"

"I promise."

"Promise me another?"

"Yes."

"That you'll remember me not as I am, but as I was."

I wept then, again, exhausted, at the end of all resistance. I saw quite clearly that she was changing, by the minute. The flesh really was flaking away around her eyes, exposing her cheekbones. The smell wasn't quite as bad now, like old, dirty straw.

"We have to go," I said.

So we went. We walked for blocks, zig-zagging in and out of streets, south and east and west and south again, past a theater where a huge, inflated green boot seemed poised to stomp on passers-by. We crossed Times Square, now frantic with early evening activity, the buying and selling of trinkets, sex, lives. We fit right in. No one noticed. No one cried out, pointed.

Only once in a great while did either of us say anything, and then it was only trivial comments, dying sparks of wit, old memories.

We seemed to spend hours window-shopping at all her favorite places, now closed.

"My credit's probably no good anymore, anyway."

She laughed. It was still her laugh.

Later, when the streets began to empty out but for a few worried stragglers and the last of the hustlers, we came to a place I recognized, where, so long before, just before the two of us were married, we had stood for what must have been half an afternoon watching a street performer in silver tights and an ebony mask defy the laws of gravity as he moved through a machine-like dance with golden balls rolling all over his body.

Sarah paused there, searching for something, but the sidewalk was simply bare.

A single twilight-gray butterfly flew around her head, lit on her shoulder, then was somehow gone.

It had started to drizzle. Traffic hissed by.

We came to a fountain in front of a huge, granite office building. We used to meet there for lunch, back when the two of us had real jobs. Now she dipped her hand into the water, and the flesh fell away like sand, and she held up gleaming white bone. The butterfly lit there, the owl-faced one, appearing for the first time, slowly opening and closing its wings, but I shooed it away and took her hand in mine— *that* hand, the skeletal one—and we walked on.

I wasn't afraid now. I tried to think. I felt an enormous sense of guilt, that we were stalling, wasting what little time we had left with trivia, that there was some important thing we had to do, to get over with before it was too late, which would give order and meaning to everything. But I had no idea what.

I tried to explain everything then, to say, indeed, I was sorry, to go over our whole lives and marriage, to pick at the scabs and make the wounds run with genuine, living blood, but she put a bare-bone finger to my lips and said, "No. Hush."

Then there were more butterflies: one, two, a swarm, fluttering against my ears, landing on her shoulders, on her head, one of them exploring the dark recesses of her ear with its flickering tongue.

She didn't seem to mind. She didn't seem to notice. She was becoming, with the arrival of the butterflies, somehow more distant. I was losing her. She was slipping away.

I remembered reading somewhere that in the Orient people believe that the butterflies they see in graveyards are the souls of the recently departed. But I knew it wasn't like that. It wasn't so simple. These were fragments of death itself, come to devour Sarah, to drag her back into the darkness from which she had come, to shorten her visit.

Angrily, I brushed them away. I tried to catch them in my hands and crush them, but it was like grasping at smoke.

There were only more of them.

Sarah walked. I followed her, into Central Park. For just an instant I thought of how reckless it was to go into Central Park at such an hour. I glanced at my watch; it was almost 5 A.M., but I couldn't convince myself that it mattered; not now, not this once.

Sarah walked on, relentlessly as a wind-up toy, and after a time she seemed, indeed, like some frail, mechanical thing. She did not speak now, even when I spoke to her. I could only follow.

A very late, sickle moon rose above the skyscrapers, flooding the park with light the color of blood, until the trees were not mere trees and the stones and paths not mere stones and paths, but stark, symbolic, almost cartoonish representations, as if we had walked into a Henri Rousseau painting and fantastic beasts lurked all around us, among the cartoon fronds and ferns and intensely black tree trunks.

The butterflies came by the thousands, surrounding us in a cloud of muted colors, all tinted red by the impossibly bright moon.

Sarah was still searching for something. I couldn't help her. I couldn't find any words at all. The whole thing was a puzzle, an extra few hours granted as inscrutably as it was miraculously, a meaning to be worked out for the rest of my life and maybe beyond. Nothing more. There were no secret words, no final, special goodbyes, none of the significant things you'd be sure you'd have to cram into the last hour of a loved one's presence.

Nothing more. No words at all.

In the end she staggered and fell and the butterflies covered her entirely, a writhing, dark blanket, but I brushed them away and took her in my arms. She wasn't even a skeleton, but a thing of tatters, an old, cardboard Halloween decoration you might see trampled on the street in the middle of November.

She spoke a little then. I couldn't make out the words. I listened for a long time before I realized she was reciting the words to an old song we both knew.

> "Go fetch me water from the desert,
> And blood from out of a stone.
> Go fetch me milk from a fair maid's breast
> That never a young man hath known."

I sang softly in reply, "When shall we meet again, Sweetheart? When shall we meet again?" but my voice broke and I couldn't continue.

The butterflies were like a wave, a flickering tide. I saw the beasts in the cartoon jungle then, great-maned lions with eyes of fire, and a zebra striped red and black, and a serpent with a human face, coiled around the base of a hill, regarding us. There were two moons in the sky now, one red, the other white, hardly shining at all, the color of white paper.

I held onto Sarah tightly, all the while afraid that I would break her, that she would crumble to bits in my arms. I felt her crumbling anyway, diminishing. It was like trying to carry a sand sculpture.

I wore a cloak of butterflies then, the sound of their wings against my ears a constant sighing like a tide, and more, rising almost into coherence, almost into words.

We walked up the hill past the blank-eyed face of the serpent. I knew this place. We stood before Cleopatra's Needle, that ancient obelisk the Khedive of Egypt had sent to the people of New York in the 19th century as a token of his esteem. It stood gleaming in the double moonlight, surrounded by benches and little placards explaining what the hieroglyphics meant. We'd been here before, many times in fact. It had been a running joke between us, when we were younger, to make up our own translations, something more interesting than just "Ra, son of Ra, Lord of Upper and Lower Egypt."

Now, I shook the butterflies off Sarah's face so she could see. I turned her head with my hand, gently.

"Look. Up at the top. It says EAT AT THUTMOE'S. There, further down, the sacred moustache cups of 'Im'otep and 'Er'otep, the only Cockney Pharaohs. And those figures, the Middle Kingdom Kickers, ancient predecessors of the Rockettes, and—"

I tried to laugh, but was sobbing instead. She made no response at all. I felt her getting lighter every instant, going away, as the butterflies somehow drew away her substance.

There was no revelation, no portentous wisdom from beyond. We two had come together by accident, been separated by accident, reunited by accident, however briefly. We merely lingered as long as we could, savoring, creating memories, filling each pitiless moment one by one, until I held only her bare skull in my hands. White bone flashed beneath the butterfly wings.

"There has to be more," I said. "No. This isn't right. There has to be more than this."

The skull wheezed. It ground its teeth. It spoke syllables, not words, in a voice that was wholly alien.

That was the one true moment of terror I felt, the helpless horror of holding something *else* in my arms, which was not Sarah nor ever had been—some devil come from Hell in this particular shape to torment me. Sarah was already gone, and I had done nothing, said nothing, made a fool of myself in this very last, crucial time, *wasted, wasted, wasted.*

The hundred million butterflies covered me, the benches, the obelisk, everything. And then, for an instant the shifting patterns of the wings formed some semblance of her face. I saw her again, and I heard *her* voice one last time.

"This was enough. You were with me. Thank you."

"No," I said. "More—"

I shook the skull. Dust and scraps of clothing fell from my arms. The butterflies swarmed, filling the air, settling again.

The skull moved. The jaw clicked up and down. Its voice was like a crow, shrieking.

"Alas, poor Yorick," it said, and the jaw fell off and the rest crumbled like paper-thin wax.

I must have slept. I awoke to the sounds of children's voices. For an instant I was terrified that I would be discovered holding Sarah's skull, but my hands were empty, blue-black from the iridescent dust of butterfly scales.

Later, I went to see Frank Rodgers, who has helped our mutual friend Sam Gilmore through his own time of difficulty and strangeness. Those of us who have experienced such things have a way of finding one another. We form a network, sharing, remembering.

So, I told him the whole story as if I were in a confessional, and he said, "That was still her at the end, with the Yorick joke. It was her way of signing off. It was the sort of thing she would do, don't you think?"

I had maintained my composure with Frank until then, but I

just broke down, and he held me as a parent might a sobbing child.

"Just a joke? Just an effing *joke?* Was that all it was?"

"Oh, it was a lot more than that, but don't you think it was a nice touch to go out on a happy note, with a joke?"

"But we had so little time."

"And it was very well spent."

It was very hard for me to understand that, but I tried, and he helped me, and eventually, perhaps, I could.

Thanks for reading!

Thanks for reading. If you enjoyed this book, please consider leaving an honest review on your favorite store's website.

§

About the Editors

Kelly A. Harmon is a best-selling author and an award-winning journalist. She is a member of the Horror Writers Association and the Science Fiction & Fantasy Writers of America. She is a former newspaper reporter and editor, and now edits for Pole to Pole Publishing, a small Baltimore publisher.

A Baltimore native, Ms. Harmon writes the *Charm City Darkness* series, which includes the novels: Stoned in Charm City, A Favor for a Fiend, A Blue Collar Proposition, and In the Eye of the Beholder. A stand-alone novel, Blood Soup, was winner of the Fantasy Gazetteers Award. Her short fiction has been nominated for a Pushcart Award and short-listed for the Aeon. It can be found in The Pale Leaves and Gallery of Curiosities magazines, Beyond Steampunk, Occult Detective Quarterly, The Best Indie Speculative Fiction Volume 1, and more.

She is co-editor with Vonnie Winslow Crist of Pole Publishing's first three Dark Stories anthologies: *Hides the Dark Tower, In a Cat's Eye, and Dark Luminous Wings, and* Pole to Pole's first four anthologies in the Re-Imagined series: *Re-Launch, Re-Quest, Re-Terrify,* and *Re-Enchant.*

Visit her website at http://kellyaharmon.com, or connect with her on Facebook.

§

Vonnie Winslow Crist, MS Professional Writing, has had a life-long interest in reading, writing, art, science fiction, fairy-tales, folklore, and legends. An award-winning author and illustrator, she is a member of the Science Fiction & Fantasy Writers of America, the Horror Writers Association, the Society of Children's Book Writers & Illustrators, and Pen Women. Her books include The Enchanted Dagger, Murder on Marawa Prime, Owl Light, The Greener Forest, and Leprechaun Cake & Other Tales. Her speculative stories can be found in Chilling Ghost Short Stories, Faerie Magazine, Killing It Softly 2, Chaos of Hard Clay, Fae Wings & Hidden Things, Amazing Stories, Cast of Wonders, and elsewhere.

Editor of The Gunpowder Review, Ms. Crist co-edited with Kelly A. Harmon Pole to Pole Publishing's first three Dark Stories anthologies: Hides the Dark Tower, In a Cat's Eye, and Dark Luminous Wings, along with the first four anthologies of Pole to Pole Publishing's Re-Imagined series: Re-Launch, Re-Quest, Re-Terrify, and Re-Enchant. For more information, visit her website: http://vonniewinslowcrist.com/, blog: http://vonniewinslowcrist.wordpress.com, Fb page: http://facebook.com/WriterVonnieWinslowCrist, or http://twitter.com/VonnieWCrist

Also Available in The Re-Imagined Series

Re-Launch
Science Fiction Stories of New Beginnings

Re-Launch reminds readers that new beginnings rarely go as planned
and danger waits for the unwary on all worlds.
http://poletopolepublishing.com/books/re-launch/

Re-Enchant
Dark Fantasy Stories of Magic and Fae

Re-Enchant takes readers down twisted walkways to discover strange
and magical places, people, and creatures.
http://poletopolepublishing.com/books/re-enchant/

Re-Quest
Dark Fantasy Stories about Magic and the Fae

Re-Quest takes readers on fantastical quests filled with adventure, magic, and danger.

http://poletopolepublishing.com/books/re-quest/

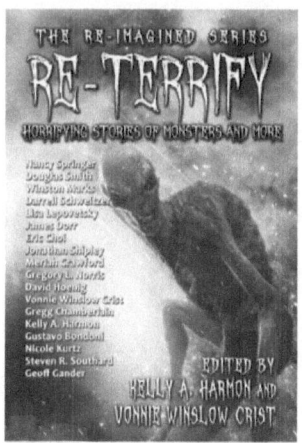

Re-Terrify
Terrifying Stories of Monsters and More

Re-Terrify reminds readers that monsters hide in the shadows and even the bravest person should beware of the dark.

http://poletopolepublishing.com/books/re-launch/

Available in the Dark Stories Series

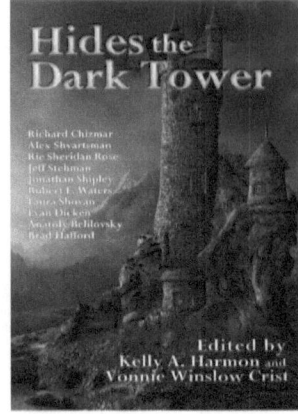

Hides the Dark Tower

Dark Stories #1

Mysterious and looming, towers and tower-like structures pierce the skies and shadow the lands. Hides the Dark Tower includes over two dozen tales of adventure, danger, magic, and trickery from an international roster of authors. Readers of science fiction, fantasy, horror, grimdark, campfire tales, and more will find a story to haunt their dreams. So step out of the light, and into the world of Hides the Dark Tower—if you dare.

http://poletopolepublishing.com/books/hides-the-dark-tower/

In a Cat's Eye

Dark Stories #2

Cat stories set in ancient Egypt, pre-history Mexico, Victorian England, space stations, grim magical worlds, during the zombie apocalypse, and a typical neighborhood give a glimpse into the mysterious lives of felines. Cat-lovers and readers of science fiction, fantasy, mystery, and horror will find a tale to sink their claws into.

http://poletopolepublishing.com/books/in-a-cats-eye/

Dark Luminous Wings
Dark Stories #3

From Icarus to Da Vinci to tomorrow's astronauts, humans have dreamt of flight. Feathered wings. Mechanical wings. Leathery wings. Steel wings. Stories of winged creatures set in graveyards and churches, bustling cities, fantastical worlds, alternate histories, and outer space reveal the shifting nature of Dark Luminous Wings. Take flight with 17 science fiction, dark fantasy and horro-filled tales from an international roster of authors.

http://poletopolepublishing.com/books/dark-luminous-wings/

Coming Soon in the Dark Stories Series!

Not Far From Roswell
Dark Stories #4

http://poletopolepublishing.com/books/roswell

www.ingramcontent.com/pod-product-compliance
Lightning Source LLC
Chambersburg PA
CBHW030305200626
46816CB00002BA/770